M

Essay on Religious Philosophy

Volume 2

SALZWASSER
VERLAG

M. Emile Saisset

Essay on Religious Philosophy

Volume 2

Reprint of the original, first published in 1863.

1st Edition 2022 | ISBN: 978-3-37500-666-2

Verlag (Publisher): Salzwasser Verlag GmbH, Zeilweg 44, 60439 Frankfurt, Deutschland
Vertretungsberechtigt (Authorized to represent): E. Roepke, Zeilweg 44, 60439 Frankfurt, Deutschland
Druck (Print): Books on Demand GmbH, In de Tarpen 42, 22848 Norderstedt, Deutschland

MODERN PANTHEISM.

ESSAY

ON

RELIGIOUS PHILOSOPHY

BY M. ÉMILE SAISSET

Translated,

WITH MARGINAL ANALYSIS, NOTES,

CRITICAL ESSAY, AND PHILOSOPHICAL APPENDIX.

VOLUME II.

EDINBURGH:

1863.

CONTENTS.

—o—

Seventh Treatise.

The Pantheism of Hegel.

It is impossible to doubt that Kant's idea of God is quite inconsistent with his system. But I cannot at once conclude that Kantism is false. For if I take this system by itself, after eliminating every heterogeneous ingredient from it, it appears to form a sufficiently united whole, and that whole is possibly the truth.

Philosophic genealogy—Kant, Fichte, Schelling, Hegel.

The last doubt which I wish to settle is connected with the question of the definite conclusion of the Kantian system. I hear it said that Kantism leads to the Idealism of Fichte, and that this Idealism itself conducted Fichte to a Subjective Pantheism, from which arose the Absolute Pantheism of Schelling and Hegel.

What is the definite meaning of the *formulæ*, Idealism, subjective Pantheism, absolute Pantheism? What is the strange genealogy which deduces Fichte from Kant, Schelling from Fichte, and Hegel from Schelling? I wish to understand all this. I wish especially to find a key to the system of Hegel, since I am assured that it contains the final conclusions of German philosophy.

Subjects of this treatise. I. Idealism. II. Subjective Pantheism. III. Absolute Pantheism, and especially Hegelianism.

I. One point which is clear to me is, that the

I. Idealism and Fichte. Two systems in Kant.

philosophical movement excited by Kant could not stop with him. I have clearly, indeed, recognised the fact, that the *Critique of the Pure Reason*, and the *Critique of the Practical Reason* do not form one homogeneous philosophy, but, in some sort, two distinct and even contrary philosophies, which no artifice of logic or of analysis can solder together.

I do not insist upon the additional fact, that Kant has written a third criticism, the *Critique of the Judgment*, which, fastened on to the two others by ingenious combinations, enriches them undoubtedly, but also complicates to excess the whole system.

Fichte considers that even the first of the two Kantian systems—that contained in the *Critique of the Pure Reason*—is wanting in unity and consistency.

But I consent to enclose myself within the limits of the *Critique of the Pure Reason*, and to forget all the rest. Has the system, thus simplified, perfect rigour and perfect unity? Such is the question which Fichte put to himself. It led him to substitute a new doctrine for that of his master, which at first he merely proposed to make more perfect. According to Fichte, the system developed in the *Critique of the Pure Reason* is essentially wanting in that logical severity which, in his estimation, is the characteristic of true science.

The system of Kant starts with an enormous concession, with a hypothesis.

The first assertion of Kant is, that nothing can be produced in thought, except as the sequence of experience and of the phenomena which strike our senses. But these phenomena, which the mind meets with and does not produce, pre-suppose a foreign principle. Thus we have, at the very outset, an enormous concession, which ruins by anticipation the whole system of Critical Philosophy. What! Science has the subject—the human mind—for its impassable barrier; and yet there exists another thing: and the first condition of science is to postulate an object which science does not know, which it cannot attain, and which is the only origin of all! Science, then, starts with a hypothesis, and with a hypothesis contradictory in its very nature. It leaves its principle outside of itself, or rather it has no principle—it does not exist.

Fichte's primary law of identity. Me=Me.

The end which Fichte proposes to himself in his *Theory of Science* is to give to science a true, that is to say, an absolute principle, reposing only upon itself, and leaving a basis to all the rest. Here, the idealism of Kant is accepted in all its rigour. There is no longer any arbitrarily supposed objective element, even as a simple phenomenon. All is severely deduced from the subject, the sole term of knowledge admitted by idealism. Fichte's problem is just this: to bring out philosophy whole and entire from the *Ego;* and this bold reasoner proposes to give his deduction a more than mathematical exactitude. Algebra rests upon the law of identity, which is thus expressed: A = A. Fichte maintains that this law implies another, the only one which a philosopher is entitled to admit without proof, and also the only one which he requires: Me = Me.

This principle is absolute both in *form* and *matter*.

When you say A = A, you intend to affirm nothing upon the existence of A. You only affirm that if A is A, A can be nothing else than A. The proposition A = A, is therefore, says Fichte, absolute only in its *form*, and not in its *matter* or contents. I know not if A exists practically and materially or not; but it matters not. I am formally certain that *given* A, A cannot differ from A, and that there is a necessary relation between these two terms. It is by the analysis of this relation that Fichte undertakes to prove the existence of the *Ego*. In the proposition A = A, he argues, the first A is not considered under the same point of view as the second. The first A, as we have seen, is laid down conditionally, the second absolutely. What reduces these two terms to unity, puts them in a certain relation, judges, affirms, and constitutes this relation? Evidently the *Ego*. Take away the *Ego*, and you take away the relation, the two terms, the proposition A = A. Above it, then, there is a higher and more immediate truth. The principle of identity is only absolute in *form;* the principle ME = ME is absolute both in *form* and matter; it alone is *truly absolute*.

Fichte's *Ego* and *Non-Ego*.

I need not follow Fichte in the course of his deduction, the most subtle and artificial which can be conceived. It is enough for me to know that he pushed to the utmost the strange idea of deducing a vast system of philosophy from this one principle, the *Ego*. Upon this needle's point he pretends to rest the entire edifice of human beliefs. Nature and God are but developments of the *Ego*. The *Ego* alone is the principle, explaining, laying down, creating all; explaining, laying down, creating itself. I know not whether I should wonder more at the excess of extravagance to which the human mind may be carried, or at the amazing richness of its resources. By Kant it was condemned to be ignorant of the universe and of God, locked up in the prison of the *Ego*. Let him alone. This one reserved point will give him back all the rest. From the furthest limits of scepticism he will even pass to the most absolute dogmatism. But a little while ago he doubted of everything. Now he vaunts, not merely that he *knows* Nature, but that he *creates* her. Nay, he vaunts that he CREATES GOD. Such are the very expressions, at once absurd and logical, of Fichte.

Yes! Fichte draws nature and God from the *Ego*. The *Ego* implies the *Non-Ego*. It limits itself. It is only itself by opposing to itself another which is not itself. It *poses* itself only by *opposing* its contrary. It is itself the link of this opposition, the synthesis of this antinomy. In fact, if the *Ego* only exists for itself by limiting itself, the faculty of self-limitation which it possesses, implies that, in itself, it is infinite and illimitable. Beyond the divisible and *relative Ego*, opposed to the *Non-Ego*, there is, therefore, an *absolute Ego*, comprising nature and man. This Absolute Ego is God. Here, then, is thought in possession of its three essential objects; here are man, nature, and God, in their necessary relation, members of one identical thought, with three terms, at once separated and reconciled; here is a philosophy worthy of the name; a rigorous, demonstrated, homogeneous science, starting from one great principle to follow out and to exhaust all its consequences.

Relative Ego, the simple antithesis of the *Non-Ego* and *Absolute Ego* =God.

Such in its general principle is the metaphysics of Fichte. His morality is a logical, though perhaps unforeseen, consequence of this. It is

Morality drawn from the *Ego*, whose characteristic is liberty.

founded upon the *Ego*, whose eminent characteristic is liberty. To preserve one's own liberty, one's *Ego*, is duty; to respect the *Ego*, the liberty of others, is another not less sacred duty which becomes the foundation of right. Hence the noble stoicism of Fichte, and that passion for liberty, which were in such perfect harmony with the masculine strength of his character and the generous part which he played in the political affairs of Germany.

But the metaphysical portion of his system the most important as the prelude to the dogmatism of Schelling and Hegel.

But the importance of the system of Fichte does not lie here. I find his greatness and originality in the extraordinary metaphysics so justly and boldly called by himself Subjective Absolute Idealism. It has this singular feature, that in pushing the scepticism of Kant to its extremest consequences, it prepares the way for the dogmatism of Schelling and of Hegel. Not only does it prepare the way for, but even begins and contains this dogmatism. Fichte openly aspires to absolute science. He explains all things—man, nature, and God. He leads German philosophy, if I may venture to say so, from the subjective to the objective by the subjective itself. From absolute scepticism he flings it into an enormous dogmatism. Setting out from a teaching so timid that it scarcely ventures to affirm one actual being, it is the prelude of that ambitious philosophy which embraces in its enormous frameworks the history of man and that of nature, and pretends to an unmeasured, unreserved, and universal explanation of all things.

II. Subjective Pantheism, and Schelling.

II. Schelling began his philosophical career by accepting the system of Fichte, as Fichte had at first adopted that of Kant. His first writing, composed at the age of twenty, has this significant title: *Of the Ego as the Principle of Philosophy*. But he was not long in perceiving the absolute impossibility of retaining philosophy within the narrow boundaries where she could not breathe. Human thought, gone astray upon the track of Fichte, had lost nature: the question was to win her back.

Schelling starts from Fichte.

Nature exists in presence of the *Ego*. This is a simple fact, but a fact which science should explain. But the example of Fichte has proved that every attempt to deduce nature from the *Ego*, the object from the subject, is radically impotent. One would succeed no better in deducing the subject from the object, the *Ego* from nature, thought from being. Thus there is no being without thought, no thought without being, and no means of resolving thought into being or being into thought. Schelling put the exact problem of philosophy to himself in these terms.

The problem as put by Schelling: No being without thought, no thought without being, and no means of resolving thought into being, or being into thought.

I can explain to myself, without much difficulty, the solution to which he was led. According to him, thought and being, the subject and the object, cannot be at once indivisible and inseparable, unless there be one principle common to both, at once subjective and objective, intelligent and intelligible, the only source of thought and being. This principle, this absolute subject-object, as Schelling calls it, is the leading idea of his philosophy.

Common principle of the subject and object =absolute subject-object. Schelling's solution.

Almost in the same way, Spinoza was led to his unity of substance. His master, Descartes, had laid down a fundamental duality, at the beginning of science. He had recognised *extended being* in face of *thinking being*. How was their co-exis-

Analogy between the modes in which Schelling and Spinoza were led to their conclusions. tence, still more, their union, to be explained? Malebranche, a precursor of Kant's idealism, had denied that bodies can be known. Berkeley, anticipating Fichte, had tried to explain extension as a creation of thought. Spinoza, feeling beforehand the uselessness of these attempts, loudly declared that the co-existence of thought and extension was only possible by an infinite substance, at once extended and thinking, at once nature and humanity.

The analogy between Schelling and Spinoza is not to be pressed too far.

The analogy is marked, but I must take care not to exaggerate it. The movement of German philosophy has a character peculiar to itself, and an originality, which, however limited, is real as far as it goes. Schelling is not merely the plagiarist of Spinoza. Yet he had read and admired Spinoza from his youth, while the fierce controversy, which divided Mendelsohn and Jacobi, and in which all the thinkers in Germany took part, was a few years earlier than the first writings of Schelling, and struck him so strongly, that in his first essay he openly expressed a hope of "one day realising a system, which should be the pendant of the *Ethica* of Spinoza." It was just what actually happened.

Analogies and differences between Schelling and Spinoza. 1. Analogies. (a.) Spinoza.

1. (*a.*) In the universe of Spinoza there are two worlds, at once united and opposed, the world of thought or of souls, and the world of extension or of bodies. These worlds interpenetrate one another. Every soul has a body, every body has a soul. Thought has its own laws, so has nature; but these laws strictly correspond. One of the main theorems of Spinoza is this; "The order and connection of ideas is the same as the order and

connection of things." [1] What is the secret of this identity? This—that thought and extension, souls and bodies, are but two sides of one and the same extension. Nature is God in extension and motion; the soul is God in thought. God being one, the laws of his development are one. Thus all existences interpenetrate one another; all is united and identified.

(β.) Schelling also set out from this duality, **(β.) Schelling.** thought or the subject, things or the object, or again, nature and humanity. Nature has laws; but a law is something essentially intellectual, it is an idea. Nature, therefore, is penetrated through and through with intelligence. On the other side, humanity also has its laws; it is free, no doubt, but it is not given up to chance. Absolute laws govern its development. There is a kindred, then, between humanity and nature. From whence does their distinction come? Because nature obeys its laws without consciousness, while humanity is conscious of its laws. In other words, there is being in thought, the ideal in the real, and there is also thought in being and the real in the ideal. The difference is that thought predominates in one direction and being in another; but, at bottom, thought and being are inseparable. There is, therefore, a common principle, which developes itself, sometimes with, and sometimes without self-consciousness. This is the God of Schelling.

2. So far, the Dutch philosopher and the German philosopher are at one. Here comes the **2. Differences.** point at which they diverge.

(α.) In the universe of Spinoza, there is an **(α.) With Spinoza,** abyss between thought aud extension. Thought

[1] *Ethica*, Part II., prop. 7.

an eternal relation of continuity between thought and being.

and extension in this system, indeed, are always represented as God, but there is no kind of union between these two portions of his being. The tide of ideas flows on one side, the tide of bodies on the other. God embraces them, it is true, but the contrary waves are never united in this infinite ocean.

(β.) With Schelling, thought and being form a homogeneous whole. The *prozess*.

(β.) It is quite otherwise in the system of Schelling. The total of beings forms one continuous and homogeneous whole, in which each form of existence leads to a higher form. Nature is not destitute of intelligence, as with Spinoza. An infinite current of thought circulates through every portion, only this thought does not at once arrive at the plenitude of its being. It is, at first, thought so *deaf* and so obscure that it absolutely escapes from itself. By degrees, it becomes clearer and falls back upon itself; first it feels itself, then it distinguishes itself, then it arrives at self-reflection, self-possession, and perfect self-knowledge. "Nature," says Schelling, "sleeps in the plant, dreams in the animal, wakens in man." This marvellous development is what the Germans call the progress or *processus* of being *(prozess)* and if we are to believe them, the idea of the *processus* is the peculiar conquest of Schelling, and his great claim to distinction. This, however, is to forget that Leibnitz, and Aristotle, two thousand years before Leibnitz, had conceived nature as a series of homogeneous forms, rising from gradation to gradation to an ever-increasing perfection. But this is comparatively unimportant, as Schelling evidently copied neither Leibnitz nor Spinoza, nor any one else. It was the movement of his own thought, it was the current of the Kantian philosophy, which led him on to the philosophy of identity.

In point of fact the system of Schelling—in one sense an extreme reaction against the doctrine of Fichte—is, in another sense, a continuation of it. Does not Fichte also admit the absolute identity of things? Did he not resolve the opposition of the *Ego* and the *Non-Ego* into a superior principle? Only this superior principle was always understood to be the *Ego*, and hence the idealistic and subjective character of the whole system. This ideality, admitted by Fichte, Schelling generalises and transforms. It is with him no longer locked up in the narrow prison of the *Ego*—it is the foundation of all things. It may be said that Schelling has taken the frames of his philosophy from the hands of Fichte; but in enlarging them he has given them infinite amplitude. He has caused exiled nature to enter into the system of Fichte, and scattered reality over it in handfuls.

Schelling's system partly a reaction against, partly a continuation of, Fichte.

3. The evolution of German philosophy could not stop short with Schelling. The system of Schelling, indeed, contained a principle, but it did not furnish any means of giving it scientific development. Schelling had conceived the sum total of things as the progressive series of the varied forms of one identical principle. But how are we to grasp this principle? how are we to find the law of its development? how are we to demonstrate it? This Schelling never did.

III. Absolute Pantheism and Hegel.

Schelling failed to bring out the identical principle, of whose varied forms all things are the progressive series.

Why does this principle develope itself? why does it become alternately gravitation, light, activity, consciousness? Are we to question experi-

His *intellectual intuition* a vain attempt.

ence? Experience only collects, but cannot explain, facts. Shall we say that the subject-object developes itself by its very nature? It will be asked, in return, what its nature is? and this Schelling in no way determines. The occult quality of an unknown principle must be admitted here. How many mysteries and hypotheses! and what end do they all serve? Take away experience, and there is no apparent mode of constructing science regularly, or even of sketching its faintest outlines. Under the pressure of this difficulty, Schelling imagined his *intellectual intuition*, a transcendental faculty which attains the absolute with an immediate grasp, without passing through the laborious steps of analysis and reflection. But Schelling was never able to throw any light upon the equivocal nature of this alleged intuition. Is it a natural gift, or an abnormal privilege of the human mind? We know not. What can be obscurer, more arbitrary, or more incompatible with the conditions of science? German philosophy must take a step further, or abandon its principle.

Hegel's logic.

Hegel took this last step.. Hegel sought for, and believed that he found, a method of constructing and demonstrating absolute science. That method he calls logic.

His principle of the "identity of contradictories."

It is no easy matter to understand the logic of Hegel. If I at all comprehend his meaning, it is characterised by two great novelties which are closely connected. First, he pushes further than Schelling had ever done, and to its very utmost limit, the principle of the absolute identity of thought and being; then, as a consequence of this very excess, he introduces a law which is the reversal of all received ideas—namely, that contradictions are identical, that being is identical with nothing, the finite with the infinite, and life with death.

The "identity of contradictories" derived from Kant's antinomies.

However strange these novelties may appear, I think that I can perceive their root in the doctrine of Kant. Suppose that Kant could have risen from his grave in 1820, on seeing what philosophy had become in the hand of Hegel, there can be no doubt that he would have exclaimed, like Malebranche when he read Spinoza, that it was *a fearful chimera*. And yet, upon closer inspection, those two strange and perilous principles—the identity of contradictories and the identity of thought and being—are already in the system of Kant. Has not Kant, in the dialectical portion of his work, set the example of opposing ideas to one another, and of proving that contradictory propositions are equally true? Is not Hegel's logic, in this point of view, the development of the antinomies?

The Hegelian idea of the "identity of thought and being" similarly derived from the Kantian doctrine, that laws of phenomena are but the forms of our intelligence applied to them.

What is still more evident, and still more important is, that Kant prepared the way for the absolute identification of thought and being.

The history of this principle, of which Germany is so proud, and in which she makes her principal reputation to consist, is an infinitely curious study. We see it *born* from Kant, *developed* in Fichte, *transformed* in Schelling, and finally grown to its *fullest maturity* in the system of Hegel. According to Kant, what we call laws of nature are really the forms of our intelligence applied by us to phenomena. The great error of philosophers is to detach these laws from their true

Traced from Kant through Fichte and Schelling to Hegel.

principle, which is the human mind or subject, to transport them into things, to *objectify* them. Kant loved to make the idea of his philosophical reform sensible, by comparing it to that which his countryman, Copernicus, had introduced in astronomy. The vulgar believe that the stars turn round the earth, which does not accord with the exact observation of facts. Reverse the hypothesis. Make the earth revolve round the sun. All contradiction vanishes. Everything is explained and cleared up. Just so; we are accustomed to subordinate thought to being, while, in truth, according to Kant, being is subordinated to thought.

From this conception to that of Fichte there is but a step. If things are only what thought makes them, it is thought which constitutes and creates things. The *Ego*, in thinking and laying down itself, creates itself. This is the absolute identity of thought and being, explicitly professed by Fichte, and boldly, but logically deduced from the fundamental idea of Kant, only that this absolute identity has the peculiar impress of Fichte's system, I mean to say, that it is purely psychological and subjective. With Fichte, being, like thought, is ever the *Ego* or a development of it. Fichte could give no other meaning to the identity of thought and being, but upon condition of going beyond his system. Schelling took up, and radically transformed the system of Fichte. In his eyes, the *Ego* and the *Non-Ego* have an equal reality; nature and humanity subsist face to face. They find their union in a principle at once ideal and real, subjective and objective, which constitutes and contains them.

The identity of thought and being, of subject and object, conceived as real and objective, is the common principle of the philosophy of Schelling, and that of Hegel, and we have seen that both one and the other are closely linked with previous doctrines. Let us now glance at the difference of the two systems. Schelling identifies thought and being only in their first principle, which is God; but below God, thought and being are distinguished without separation. There is more being in nature, more thought in man. If it be so, thought and being are two different things, and the principle of identity is at fault. Logically, if thought and being are one and the same essence, thought should not only be found wherever being is, but it should be met with in the same proportion. Why is this equilibrium broken, and how is it possible that it should be broken? Why is God more in humanity than in nature? The question is, no doubt, a rash one, but it is one which he, who is bold enough to maintain that absolute science is possible for man, is imperatively called upon to answer. But this question Schelling does not, and cannot, solve. He is thus convicted of inconsistency. He proclaimed the principle of the identity of thought and being. He cleared it from the relative and subjective character, which disfigured it in Fichte and in Kant, but he did not dare to develope it rigorously. And thus his philosophy only propped itself up by hypotheses, or by disguised loans which he made from experience.

Hegel makes it his special glory that he was bolder and more consistent than his predecessor.

The ultimate Hegelian idea of truly absolute identity.

He professes to draw from the principle of identity what neither Schelling, nor any other philosopher had been able to make it yield—a science of the development of things.

Hegelian principles.

Thought and being = idea. Idea=God. Development of idea = reality. Knowledge of development = science. Science of idea=logic.

Thought and being are one. But why two words to express one thing? Let us not say thought and being; let us say, the idea. The *idea*, here is Hegel's *God;* the *development* of the idea, here is *reality;* the *knowledge* of this development, here is *science.* The science of the idea is called *logic*, and thus metaphysics and logic are confounded.

Science thus becomes possible through a knowledge of the laws of the idea.

Thanks to this truly absolute identity, science becomes possible. It is reduced to determining the necessary relations of ideas. In the theory of Schelling, we were forced, sometimes to rest upon experience to describe the movement of being in nature (which did not afford a real science), sometimes to give scope to the imagination, and to present hypothesis disguised under the sounding name of *intellectual intuition.* This arose from the fact that the essence of the first principle remained undetermined, and that an arbitrary distinction was admitted between the objects of thought and thought itself. But now that we know that this first principle is the idea, and that nature and humanity are nothing but the development of the idea, the law of the idea once known, science is found.

The laws of the idea deduced from the law of the identity of contradictories.

I ask Hegel how the laws of the idea can be determined. He answers this question by his logic, which is the scientific determination of the laws of the idea. They are all deduced from one fundamental law, the law of the identity of contradictories. According to Hegel, all thought, all being, every idea encloses a contradiction. This contradiction not only exists in things, but constitutes them. Life is essentially the synthesis and union of two elements, which together are mutually exclusive, and require one another.

At first sight Hegel owns that this doctrine is repugnant to common sense, and appears favourable to scepticism. The Pyrrhonists triumph in the opposition of ideas; but this opposition is not at all embarrassing to the true philosopher, who sees in it the condition, and the very movement of life.

Which is witnessed to by common sense. In Metaphysics and Theology.

Common sense, far from rejecting the principle of the identity of contradictories, is perpetually witnessing to it.[1] Does it not maintain firmly, from age to age, the difference and identity of the soul and the body, the co-existence and opposition of God's foreknowledge and man's free will? To abandon one of these truths for the other, under the vain allegation that they are contradictory, would be to fail in common sense. Examine common sense in its highest form, religion. Does not the religious soul adore a God at once Personal and infinite, a God at once immoveable and living, visible and invisible? The sceptic believes that he triumphs in opposing these

[1] Hegel's law of the identity of contradictories has been anticipated by Heraclitus. "When extravagant wits and pretenders to wisdom shall assert things evidently repugnant to sense or reason; that snow and coal have the like appearance (as did Anaxagoras): that all motion is impossible (as Zeno): that *contraaictory propositions may be consistent* (*as Heraclitus*"). Barrow, Sermon viii. "The Being of God proved from universal consent," in "The Christian Faith, explained and vindicated." 'Ηρακλεῖτος τὸ ἀντίξουν συμφέρον καὶ ἐκ τῶν διαφερόντων καλλίστην ἁρμονίαν καὶ πάντα κατ' ἔριν γίνεσθαι.—*Arist. Ethic. Nic.*, lib. viii. 1.]

attributes to each other: it is because his reasoning has extinguished his reason. While he is tormenting himself by turning from one of these contraries to the other, an elevation of the heart to God unites them. Has not the Christian religion, the most reasonable of all religions, been teaching men for the last eighteen hundred years, that God made the world out of nothing, that God was made man? Are there not there just as many contradictions as there are propositions, but contradictions full of reason, life, and truth?

In science. The sciences present us with a thousand examples of the identity of contradictories. In physics, do we not admit without difficulty that light supposes darkness? Imagine a light without a shadow. Objects equally illuminated can no longer be distinguished, and this uniform day is precisely equivalent to night. Thus light implies its contradictory, obscurity. Not only does it suppose, but it bears darkness within itself and engenders it: and on the other hand, while producing it, it realises itself. The product is effective light, colour.[1]

From these quaint but simple examples we may form a general idea of the system of Hegel.

Three *moments* of every idea. Every idea encloses three elements, or to use the orthodox Hegelian language, three *moments*. It may be considered *in itself*, in its *opposition* to the contrary idea which it implies, or finally, in the *union* which conciliates them.

The first moment is that of the idea *in itself;*

[1] ["Erit igitur lumen quasi coloris color."—*Jul. C. Scalig. De Subtil, Exerc.* lxxi.]

the second, that of the idea *out of itself;* the third, that of the idea *in itself* and *for itself.* The idea first exists simply and immediately; then it is divided and opposed to itself; then, finally, it reduces its two members to unity. The moment of unity is that of life, of concrete, individual reality. He who only considers the idea in its earlier moments knows nothing but abstractions, and this is the common weakness of the vulgar, and of those philosophers who follow the logic of the schools. The vulgar holds to that first view of things which makes us know them in a state of mixture and confusion. This is the perception of the *senses.* The *understanding* is applied to this gross matter, divides and decomposes it. Here oppositions come out conspicuously. All things appear contrary. Life and death, motion and repose, soul and body, fact and right, society and nature, philosophy and religion. Minds which fasten upon these oppositions cannot fail to fall into scepticism; an absurd extreme, as far removed from common sense as it is from true philosophy. But to stop short at scepticism is to know very imperfectly the nature of things and the power of thought. The *understanding* is above the *senses*, but *reason* is above the understanding. What the *understanding* separates, the *reason* unites. Things which seemed incompatible appear united. Confusion is succeeded by order, war by peace, doubt by faith, the anguish of the soul and the hesitations of reasoning by the serenity of an affirmation, which is sure of itself, and the fulness of a perfect comprehension. Life and death are but the two moments of

First moment=idea *in itself.*
Second moment=idea *out of itself.*
Third moment=idea *in itself, and for itself.*

existence; fact and right, the two aspects of one necessity; society, an advance made upon nature; philosophy, a finished development of religion.

I can see how Hegel may have been led to the principle of his logic and of all his philosophy, the identity of contradictories. His constant method is to find in every idea a contrary idea, and to unite them in a third idea; to oppose thesis and antithesis, and reunite them in a synthesis; to consider the idea successively *in itself*, *outside of itself*, and *for itself*. We thus arrive at a new idea, which is nothing but the first idea, vivified by the very opposition which it has met, become concrete and living, instead of dead and abstract. The same idea thus transformed, meets with a new contradiction, a new opposition, to come out victorious from it, and so on, *ad infinitum*, from the simplest idea which contains the germ of all the rest, to the most compound, which expresses its fullest development. The chain of these oppositions is science. It consists in bringing out the universal identity. Setting out from a primitive idea at the lowest degree of thought, it finds this at the summit, and all the intermediate ideas are nothing, but the same idea unfolding itself infinitely.

Method of Hegel.

Science, according to him.

Tripartite division of Hegelian philosophy.

This general view enables me to take my bearings in the midst of that vast edifice of accumulated abstractions, where the thought of Hegel plays with unparalleled subtlety and fertility. Nothing remains external to this system, and I am not unwilling to allow that there is in it an immense effort to embrace and explain all things.

The work of Hegel comprises three parts:

logic, properly, so called; the *philosophy of nature;* and the *philosophy of mind.* The first and last principle of things, which Hegel calls the *idea*, should first be contemplated in itself, in the depths of its yet unmanifested essence, in those necessary and primitive laws which constitute it, and which at a later period are reflected in all its works.

Logic, philosophy of *nature*, philosophy of *mind.*

The science of the idea in itself is *pure logic*, the key-stone of the whole system.

The idea—by a necessary sequence of its nature, such as logic has described and explained it—developes itself; or, to use a better expression, splits itself and lays bare the element of contradiction which was enfolded within it. It was God in Himself; it becomes nature; eternal and immutable, it falls under the conditions of time and change. The *philosophy of nature* developes for us the series of necessary movements which carry the idea across all the degrees of the scale of sensible beings. The laws of mechanics, chemistry, and physiology resolve themselves into a series of oppositions. But the final principle, which presides over this development, decides that the contradiction necessarily assumed at the outset should be necessarily destroyed in the sequel.

Science of the idea in itself=*pure logic.*

Science of the series of necessary movements of the idea =*philosophy of nature.*

The idea, which in nature was ignorant of and denied itself, returns upon itself and becomes mind. The science of the return of the idea to itself is the *philosophy of mind.* Religions, arts, systems, social institutions, are but different phases of that evolution which is regulated by an eternal and inflexible geometry. The history of humanity reflects that of God. It is a living logic. It is God who realises Himself; who,

Science of the return of the idea upon itself =*philosophy of mind.*

setting out from Himself, returns to Himself, thus closing the infinite and eternal circle.

I resume these three great divisions. Logic, in the system of Hegel, occupies the position which in ordinary systems is assumed by Theodicea. It is the science of God, considered in Himself before creation (at least, if the words God and creation have any meaning here). Strange *Theodicea* truly! where, in place of the sublime attributes of eternal justice, infinite goodness, pure and unmingled beauty, I find a dry enumeration of abstract ideas—being, nothing, quality, quantity, measure, identity, difference.

These ideas form a chain whose first link is the idea of being; all the others presuppose it, while it presupposes none of them. But the idea of being or being—for Hegel here identifies these two things, as he always does—is identical with nothing. What is being considered in itself? It is absolutely undetermined being, neither finite nor infinite, neither mind nor matter — that which has neither quantity, quality, nor relation. All this may be affirmed of nothing. To think upon nothing is to abstract from all the forms of existence, which is consequently the same thing as to think upon being in itself. On the other side, Hegel does not deny that being and nothing, the existent and the non-existent, are two contradictory terms. They are at once contradictory and identical. Contradiction in identity is the supreme law of thought and things.

Thus, from the idea of being, the primitive matter of things, comes out the idea of nothing. But being and nothing do not remain as they are.

Being at once excludes and call for nothing. This double movement excites a third idea, which Hegel calls becoming, and which reconciles the other two. Becoming is the idea of development, by which a being becomes that which it was not before. This idea implies simultaneously that of being and that of nothing; it is their synthesis. We are now free from the confused abstraction, where all is lost and mingled. We set foot upon the solid ground of reality. We have to do with determined being, with *quality*.

The Hegelian trichotomy carried out through all science.

Athwart this endless deduction, which I shall make no attempt to follow out in detail, the leading idea of Hegel's system is maintained with singular firmness. In all cases, the idea traverses three necessary moments. It is first the confused identity of contraries, then it divides itself to go back finally to its primitive identity, illuminated and quickened. This is the dominant law of all spheres of thought, not only physics, astronomy, and the natural sciences, but also psychology, morals, jurisprudence, the history of civilisation, of religions, and of philosophies.

Applied to anthropology.

There are three faculties in the human mind: *sensation*, which gives ideas confusedly; the *understanding*, which disentangles and opposes; the *reason*, which unites them.

Man is first for himself a confused unity of a soul and a body. This unity is split by reflection. The soul opposes the body, but it perceives that the body is still itself, and then it refers it back to itself as a necessary moment of its existence.

In man, all at first is mingled—*instinct*, *will*, *reason*. The man already exists in the child without doubt, but in an abstract and undetermined way. He is *in himself*, not *for himself*. The age of reflection comes. An opposition emerges between instinct and reason, nature and will. Hence evil, but hence also good. Good supposes evil; for he who does good without struggle, solely by the impulse of an excellent nature, is not truly good. Here, according to Hegel, is a brilliant verification of the principle of his logic. We cannot conceive good without at the same time conceiving evil. Good, in one sense, therefore, implies evil, and yet excludes it. This is the contradiction to be solved. Hegel believes that he attains the solution by demonstrating that at botton instinct and reason are identical. Instinct is reason which is ignorant of itself. After being opposed to itself in the struggle between the will and nature, it recognises their identity, and henceforth all becomes order in the pacified soul. Instinct understands that to obey reason is to be faithful to oneself. Reason understands that it is not destined to extinguish or violently suppress instinct, but to guide it; and the intelligent and voluntary harmony of instinct and reason is virtue, the source of happiness. People imagine that virtue and happiness are two different things, but that is a narrow philosophy of the understanding. Reason identifies what the heart of the honest man never separates, well-doing and well-being, virtuous action and felicity.

Further developments of the principle of the identity of contradictories.

Everywhere, on the surface, are contradiction and difference; everywhere, at bottom, are harmony and identity. What, apparently, can be more opposed than philosophy and religion? What more different than various religious worships? What more contrary than philosophical systems? Yet, in reality, all these religious institutions, whose variety confounds and whose opposition astonishes us, are but members of one body and moments of one idea. The idea which is developed in the harmonious course of religions, is the same which, under clearer forms, displays its ever-diverse, yet ever-identical, nature in the regular movement of philosophic systems. The laws of logic, everywhere present, because they are the foundation of all, determine and preside, with sovereign power, over this twofold evolution.

Applied to three great religions.

Hegelian view of Christianity.

There are three great religions—the Oriental religion, the Greek religion, and the Christian religion, which correspond to the three necessary moments of the logical idea. The *Oriental* religion is the idea of God in its first moment, comprising all the rest in their confused unity. Man adores God, but without knowing Him and without knowing himself. The universe, man, and God, form as yet but an indistinct whole, nature. The Greek religion is the idea of God at the moment of diremption and contradiction. God is divided, so to speak, ramified into a thousand branches, opposed to man and to Himself. The infinite is lost and dissolved in the finite. The Christian religion, in its very essence, is the religion of reconciliation. The daughter of the East and of Greece, Christianity reproduces and identifies them. God, who was ignorant of Himself in the obscure symbols of India, who, in a certain sense, wandered out of Himself in the prodigious variety of contrary divinities in Greece and Rome, came back to Himself, and took clear consciousness and perfect possession of Himself in Christianity. Thus Christianity is the sole, complete, true, self-evident religion; it is God knowing Himself, and affirming Himself to be God.

What are called the mysteries of the Christian religion are the absolute laws of things, obscure to the senses, to the understanding absurd and contradictory, to the reason clear and harmonious. Is not the first of these mysteries that of the Holy Trinity? But the Holy Trinity is the very principle of logic under the form of a symbol. The Father is the idea *in itself;* the Son is the idea *out of itself*, in its visible manifestation; the Spirit is the idea *in itself* and *for itself*, arrived at the ultimate term of its movement, recognising itself as identical in all the degrees which it has traversed. In the bosom of the Father are found the three moments of the idea, but as yet in a purely ideal form; being or power, the object of thought; the word, or intelligence, or again, thought engendered by being; finally, love, which proceeds from and unites the two. This purely ideal trinity is realised by creation, the kingdom of the Son; but, to fasten creation to its principle, the finite must know itself infinite, man must know himself God—this is the kingdom of the Spirit. To philosophy it pre-eminently belongs to realise the kingdom of the Spirit upon earth. Philosophy, in fact, it is which, by linking the symbols of Christianity to the laws of thought, explains and demonstrates that which religion could only assert—the intimate union of God and man. The first form of this union is found in the Christian community of the Church in its cradle; the second has been the organised Church; the last will be the State, to which all religious creeds are invited to ally themselves one day under the law of reason and of liberty.

Weakness of German philosophy.

I must frankly confess that my first sentiment, as I leave these strange speculations of modern Germany, is one of astonishment that, in the country of Leibnitz, they should have been able to enthrall men's minds so long.

The belief that absolute science is attainable by the human mind the πρῶτον ψεῦδος of German philosophy.

Unless I am much deceived, German philosophy, for the last half century, has been under the dominion, and, as it were, under the spell of an illusion, that of believing that absolute science is possible for the human mind. Absolute science—by which term I mean to denote the universal and adequate explanation of all things—is the chimera which German philosophy has been pursuing since the time of Fichte, and each of the systems to which it has by turns given birth is merely an effort to seize the elusive phantom.

This haughty belief does not arise merely from the speculative genius of the Germans;

It is said that this unmeasured confidence in pure theory arises from the speculative genius of the Germanic race. This explanation is true, as far as it goes; but insufficient. For this land of enthusiasm has produced such great critics as Wolf, Heyne, and Paulus. This chimerical race has given birth to Kant.

rather a reaction from the excessive scepticism of Kant.

I should rather be apt to believe that it is the very excess of doubt, in the doctrine of Kant, which has produced, in that of Hegel, the opposite extreme of dogmatic pride. In philosophy, account must be made of two essential elements.

On one side, there is the human mind, with its nature, its limits, its weaknesses of every kind. On the other, there is the sum of things, their essence, and their relations. To reduce the human mind to the sole knowledge of its own constitution, in forgetfulness of the nature of things, is to deny science. To conceive science as independent of the nature of the human mind, its constitution, laws, and limits, is to deny it again; for it is to make it impossible and contradictory.

Kant's extreme scepticism and Hegel's extreme dogmatism.

German philosophy affords the spectacle of these two opposite extremes. Kant begins by recognising the fact that in science philosophers have not given sufficient weight to the human mind, to the subject. This is a profound as well as solid view, from whence an incomparable analysis of reason has arisen. But soon, dragged on by his own principle, this wise thinker forgets his wisdom so far as to debar the human mind from all access to the reality of things. Hegel flung himself into the opposite extreme. The author of the *Critique of the Pure Reason* scarcely ventured to affirm the existence of external objects; the author of the *Logic* professes to know them thoroughly, and to demonstrate their origin, essence, and laws. The father of German philosophy pared down Theodicea to a suspicion of the possibility of God. To the last inheritor of that philosophy, the Divine nature has no mysteries. The number and order of His attributes are discovered with the same clearness as the properties of geometrical curves. Kant imprisoned reason in the circle of experience. Hegel refuses all scientific authority to experience; all must be demonstrated in philosophy, that is to say, deduced from pure ideas. For the master, the highest conceptions of the human mind had a merely relative and subjective value; if we believe the disciple, nothing relative and subjective has any place in the frameworks of science.

Common point in Fichte, Schelling, and Hegel,—their belief in the possibility of absolute science.

Thus, of the two necessary terms of all knowledge—the human mind and things—Kant suppresses the second, Schelling and Hegel narrow the first, Fichte marks the transition from one extreme to the other. In fact Fichte, even while exaggerating Kantism, pursues the chimera of absolute science; but it is in the *Ego* that he flatters himself with the hope of finding it. Like Kant he suppresses things, but he preserves their ideas, and prepares the future transformation, which is about to construct things themselves out of these ideas. Thus Fichte, Schelling, and Hegel (and one might add to these eminent names those of all the philosophers of modern Germany) have this common point through all their differences, viz., that they believe that absolute science is possible, that they search after, and attempt to construct it.

Their common method—the suppression of experience.

Hence *their common method*, which is as chimerical as the object which it pursues. Its distinctive feature is *the suppression of experience*, or at least its complete subordination to the *data* of pure reason. Germany has the most complete contempt for observation. To attend to facts is, in its estimation, to fall into empiricism, the lowest stage of intellectual degradation. Science is essentially the explanation of things. But experience explains nothing. Science in explaining demonstrates. Experience can demonstrate nothing.

It is enclosed in necessary limits. It knows what happens at a given time or place. But science must have universal and durable results. Experience is the work of a finite mind, and consequently always relative and subjective. Science is, by its very essence, absolute and objective.

Absolute science involves an *à priori* method.

Evidently, if philosophy pursues absolute science, the philosophic method is the *à priori* method, founded upon pure ideas, following the order of things, explaining and deducing everything, despising experience, recognising no limit and no condition. By such a science such a method is absolutely required. These two chimeras are made for one another!

The most dangerous Pantheistic principles of Schelling and Hegel come from the ideas of such a method and such a science.

If I am not much mistaken, the secret of all German speculation is here. The double illusion which I have just pointed out appears to have for its necessary consequences—(1.) The principle of the identity of thought and being, the common foundation of the system of Hegel and Schelling. (2.) The still more dangerous principle of the identity of contradictories, of which the Hegelian logic is a perpetual application. (3.) The eminently Pantheistic idea of the *processus* of things, which makes of the human mind the ultimate term, in which the successive developments of existence are at last concentrated and reflected.

Absolute identity between ideas and things required for absolute knowledge.

For the construction, indeed, of absolute science, it is not enough that the order of ideas should express the order of things. The ideas must embrace, penetrate, and constitute the things. The ideas must be the things. Suppose that things are separated, or only distinct from ideas, a doubt is possible as to the perfect conformity of the ideas to the things. The essence of things is surmised, perceived through a medium; it is not grasped and thoroughly mastered. Absolute science is overthrown, if there is not a perfect identity between ideas and things.

Absolute science must start from the idea of undetermined being.

Absolute science must start from a first idea, and deduce all others from it. What can this idea be? The vaguest and most comprehensive of all, the idea of undetermined being. But how are we to pass from undetermined to real being, from the abstract to the concrete, from the negation of existence to life? There is a contradiction there. Well! Instead of concealing it, let us boldly accept it.

From thence will follow the principle of the "identity of contradictions," and its conclusion down to "nothing become God,"

Contradiction then will be at the very origin of things. Let this primitive contradiction become the fundamental law of thought and being. Let it be found again and again in all nature. Let it be the hidden force by which ideas come out, one from the other, from the poorest to the richest—so that definitively nothing is the principle, God the term, and nothing becomes God.

and to man divinized.

But how can the human mind know and describe this vast and marvellous evolution? On one condition only—that the human mind be the superior degree in which everything ends, the final circle which envelopes and penetrates all the rest—on condition that the human mind is all, that Man is God. *Man divinized*—such is the last word of German philosophy.

Pantheism of the systems of Schelling and Hegel.

Schelling says that God is the absolute subject-object. Hegel says that He is the idea, infinite mind. But we must understand each other clearly. The subject-object, considered prior to its development, is but an abstraction, an empty identity. I say as much of the infinite mind, of the idea in itself. Hegel himself declares that the idea in itself is identical with nothing. If this be God, it is necessary to explain it frankly. But it is not so. The God of German philosophy is not at the commencement, but at the end of things. This God is the human mind; or rather, God is at once at the origin, at the end, and in the middle; which is just tantamount to saying that there is no God distinct from things.

How far are these doctrines original?

In default of more solid merit, have these strange doctrines that of novelty? Here again is one of the illusions of German philosophy.

German pretensions to originality.

Nothing can be more artless than these pretensions to originality on the part of our neighbours beyond the Rhine. In the Hegelian school especially they have been carried to the furthest point. Hegel, in his *Lessons on the History of Philosophy*, only recognises two great epochs—the Greek epoch and the Germanic epoch. But it is a matter of course that German philosophy is comprised between Kant and Hegel. This is to erase, with one stroke of the pen, from the annals of human thought, scholasticism and French philosophy, such names, for instance, as those of Abelard and Descartes. We can understand that Germany should treat French philosophers with this haughty contempt. But is it not the extreme of ingratitude thus to humiliate Leibnitz?

Hegel's two epochs of philosophy.

The greatest ideas of German philosophy are not original.

This is the more revolting, inasmuch as these proud contemners of the philosophy of the seventeenth century have not disdained to borrow from it its most original views.

They come partly from Leibnitz.

The following great ideas, which constitute all the force and riches of Schelling, come from Leibnitz:—

(1.) The principle of the *universal homogeneity* of substances.

(2.) The law of *continuity*, according to which all beings are interlinked and placed on the scale.

(3.) The inner *dynamism*, which all through nature makes itself felt, under the apparent *mechanism* of its phenomena.

(4.) The profound *analogy* between the laws of the universe and the laws of humanity.

Partly from Spinoza.

Has not another Cartesian, Spinoza, a large part to claim in the speculations of Germany? I have formed a positive conclusion, that the principle of the identity of thought and being, is the very fundamental doctrine of Spinozism. Hegel accuses the Jew of Amsterdam of having mistaken the occidental principle, the modern principle of personality—of having made of God necessity, or absolute existence, without recognizing in Him the subject, the person. But is it becoming in Hegel to raise against Spinozism such an accusation, however well-founded in other respects? Has *he* respected in God or in man the personality which he invokes—*he*, who from the summit of being to its lowest gradation, has seen nothing but the rigorous geometry of the idea? While distinguishing himself from Spinoza, Hegel nevertheless recognizes a great precursor to German philosophy. Who, in the name of wonder? Not

Spinoza. Perhaps Descartes. No; it is a German of the sixteenth century, the chimerical author of the *Dawn of Morning*, the philosophical cobbler of Gœrlitz, Jacob Bœhme!

Hegel's boast of the originality of German philosophy.

I let Hegel himself speak: "We shall see," says he in a celebrated discourse, "that amongst those nations of Europe where the sciences are cultivated with zeal and authority, philosophy has been left nothing but the name, the idea of it has perished, it only exists in the German nation. We have received from nature the mission of being the preservers of this sacred fire, as to the Eumolpidæ of Athens was confided the preservation of the mysteries of Eleusis, and to the inhabitants of Samothracia that of a higher and purer worship; as in still older times, the universal spirit had given to the Jewish nation the consciousness that he would come forth renewed from her."

What astonishes me most in the artless vanity of these words, is that the history of philosophy, which has been cultivated so deeply and patiently by the compatriots of Hegel, and by Hegel himself, has not in the slightest degree altered the serenity of their speculative pride. Without going back to the early times of Greek philosophy; I find about the time of the decline of Greek and Roman civilization, a philosophical movement, full of striking analogies with that which has agitated Germany for sixty years, I speak of the Alexandrian philosophy. It also had been preceded by a radical scepticism, that of Œnesidemus, of Agrippa, and of Sextus; it also flung itself into the contrary extreme, to embrace the phantom of absolute science. Like Hegel, Plotimus disdains experience; like him, he pretends to seize the absolute order of things, and not only to seize it, but to deduce it, and to demonstrate it; both admit a dialectic movement in being which is reflected in science, and which identifies reason and being in the idea. At Alexandria as at Berlin, the mysteries of the divine essence are clearly discerned, they are analysed into three elements, at once distinct and inseparable, a primitive trinity which is found at the bottom of every thing, and of every thought. This trinity becomes to these two schools a sort of magic wand, which removes every veil, lights up every obscurity, and effaces every difference. Philosophical systems are brought together, religious symbols are confounded, everything is interpenetrated and united. At the summit of this trinity, beyond all the determinations of thought and being, reigns the absolute unity, the identity of existence with nothing, the abyss where human thought, after having run round the necessary circle of its revolutions, comes to seek repose in the annihilation of consciousness and personality.

The Alexandrian philosophy a precursor of the German, as well as that of Leibnitz and Spinoza, as above indicated.

Thus, in both cases, there is the same principle, the search after absolute science: the same method, purely rational speculation: the same results, the identity of contradictories, and man made one with God.

This, then, is the beginning and the end of German philosophy; it begins with scepticism, it ends with Pantheism. And these are the two springs where the rising generations are to drink and be satisfied. Kant pours them out scepticism, Hegel pantheism, and these two currents of ideas meet in the doctrine of an impersonal God.

Thus in vain have Descartes and Malebranche, Newton and Leibnitz, exhausted their genius, to organise into a system the universal belief of the human race. The Personal God, the God of common sense, the God of spiritual philosophy, must give way, and in His stead scepticism and Pantheism leagued together must introduce the undetermined substance of being. Once for all I pause, and ask myself seriously: Must I come to this at last? Is this result the answer to my long historical researches? I have read enough, I have talked enough, the age of maturity comes, I will shut my books, I will fold myself within myself, and consult henceforth my reason alone.

The scepticism of Kant and the Pantheism of Hegel conspire to introduce the doctrine of an impersonal God.

---

[1] [The question of the consistency of Hegelianism with Christianity has been anxiously discussed. There appear to be three parties in the Hegelian school. The *droit* is occupied by such men as Bauer who, holding the Hegelian doctrine of God in man, receive the Gospel history. The *milieu* has for its exponents those who, like Rosencrantz, *only* deny deny the supernatural events of the Saviour's life. The *gauche* is represented by Strauss, who, with the anti-historial spirit of all thorough Pantheists, evaporates the whole life of Christ into the "meteoric regions of idealism," and who agrees with Hegel himself that "the Christian idea of God's oneness with mankind as a sensible history is abolished, and degraded into a distant, dreamy vision." (*Hegel et L'Hégélianesme*, par M. Edmond Scherer, cf. Michelet, *Geschichte der Systeme der Philosophie*, II., pp. 638-659. Mill on the *Mythical Interpretation of the Gospels*.)

The Hegelian trichotomy, applied to the Gospel history by Strauss, runs thus. The moment of confusion has a spontaneous expression in the evangelists. The moment of contradiction is supplied by the negations of history and of science. The moment of identity is found in the combination of faith and science in the school of Hegel! Christ has disappeared as person and fact; He abides as idea, and the union of God and man is realised in humanity. I need scarcely observe that Neander, Tholuck, and Olshausen, have overthrown this unhistorical scheme; an admirable criticism of Strauss is to be found in Dr. Mill on the *Mythical Interpretation of the Gospels*. There are just two points to which I would allude in this note. (1.) The most original portion of Strauss, his "ideological Christology," is really in the New Testament, in such texts as, "crucified with Christ," "risen with Him," appearing with Him in glory." The points of difference are, that the "ideological Christology" of the New Testament only applies to *regenerate* humanity; and, still more, that that ideology is based upon distinctly historical grounds by those who first preached it, and who, having a really ideological version of the Resurrection before their eyes, pronounced it to be a "babbling," and a "gangrene." (2.) The *character* of Christ is a knot which the Hegelian Christology can never cut. Either Christ created the Church, *or*, the Church created Christ; but the Church could not have created Christ, therefore, Christ created the Church.

The ablest exponents of Hegelianism consider his system equally inconsistent with man's immortality. Mankind, with Hegel, is mathematically immortal, because new generations supply the place of those which perish; like a spring which at any moment we term *analogously* the same with that which has existed in the same place, because other waters pour in with pauseless rapidity; or, like a tree, which is *figuratively* styled perennial, while the apparently permanent green with which it is invested is made up of successive generations of leaves. But in the immortality which Scripture reveals, each leaf upon the tree, and each drop in the river is immortal and imperishable.—Cf. August: *De Civit: Dei*, XXII., I. (See also VI.)]

Part II.

ESSAY ON RELIGIOUS PHILOSOPHY.

MEDITATIONS.

First Meditation.

Is there a God?

I REFLECT within myself and say, "Whence comes it that I must always think of God? I exist, I live; existence and life are dear to me. I find around me a thousand objects which please and interest. What need I more to fill my soul? and why do I seek something beyond? Why? Because I feel but too well that I am imperfect, and set in the midst of imperfection. When I consider my being, I see it pass away like a rapid stream. My ideas, my sensations, my desires, all change every hour; and, in the same way around me, there is no being that is not passing from motion to repose, from progress to decay, from life to death. Amid these vicissitudes, like a wave borne on by other waves, I roll in the immense torrent that bears all things to the unknown shore. This change—this perpetual change, is the universal law—is my condition.

Why do I think of God?

And the more I reflect, the more I see that this condition belongs to the very nature of things. Within me, and without of me, being is ever changing, because it is limited. I find myself confined in a corner of space and time. In vain I strain

I am led to do so by change and imperfection.

all the springs of my frail corporeal machine; I can only lay hold of the few objects that are within my reach. I think, but among the numberless truths

Man,

that I perceive I can but seize some, and these only on condition of concentrating my thoughts in a narrow circle, beyond which I see dimly, or not at all. I

And all nature.

love, but my power of loving, which turns with a sudden impulse towards all which contains some evident or secret perfection, can only cling to frail, perishable, changeable objects, not one of which fulfils the promises it made. Everywhere there is a limit. I change its place, but I cannot destroy it: still I feel it, still it weighs me down. There is in me an indefinite power of development, which aspires to unfold itself in a thousand different ways, and which, meeting everywhere with obstructions, now strains violently against them, now falls back upon itself, weak and weary, discouraged. And the reason of this continual change within and around me is this: we all, inhabitants of this world, great and small, thinking atoms, blades of grass, grains of sand, are, in our different degrees, and under forms infinitely various, imperfect beings, striving after perfection, but only reaching it in an imperfect manner.

Why am I? My reason of existence is not in myself.

But why am I imperfect? why do I bear such a form, in such a manner, at such a time, or in such a place? Why do I exist at all? I know not, and this proves invincibly that the reason of my own existence is not within myself, that my being is not a first being, but a borrowed and relative existence.

Now, whenever I contemplate my being thus, as radically imperfect and incapable of self-existence, there arises in my soul the idea of the perfect

Being. I conceive Him perfect in all the infinite powers of His being. Whilst I am endeavouring, across the waves of time, to gather the broken fragments of my life, and to develope imperfectly some one of my powers, He, concentred in an immutable present, enjoys the absolute plenitude of His existence in its eternal expansion. I find everywhere limits, either in the beings who surround me and press upon me, or in the form and degree of my own powers. He is the being without limits, the only being of His kind, the being to whom nothing is wanting. All the powers of life are concentred in Him, those that I know as well as those infinitely more numerous, of which I have no idea. In imperfect beings, limited and unequal, they are subject to strife, to negation, to discord. In Him all is infinite, positive, full, equal, alone, harmonious. This plenitude, this harmony, this unity of all the powers of being, is the supreme good, is the absolute beautiful, is the Being of beings, is God. This idea of the perfect being charms me. How vast, how sublime it is! but is it not too far from me? On the contrary, it is as near as possible. Plunged in the whirl of passing things, I may, for an instant, be seduced by their charms. I may, falling in love with myself, be sometimes dazzled and intoxicated with a feeling of my own strength, but it is because I only look at the surface of things. As soon as I return to myself, as soon as I examine the depths of my nature, I am terrified at the weakness, the inconsistency, the incurable fragility of my being, and I feel that it would vanish away if it were not supported by the true Being. There is no effort of the mind in this, no circuitous thought, no reason-

Idea of the perfect Being.

ing process; there is a sudden, spontaneous, irresistible impulse of my imperfect soul, turning to its eternal principle, feeling itself live and exist in Him.

The existence of God, like our own, not the conclusion of a syllogism.

The primary objects of thought—imperfect and perfect being.

When I come to reflect and to reason on these two objects of my thought—the imperfect being that I am and the perfect Being by whom I exist—I see that it would be madness to suppress one or other of these two terms. I find them at the end of all my analyses, at the beginning of all my reasonings. They compose, in their indissoluble union, the permanent foundation of my consciousness.

Thought of duration leads to eternity, of space to immensity, of finite to infinite.

Can I think on duration which passes away, always preceded and always followed by another duration, without conceiving eternity? Can I represent to myself a certain space, surrounding a smaller space, and surrounded by a larger, without conceiving immensity? Can I contemplate a being finite, changeable, in process of development, without conceiving the Being who is infinite, immutable, perfect? These two ideas call one to the other, and are linked by a necessary connection. But am I not the dupe of a fortuitous reciprocal relation, which is, perhaps, only in words? Nay, how should it be in the words if it were not in the ideas, and how in the ideas if it were not in the things? Besides, is not this connection most simple? Before the imperfect being there must be the Perfect Being; before that which only exists in a temporary, local, and relative manner, there must be that which exists fully and absolutely. This is simple, clear, evident; it is a natural axiom; it is the first of axioms; it is the supreme law of my reason.

Shall I endeavour to destroy, by an artifice of reflection, what nature has so deeply engraven in my consciousness? I have tried it more than once

The idea of the infinite cannot be destroyed by reflection.

without ever being able to succeed. Supposing that there is no perfect being, how should I have the idea of one? Could I have created it? But with what elements and after what model? I might accumulate ages and spaces, I should never make immensity or eternity. In vain should I heap size upon size, in vain should I choose among existences all their powers, all their features of beauty or perfection: these accumulated masses, these beauties, these powers, ever increased, purified and combined by the most powerful imagination, would never give me the infinite, the absolute, the perfect. Moreover, what are ideas in general? They are forms of thought; and what is thought in general? What is its essence? It is to represent that which is. How, then, should it represent that which is not? Finally, if I were to analyse the idea of an imperfect being, I find that the imperfect being is one who has not within itself the reason of its own existence, and supposes, consequently, something beyond itself. If, then, I were to conceive the imperfect being as exhausting all existence, I should conceive it at the same time as supposing, and not supposing something beyond itself, which is a palpable contradiction.

Contingent and imperfect implies necessary and perfect being.

I could bring forward many more reasons and show that I cannot deny the perfect being without being liable to a *reductio ad absurdum*. But that is useless. I am in a region above reflection and reasoning—in the region of primary ideas and evident principles. I lay down, then, as a principle, as a truth self-evident and anterior to all other truth, that my contingent and imperfect being, and every other analogous being, has its reason in the necessary and perfect being.

Second Meditation.

Is God accessible to Reason?

Proof that the Perfect Being exists by Himself.

I KNOW that before this universe of which I form a part, and which is a moving collection of fragile and imperfect beings, there is the perfect being who alone exists by Himself. This is the first ray of light that breaks upon my night; and I scarcely perceive it, when it seems to vanish, and leaves me involved in darker shadows. For what is the signification of these words; God exists by Himself? I find a profound mystery in the very evidence they afford. I cannot doubt that the Perfect Being necessarily contains in Himself the principle of His own existence. Otherwise God would not be God, the perfect being. For not existing by Himself, He would exist by some anterior principles, He would only have a communicated, perishable, dependent existence. And this extraneous principle, whence He must draw His being, would be the true God, unless, in its turn, it depended upon some other principle, and so on, infinitely; and thus there would be no first principle, no God. Therefore, it is certain that the perfect being must exist by Himself.

Negative notion of Being by Himself.

Yes, it is evident enough, but that does not make it more easy to understand, for what is the meaning of self-existence? If a negative notion were sufficient, I should say, To be self-existent is to have no need of a beginning. I understand this well enough, for I have only to look at myself, or at any other being whatsoever in the universe, to know what it is, to need a beginning. I know negatively what it is, to be self-existent, but when I want to form a positive notion of the self-existent being, I feel myself face to face with an insoluble enigma. Were I to say that God creates Himself, it would be using mere words, for if I accept this explanation seriously, it signifies that God is both the cause and effect of Himself, He was then before He made Himself, He was then before existing: two contradictions—so we are reduced to say that God has no need of a Creator, that He is uncreated. I fall back upon a notion purely negative and indirect.

Does God create Himself?

Is God's perfection the reason of His Being?

Were I to say that God is perfect, and that His perfection is the reason of His existence, even this thought which had appeared to me solid, and profound, is an illusion. No one has yet succeeded, perfection being given, in deducing existence from it. Who shall attempt it where so many have failed? If the perfection of God is the reason of His existence, we must say, to speak rigorously, that God is perfect before existing, which is a contradiction. Reason being so constituted that she submits every conception to the conception of existence, that she can conceive nothing anterior to existence, we must here invoke some human faculty superior to reason, some unheard of esctatic intuition.

But perhaps I am wantonly making difficulties

Shall we say, Being must exist? We are met by the answer, Why not *nothing*?

for myself. God is being itself. Is it not quite plain that being must exist? No, it is not quite plain; for how many times at the end of all my reflections on the origin of things have I met with this problem. Why is there anything rather than nothing? I mean rigorously nothing, neither imperfect being nor perfect being, neither finite being, nor infinite being, neither God, nor universe, neither man, nor space, nor time, nor movement, nor number, in fact, absolutely nothing.

Our ignorance of God.

I shall be told that this supposition is contradictory, and that trying to conceive absolute nothing, I myself destroy the conception, for I at least exist who conceive the nothing. It is true, I cannot evidently draw out the hypothesis of nothing, as an hypothesis actually realised; but that does not prevent me from conceiving nothing as possible, having abstracted myself as well as everything else. What matters it that I have no positive idea of self-existence? If I could conceive it, I should know how and why it exists, and I need not ask, Why is there anything? This question shows me the depths of my own incurable ignorance; it shows me my absolute incapacity of attaining God in His essence. I know that God is: I know not why He is. His essence escapes me. I can say what it is not; I cannot say what it is.

God *inconceivable* as well as *incomprehensible.*

It is not enough to say that God is incomprehensible. God in His essence, God as self-existent, is absolutely inconceivable to any other being but Himself. When we say that all in God is infinite, and, consequently, infinitely disproportioned to man, and consequently incomprehensible, we speak the truth. When we say that there is in God an infinity of perfections, an infinity incomprehensible to a finite being, we speak truth again; but we speak the whole truth when we say that the essence of God is wholly inaccessible to us; and it is quite conceivable to say that the essence of God is incommunicable; God alone is God. We must be God to understand what God is in Himself, and why He exists; where is the root of His perfections, and what mysterious tie unites them.

Then it avails me nothing to have found God, since this knowledge only shows me the infinite depth of the abyss of ignorance, where my thought is lost. But let not my soul therefore despair. Let me examine closer. We cannot know the essence of God, but it does not follow that we can know nothing about Him. We cannot know His essence because it is incommunicable, but evidently all in God is not incommunicable, for we exist, we think, we love, we act. And thought, and life, and activity, and love, are everywhere diffused around us. God has not then remained within Himself, enwrapped in the mystery of His essence: God has manifested Himself, God has communicated Himself. Why, how, we know not, but the fact is certain, the universe is there. There is then something incommunicable in God, namely the essence of His being. There is also something communicable, namely the powers of His being, thought, love, joy, and life.

Yet no need of despair or scepticism.

Somewhat in God is communicable.

We know besides that God is perfect. Without understanding, without even conceiving the first foundation of His essence, we know that all that is in Him, is there under the form of perfection, that is to say, under the form of immensity, of eternity, of absolute plenitude, and of entire completeness. Why, then, should we not know God according to the measure of our needs and earthly condition? Without indiscreet haste, or timid mistrust, instead of groaning over the weakness of our nature, let us walk by its light, and to strengthen our steps let us make use of what we know best in the world, our own thought.

Our thought leads us up to Perfect Thought.

We think, doubtless weakly, sometimes well, sometimes ill, always much worse than we wish, but as a matter of fact we think. Among all beings, we have the privilege of exerting that superior power of thought which is called reason, and which has truth for its object. We know very clearly what constitutes truth. No doubt we do not always attain to it, but we know always that it consists in the agreement of thought and being.[1] Without being, there is no thought, without thought the being escapes from itself, it is as if it had not been. Thought reflecting being, being laying hold of itself by thought, this is truth. Now, why is thought imperfect? Because it is limited, either in its object, or in itself. Being escapes it, and often in its effort to seize it lets it escape. Because it pursues with too much ardour, it is always trying to embrace a larger quantity of being, and to lay hold of a higher degree of purity, and it never attains its object. Thought is an incomplete power, which attains

[1] ["Veritas est affectus orationis conveniens menti, et affectus mentis conveniens rei . . . falsitas erit in *notionibus*, quæ sunt in animâ, propterea quòd eæ rebus adæquatæ non sunt."—J. C. Scaliger, *De Subtil.*, *Exercit.* II.]

action only by effort, aided by time, across a thousand intermediaries, a thousand obstacles, a thousand mistakes. And even when it attains some particular truth, it cannot stop there. It perceives immediately another distant truth which attracts it, so that having taken breath, it dashes forward again, always restless, desirous, greedy of truth, never satisfied. This aspiration ever disappointed, teaches us to conceive the ideal of the perfect thought, I mean thought in a state of absolute completion, embracing all being, embracing it with a sure hold, and with a single glance, without effort, without intermediary, without succession, without limit, without weakness, without the least imperfection. O, we cry, what a sublime ideal were this! With what ineffable joy should we follow such a possession of truth! and we say well, for living truth, truth laying hold on itself, and enjoying itself, perfect joy in the full possession of truth, is God.

What if this be a delusion?

But what if all this is but a delusion, a chimera of my reason, which gives reality to that which it desires. What if, making a God in my own image, composed of all that is best in myself, I have invented a God who has no existence but for me alone? I said just now, and I thought I demonstrated, that between God and man there is a difference which is absolute, and not relative; a difference of nature, and not of degree.

Finite and infinite thought.

It is true the finite has no proportion with the infinite; but let us weigh this well—between the intellects that we possess and the complete intellect, there is the infinite. Our thought, and every imperfect thought, is a power in the way of development; this is its essence and its necessary law. Divine thought is a thought fully developed, which by its essence is anterior to all development. Finite thought implies effort, infinite thought excludes it. Finite thought is displayed under the form of time, infinite thought subsists and is maintained under the form of eternity. It knows none of the conditions of an imperfect intelligence, nothing of limit, or time, or space, or succession, consequently nothing of memory, or reasoning, or induction, or any of those human intermediaries between an infinite truth and a finite thought; nothing of those laborious operations which are the torment and confusion of our reason. It is but the pure essence of thought, thought adequate to being, intuition having consciousness of itself, thought taking hold of being, and taking hold of itself. On one side an indefinite virtuality, tending towards action without being able to reach it, on the other the absolute infinite act, excluding all virtuality, all effort, all measure, all degree, all interval between itself and its end. The difference is not of degree, but of nature and essence; it is the difference between time and eternity, between the finite and the infinite, the relative and the absolute.

God has intelligence and consciousness.

Also, since God is the universal Being, the Being to whom nothing is wanting, He must possess intelligence. There could not be less in the Perfect Being than in the imperfect, in the cause than in the effect. God could not be the source of being and yet not be the source of that intelligence without which being would be as though it were not. And if God be intelligent He must perform acts of intelligence, He must have intuition and consciousness of Himself. For in reality to imagine a thought without intuition, and without consciousness, would be to keep the name while taking away the thing; unless I should venture to say that there is nothing in common between divine thought and human thought. And then these words, God thinks, would have no sense to man. The consciousness of thought would be an imperfection, sleep would be better than waking, and God, as said one of the ancients, would be like a man asleep. Where would be His dignity? "No," cries another sage, "no, by Jupiter! they will not persuade me that thought, a soul, motion, and life, do not belong to the Absolute Being; that this Being neither lives nor thinks, that he remains motionless, immutable, a stranger to the august and holy powers of intelligence."

God is not absolutely incommunicable.

And the sages were right. God is not an absolutely incommunicable being, having no relation with that which proceeds from Him. If there be in His essence a mystery which baffles me, there is also in it a dazzling light which shines to the eye of my reason, and charms it.[1] He is reason itself, eternal reason; not the dark

[1] [It has been said that "not our logical mensurative faculty, but our imaginative one, is king over us," and that "a symbol is ever, to him who has eyes for it, some dimmer or clearer revelation of the God-like."—Carlyle, *Sartor Resartus*. The opposite aspects of the infinite God are thus revealed to us under apparently contradictory symbols in the Bible: "The Lord said that He would dwell in the thick darkness;" yet "He dwelleth in the light which no man can approach unto."—1 Kings viii. 12; 1 Tim. vi. 16. What is the conclusion of philosophy, as indicated above, but the translation into modern language of God's "dwelling in thick darkness," yet "in light unapproachable."]

germ of thought, but thought complete; not abstract truth, but truth substantial and active, which diffuses itself and communicates itself infinitely. Rejoice, my soul, thou hast found God, the living God, the true God.

OBJECTIONS OF A PYRRHONIST.

I was resting joyfully in the idea of eternal truth, the divine harmony of being with thought, the complete type of the perfect life. I said to myself, Here is a certain victory; here is a first step made on firm land. I may advance in safety, and I congratulated myself on having set aside books, systems, the disputes of the schools, and permitted my mind to give itself free scope, and to taste at will the pure luxury of free thought. But it is all in vain. Books follow me; they fling themselves in my path, and force me to stop in spite of myself. Sometimes Kant impedes my way, sometimes Spinoza. And when I succeed in putting to flight the illustrious dead, their living disciples rush to the assault. I cannot take one step out of my retreat without meeting with scepticism or pantheism, in the person of some one of my friends.

Scepticism—especially in the Hamiltonian form.

To-day it is a sceptic with whom I have to do. His opinions are in general quite in accordance with those of Sir William Hamilton, the great Scotch critic. Like him he has passed the Rhine, and been initiated in the German philosophy, whose darkest labyrinths have no secrets for him. It is especially the doctrine of Kant that has seduced and fascinated him, so that in the recent attempts of Schelling and Hegel he sees only an added proof of the impotence and the incorrigible pride of reason.

"I confess God as well as you, says he, but I believe in Him in another manner. God is not to me an object of science, but an object of faith; I speak of that natural faith which has been refused to no man, and which has a more extensive circle than reason. The visible world, the finite, or, in more precise terms, 'the conditioned in space and time,' is the domain where reason and science display themselves; that which is beyond it escapes them. I agree, that 'the very consciousness that we have of our impotence to conceive anything beyond the finite and the relative, inspires us by an astonishing revelation with faith in the existence of something unconditioned, beyond the sphere of comprehensible reality.'[1] But do not triumph in this confession, for this unconditioned, this absolute, although real and certain, is not the less outside of science. Science is composed essentially of positive and determined notions, and the absolute is to the human mind only a negative idea absolutely undeterminable.

Revelation of the infinite; which, however, belongs to faith, not science.

"See what happens when you dare to determine the nature of God. Your God is, you say, the Being of beings; that first principle which philosophers in France call the perfect Being, and in Germany the Absolute. Pray what is the absolute? As long as you confine yourself to negative determinations you are all right. You say the absolute is the infinite, the eternal, the immu-

The absolute.

[1] Sir W. Hamilton's *Discussions on Philosophy and Literature.* See especially Appendix I.; *Conditions of the Thinkable.*

table, the one, the simple. That means that God has no precise limits; that He is neither in space nor time; that He is incapable of motion, of variety, of difference, which are all void and negative notions. To speak thus is not only to say nothing about God, but it is to acknowledge, without knowing it, that He is inaccessible to man. Man, in fact, by his nature, is subject in all his acts to the laws of space and time. This is why his reason cannot exercise itself on any object without imposing on it this double condition. To say that the absolute is without relation to space and time, is to say that He is without relation to human reason; that He will always be to it an algebraic X, the X of an insoluble equation.

Sceptical objections to positive determinations of God. You are protending and magnifying your own humanity.

You feel this yourself, and you try to comè to positive determinations. God, you say, is intelligence, consciousness, reason, truth; and, if we let you go on, you will tell us presently that He is love and joy, active power and liberty, wisdom, justice, foresight, holiness, anything you please. But do you not perceive that you are the dupe of a play of the imagination, which is thus making to itself an idol of human elements? Thought, love, joy, and liberty, are but modes and relations of your particular being; that is to say, the accidental and changeable forms of a little being wandering in a corner of the earth, in the midst of infinite space. Can you call that atom, more or less amplified, God? And what an extreme of pride to see only man in the universe? Is not God the God of all beings? why confine Him and cut Him down to the proportions of man? Why not say He is matter when you aver He is spirit? By what right do you give Him thought, and deny Him motion? And then in the narrow circle where you want to contain Him, why choose that which suits yourself; why accept this, and refuse that, while all modes of life are one and inseparable? God possesses joy according to you; He must then suffer sadness. You attribute to Him thought and consciousness; He must then think as man thinks. He must recollect, reason, and conclude; He sees and hears. He must have eyes and hands. You are ashamed of this idol, which is your own creation, and you try to make it a little less material. You take away first the senses, then memory, then reasoning, till, by refining and retrenching, you have nothing left but an empty abstract thought, a thought which does not think, a nothing.

Proof that the absolute is accessible to thought.

"The strength of your reasoning is this principle, that all that is in the effect must be in the cause. But this principle is false; for otherwise we must transport into God not only finite forms of existence, but also duration, succession, and extent, without which these forms vanish.

"You would attach yourselves to the idea of Divine thought, no doubt, because you think this safer ground than any other. Well, let us try it. Assuredly if there is a truth that contemporary philosophy has put in a strong light, it is that all truth supposes the distinction of the subject and the object. There must be a subject who thinks, there must be an object who is thought; there must be a relation between the two terms. Nothing is plainer. Well, do you know what follows rigorously from this admission? This—that the Absolute is absolutely inaccessible to man; further, inaccessible to Himself. In a word, the Absolute is a contradiction to the laws of thought. How, in fact, should the Absolute admit of thought, since He is absolutely one, and thought implies a division and a difference? Besides, thought is only real when it seizes itself. It supposes, then, consciousness, the *Ego*.

From the nature of thought.

"If God thinks, God has consciousness, God says I. Now to say I, is to distinguish oneself from something else; it is to place an extraneous object before oneself. The I, consciousness, can only belong to a particular finite being, limited by other beings. This is the meaning of the celebrated formula, 'The *Ego* supposes the *Non-Ego*.' Then to suppose an Absolute being who says I, is evidently to deny His being absolute; it is to deny Him while you assert Him. We must believe, then, one of two things: either that God thinks without consciousness of His thought—that is to say, that He thinks without the necessary conditions of thought; or thinking really that He has consciousness, that He says I; and then He is no longer God.

Can the absolute be thought by man? Schelling's ecstatic intuition.

"The Absolute, then, considered in itself, is not, and cannot be, intelligence and thought; it cannot think itself; can it be thought by man? No. For to think the absolute, is to take the absolute for the object of thought; therefore to distinguish oneself from it, to set oneself outside of it. But according to its definition, the Absolute is that which embraces everything, and outside of which nothing can exist, or be conceived. Schelling understood perfectly the contradiction which exists between the Absolute and the laws of thought; and he admits, in God, a thought absolutely undetermined, a thought which is mingled with His being, and which he calls the absolute indifference of these two terms. Such a thought is equivalent to the annihilation of thought. But better still—Schelling goes on to ask, how man can think the Absolute. He knows and acknowledges that the Absolute cannot enter into human consciousness, the Absolute being one, and consciousness implying opposition between the subject and the object. So what does he do? he imagines a human intuition of the absolute, which is accomplished outside of consciousness, and which he calls *contemplation* or *intellectual intuition*. It is, says he, a flash of lightning, a sudden rapture. Ask him not to describe it; it avoids analysis, for it avoids reflection and even consciousness. In this mysterious act every distinction vanishes between the subject and the object of thought. It is not God on one side and the soul on the other. God and the soul are identified. We are in thorough mysticism.

"But we do not escape from the discussion by taking refuge in mysticism and ecstasy. For if we place ecstasy outside of reason and knowledge, we confess ourselves conquered, and if we accept the discussion we are reduced to say that there is a thought which is in contradiction with the essence of thought. Nor if we admit this thought are we any better off, for since it is outside consciousness, it is outside memory. 'We come out of intellectual intuition,' says Schelling, 'as out of a state of death; we come out of it by reflection.' This is impossible,—we cannot reflect on that which does not come within the range of our consciousness; we cannot recollect that which we have not perceived and felt. Supposing the act of intuition to be complete, having no possible relation with our consciousness, it would remain entirely extraneous to us.

Dilemma.

"This, then, is the state of the question, If you confine yourself to excluding from God all the forms of finite existence, all positive determination, you confess that God is indeterminable, and that the science of God is a void and negative science. If you try to determine positively the nature of God, either you have a god made in the image of finite being, a false god, an idol, or else you give to God contradictory attributes; as, for instance, thought without the necessary conditions of thought. Then adding to thought, love, joy, and liberty, but love without need, joy without sadness, liberty without effort, you think you advance in the knowledge of God, and that you make His nature to consist of an harmonious union of all perfections, while all the time you are making of Him a monstrous assemblage of all contradictions.

History must be consulted.

"In point of abstract reasoning, this is what logic says. In point of fact, there is but one way of solving the question, that is to consult the history of systems, and the history of religions. What, in fact, is any doctrine, philosophical or religious, but a manner of conceiving the origin of beings, that is to say, of determining the Absolute? One philosopher conceives the Absolute as substance, another as cause, another as unity; and all are persuaded that they possess an Absolute perfectly pure, unfettered by any condition or relation—the true Absolute. Now substance is not the Absolute, for it implies modes. Cause is not the Absolute, for it is relative to its effects. Intelligence is not the Absolute, for it is only realised by consciousness, difference, and opposition. Unity even, is not the Absolute, for it necessarily engenders variety; and if it does not engender it, it expresses nothing, and itself vanishes in absolute indetermination. There is no middle way; there must be either a determinate, conditional, relative God, or an undetermined God, who may be reduced to these three syllables the Ab-so-lute—and then follows the logic of Hegel, which identifies this Absolute with nothing. One of his own disciples, Oken, has given the real formula of this *God-nothing* of Hegel, namely Zero.[1]

"Religions," says this school, "so many forms of imagining the Absolute."

"This is the mere play of scholastic acuteness, but let us consider now the beliefs of human science. There is at least one incontestable fact, which is, that all men savage and educated, have

[1] [Mr. Mansel, several years ago, gave a summary of these opinions with equal learning, acuteness, and wit,—

"The land that produced one Kant with a K,
 And many Cants with a C.
Where Hegel taught to his profit and fame,
That something and nothing were one and the same;
Where, rear'd by Oken's plastic hands,
The 'Eternal Nothing of Nature' stands;
And Theology sits on her throne of pride,
As 'Arithmetic personified;'
Where Feuerbach shows how Religion began
From the deified feelings and wants of man,
And the Deity own'd by the mind reflective
Is Human Consciousness made objective."—

Phrontisterion—Scenes from an unfinished Drama, pp. 13-14.]

alike felt a need of thinking of God, of making to themselves some image of Him, of introducing the Divinity into their homes and their consciousness. Thence all religions—thence Fetichism, Polytheism, Manicheism, Monotheism, which are so many different forms under which man strives to imagine the Absolute. An endeavour touching and sublime, but ever impotent, ever infinitely beneath its object. This is why religions die, after having lived, and are continually renewed with time, places, races, nations, and the great movements of civilisation. Consider the last and the most philosophical of human religions, Christianity. You will find in it, amidst the purest symbols, the proof of the vanity of all symbols. When the God of holy writ describes Himself, He lets fall from His lips only that grand ironical sentence, 'I am that I am.' The New Testament, it is true, is given to complete the Old. God becomes incarnate in man, but how is this incarnation taught to the Christian? Is it offered to his reason to understand, or to his faith to adore? The Word made flesh is, we are told, a mystery, the great mystery. It is, in fact, the expressive mystery, for God made man, is the Eternal fallen into time, the Absolute become relative, the Infinite finite. This is the common foundation of all religions, and the eternal despair of all philosophy. All religion is the development of a symbol, and it is of the nature of a symbol to represent under a form that which is independent of all form, as it is of the nature of a system to define that which is independent of all definition. This does not mean, in the least, that philosophy and religion are without object, and without truth, or that we must be sceptical, or impious, or atheistical; for philosophy and religion are in the first place legitimate, inasmuch as they have their roots in the superior elements of human nature, and in the second place, they are efforts of ever increasing strength and happiness to reach to purer symbols, and formulas that are larger and more exact. Philosophy and religion bear witness to the origin and the Divine destiny of man. They bear him beyond the borders of the real, and transport him into the boundless realms of the ideal. They are true in their essence. But they cannot be worth more than man himself, and man is subject to change, the supreme law of all that is imperfect and finite. Man must not set himself in the place of God; to God belongs absolute truth, to man the immortal search after truth."

This scepticism is untrue—a reaction.

Such are the arguments which I hear every day, from men in whom a scepticism more or less confessed is united with the most brilliant intellectual gifts, further enhanced by a noble independence of character. I hear them, I admire and I contradict them. My profound conviction is, that this negative philosophy is a disease of our times, a bitter fruit of our philosophical disputes, a perhaps natural enough, but certainly most exorbitant reaction against the daring of speculative pride. In a word, I see in this scepticism, which is most frequently concealed, a little truth mingled with a great deal of error.

It is easy to single out the little truth that it contains—namely, the very simple fact, that the

True part, that theology has mysteries.[1]

science of things divine, as much and more than any other science, has its shadows and its mysteries. I begin, then, by confessing that not only the Absolute is incomprehensible, and also the Infinite; but even that, considering Him in His essence, in what He is of Himself, He is inconceivable to man. We know that He is. We know neither why nor how He is.

Untrue part, why God's existence cannot be demonstrated.

This comes from the weakness of the human intellect, which is the real meaning of that principle of the incomprehensibility of God that we use and abuse so much. In fact, ours is a communicated being; the being in God is of another nature. He exists of Himself. God is then different from us. The Being is His sublimest name, and yet He has no name; for there is beyond His attributes something which establishes them, and constitutes them, and this something is inaccessible and ineffable. For this reason the existence of God, notwithstanding the genius of Saint Anselm, and the accumulated efforts of Descartes and Leibnitz, has never been rigorously proved *a priori*. God alone knows why God exists, and demonstrates eternally to Himself His

[1] [It is often assumed that there is something in the very conception of a *mystery* as such, which at once baffles evidence, and precludes examination. Unquestionably there are propositions which either convey no ideas (*e.g.* those in an unknown tongue), or which are palpably self-contradictory. It is important to bear in mind (and it is a principle which cuts very deep in our controversy on the two opposite sides of Romanism and Socinianism, that a *mystery*, far from involving contradictions, or presenting no tangible truth, is an idea whose *general* outlines are traced with sufficient distinctness, while the particulars are concealed. Thus *mysteries, in general*, are possible, but the truth of a *particular* mystery must be decided by its evidence. Leibnitz says, "*Possibilitatem* mysteriorum contra insultus infidelium et hæreticorum à contradictionibus vindico; haud quidem *veritatem*, quae revelatione solâ stabiliri potest."]

own existence, because He knows the how of it. God alone sees in the idea of God, or as Leibnitz would say, in the simple possibility of God, the reason of the existence of God. It is not thus that men know the Divinity. They only know it as the reason of their own existence and of that of the universe. Nothing more.

True conclusions from man's incapacity of conceiving God.

What inference may be drawn from this? That we must bow down before the eternal mystery? I willingly do so. That we must take down the pretensions of Pantheism, that proud and foolish philosophy which pretends to penetrate to the Divine essence, to set out with the adequate definition of God, and to deduce from it the complete system and the universal evolution of beings? I assent to this also. But when, from the inconceivability of the essence of God, it is concluded that we know nothing at all about God; when instead of comprising in precise limits the science of things divine, that science is set aside altogether; I can go no further, and I enter my protest in the name of common sense. "The heavens declare the glory of God," this is the voice of common sense, and science in the depths of its analysis finds this principle, that the imperfect being has its reason in the perfect Being, and consequently that there must be in the perfect Being something that may be communicated to the imperfect being, and be to it a natural revelation of its principle.

Not that we know nothing of God, and are to annihilate theology.

God manifested.

To say that God has never manifested Himself, is to say that He is by His nature absolutely incommunicable. Now, if God were incommunicable, not only in His essence but in all that He is, God would then be the only possible being.

Not only the sceptics, but even the idealists and the mystics, those who deny life altogether, would be right in that case. Life is everywhere; I feel it in myself, I see it in the universe; and of all the forms under which it appears, the clearest, the most certain, and the purest, is intelligence. Intelligence is displayed in the whole universe. It is manifested among inferior beings by the laws which direct them unknown to themselves. It begins to work in the plants like a dim glimmer of life. It has the sentiment of itself in the beast. In man, finally, it knows itself, it possesses itself; it shines, and is resplendent. But even in man it acknowledges itself subject to the law of development and change, to ignorance, to error, to endeavour; and is consequently incapable of existing or subsisting by itself. There is then, above nature and man, a first principle of intelligence, and this principle must be intelligent, otherwise there would be less in the cause than in the effect, which would be inadmissible. All that is positive and real in the effect can only come from its cause. Properly, there belong to the effect only limits and relations. Now there is nothing more real, more positive, or more clear than intelligence. God is therefore absolute intelligence, perfect thought, truth in itself.

God is absolute intelligence.

As a general thesis, as truly God is incomprehensible in His essence, so truly He is accessible in His manifestations. I ascend to Him from the bosom of my own imperfection; and knowing that all that is real and positive in the imperfect being has its reason in the Perfect Being, it is enough for me to conceive aright the communicable

God is accessible in His manifestation, though incomprehensible in His essence.

powers of the Divine nature, to conceive them in all their plenitude under the forms of immensity and eternity.

Objections: I. To say that God's attributes are to be conceived under these forms, is to admit that they are inconceivable.

But, I am told, this is just what cannot be done. You forget that the human mind can conceive nothing that is not in space and time; therefore, to say that the attributes of God must be conceived under the form of immensity and eternity, is to say that they are in fact inconceivable. I acknowledge that space and time are the forms of imperfect existence, this is why reason can only conceive it under this double condition; but I say that reason has other objects, that while imposing on all the beings in the universe, the laws of time and space, she acknowledges herself independent of them. The proper objects of reason may be characterised as universality, eternity, and infinity, so that to submit reason and its objects to the laws of space and time is to deny reason and truth. Can we not conceive mathematical truths, and moral truths, as eternal and universal? Do we not know that before there were men injustice was an evil, and justice a good, as before there were circles the radii of a circle were equal? You will say that I, who think these things, think them in time, that if geometry be eternal, the geometrician is not so. True, but the privilege of this geometrician of a day, is to conceive distinctly eternity from the bosom of time; is to place himself beyond the finite by the contemplation of universal truths; is to perceive above the universe, beyond time and space, the divine type of the Eternal Geometrician.

2. Objection: We cannot understand an intelligence in action which is not conditioned by time.

2. If it be said that we cannot understand an active intelligence which is not subject to the conditions of time, I deny it. Thought in man, no doubt, is prevision, is recollection, is to reason, to reflect, to abstract, to pay tribute to time in every way. But these are only discursive operations, that is to say, means of assisting the weakness of our intuition. The essential of reason is intuition *sui conscia*. To see, and to be aware that we see, is the type of knowledge, is the divine model of which human thought is a feeble image. Thought in itself is then independent. Not only it has nothing in it repugnant to the nature of God, but it expresses, with a singular precision and clearness, the incomparable perfection, and the radiant beauty of that nature.

3. Objection. If we have a right to transfer to God all that is real and positive in being, we have no right to pick and choose.

3. At this rate, I am asked, if human reason can transport into God all that there is real and positive in imperfect beings, why choose this and reject that? Why not transport into God extension and duration, time and space, which are also surely something? I reply, that time and space are not real things, but ideal things; and as to duration and extension, I do not dispute that they are founded in reality, but they must not be confounded with the effective properties of beings. They have only an accidental and relative value, the proof of which is, that they cannot be thought as absolute. When you conceive time as absolute you must cut off its succession and so destroy it. On the contrary, when you conceive thought as absolute, you only take away its limits; you conceive it as a perfect intuition, that is to say, in all the purity of its essence.

This brings us to the end of the matter. There is a timid scepticism which, proclaiming God as indeterminable, fears to carry out its opinion, and dares not acknowledge either its first principle or its final consequence. Leaving these uncertain spirits, let us inquire of more daring reasoners whence they set out, and where they mean to end? This is their first principle, that thought never goes beyond the relative, and the necessary consequence is that the Absolute is absurd and contradictory.

First and last principle of thoroughgoing scepticism.

Hear Hamilton and his disciples, they will tell you that the law of thought and being is determination, and, consequently, negation and relation. A thing only exists on one condition, which is to be so and so, and to be conceived in such and such a relation with him who thinks. Thence it follows that every thinkable object must contain some negation, for, in order to be this, it cannot be that—some difference, for in order to have such a property, it must differ from that which has quite another property—and some relation, for, in order that I may think of an object, it must be present and within my reach. This being established, the Absolute, by its very definition, is unthinkable and impossible; in fact, the Absolute is that which eludes all negation, all difference, and all relation.

Error in Hamilton's proof that the absolute is unthinkable.

If I do not mistake, the whole system of these reasonings rests on an error common to scepticism and Pantheism, which formerly misled, and still deceives, many a superior mind. This error consists in imagining that every determination is a negation. *Omnis determinatio negatio est*, says Hamilton after Spinoza. Nothing can be falser

Falsehood of the principle "omnis determinatio negatio est.

or more arbitrary than this principle. It arises from the confusion of two things essentially different, namely, the limits of a being, and its determinate and constitutive characteristics. I am an intelligent being, and my intelligence is limited; these are two facts equally certain. The possession of intelligence is the constitutive characteristic of my being, which distinguishes me from the brute being. The limitation imposed on my intellect, which can only see a small number of truths at a time, is my limit, and this is what distinguishes me from the Absolute Being, from the Perfect Intelligence which sees all truths at a single glance. That which constitutes my imperfection is not, certainly, my being intelligent; therein, on the contrary, lies the strength, the richness, and the dignity of my being. What constitutes my weakness and my nothingness is, that this intelligence is enclosed in a narrow circle. Thus, inasmuch as I am intelligent, I participate in being and perfection; inasmuch as I am only intelligent within certain limits, I am inperfect.

Arising from the confusion of the *limits* of a being with its *constitutive* characteristics.

It follows from this very simple analysis that determination and negation, far from being identical, differ from each other as much as being and nothing. According as a being has more or less determinations, qualities, and specific characteristics, it occupies a rank more or less elevated in the scale of existence. Thus, in proportion as you suppress qualitiesand determinations, you sink from the animal to the vegetable, from the vegetable to brute matter. On the other hand, exactly in proportion as the nature of beings is complicated, in proportion as their bodies are enriched with new

So that *determination* is radically different from *negation*.

functions and organs, as their intellectual and moral faculties begin to be displayed, as more delicate senses are added to their grosser senses, to sensation, memory, to memory, imagination, then the superior faculties, reasoning, and reason, and will, you rise nearer and nearer to man, the most complicated being, the most determined and the most perfect in creation.

If man were to lose his intelligence, I ask you, would he thereby win perfection? Apparently not, and yet he would have one determination less. Do you find that the progress of human life, from infancy to virility, consists in the ever-increasing indetermination of its faculties? Quite the contrary. Perfection in man is the increase and development of faculties, the passing from power to act. Which is then the least real being? the being, so to speak, which is least a being? The most indetermined being; and, consequently, which is the most real being, the most perfect being, the being who is most a being? The most determinate being. In this sense, God is the only being absolutely determined. For there must be something indetermined in all finite beings, since they have always imperfect powers, which tend toward their development after an indefinite manner. God alone the complete Being, the Being in whom all powers are actualised, escapes by His own perfection from all progress, and development, and indetermination. It would be a pure illusion to imagine that different determinations could, by any chance, limit or contradict each other. Could intelligence prevent liberty? or the love of the beautiful extinguish the love of the good, or truth, or beauty, or happiness be any hindrance, the one to the other? Is it not evident, on the contrary, that these are things perfectly analogous and harmonious, which, far from excluding, require each other, which always go together in the best beings of the universe, and when they are conceived in their eternal harmony and plenitude, constitute the living unity of God?

Now, let us hear our sceptics. They say the Absolute excludes all limits, and, consequently, all determination. I reply, the Absolute has no limits, it is true, that is to say, that His being and the powers that are in Him are all full, complete, infinite, and eternal; but far from these determinations limiting His being, they characterise and constitute it.

But does not *determination* imply *relation?*

Does not every determination, say they, imply relation? By no means. If you call determination that which in imperfect beings belong to their original limitation, such as their duration, their material figure, their distance, I agree that these determinations are relative, and that an absolute duration, an absolute extension, an absolute distance are contradictory ideas; but if you come to intrinsic characters, to the constitutive qualities of beings, such as thought and activity, there is nothing here which implies a limit or a boundary—nothing, consequently, which is repugnant to the nature of the Absolute.

Thought in God is not a contradiction.

What, says Hamilton, is not the Absolute one, and does not thought imply diversity? Does it not suppose the difference between the subject which thinks and the object thought? not to mention several other conditions. I reply, you confound the real unity of God with the abstract unity of your imaginary Absolute. Doubtless, thought—living thought, real thought—implies the difference of subject and object. In this manner there is diversity in the divine thought; but this variety does not exclude unity, for in God the subject and the object are identical. A perfect being who thinks himself is not one in the sense of the unity of abstraction. He lives, he revolves upon himself; he has in him a sort of spiritual motion. But as this consciousness that the Perfect Being possesses this contemplation that He enjoys, supposes no separation between the subject and the object, no disproportion, no interval, no effort, no succession, there is nothing in it opposed to the most rigorous unity.

"To think of God is to limit Him"—this is untrue.

Hamilton proceeds: You agree that the essential condition of thought is the distinction of the subject and the object. The subject lays itself down on one side as the one who thinks, and it is opposed to the object which is thought. It follows that the Absolute escapes the grasp of the human mind for the human mind thinking the Absolute, as the subject places itself outside of it, and as the object places it in opposition to itself. Thus it destroys the Absolute. I grant that when a man thinks about God he makes himself distinct from Him, but to make oneself distinct from Him is not to be separated from Him. I think God as different from myself; that is not to think Him as finite, as limited by me, or relative to me. I think God as other than myself, but as the reason of my being. I distinguish myself from Him, but, at the same time, I link myself to Him.

You tell me that Schelling has admitted the

Pantheistic undetermined absolute is in contradiction with the fundamental laws of thought—not the determined and living God.

absurdity of such an intuition, that he has confessed that the notion of the Absolute, under the condition of consciousness, is a contradiction, and that the only method of knowing the Absolute is to be oneself absorbed into it. I give you up the intellectual intuition of Schelling and the Absolute of the Pantheists, which is an undetermined Absolute. I admit that such an Absolute is in contradiction with the fundamental law of thought and being, that it is unthinkable to the human mind and to itself. But then, this is but a vain abstraction, not the determined God, not the living God, who is intelligence, truth, and the eternal consciousness of thought.

Reductio ad absurdum of Hamilton.

You triumph when you see M. Schelling compelled, in order to justify his idea of the absolute, to invoke some strange ecstatic intuition, and to fall into a wild mysticism. But you are hastening yourself to an extremity quite as dangerous, quite as far from common sense. For after having proved that the Absolute, such as you understand Him, is indeterminable, you conclude that he is absolutely unintelligible. What does this conclusion signify? In plain words it signifies that the notion of God is absurd. You began by telling us that the human mind must believe in something unconditioned and Absolute, that the existence of God is consequently certain, that common sense has a reason for being religious, that all religions have their foundation in truth, and now you tell us that human thought can only think the relative, that the relative only can exist and be thought, and that all determination of the Absolute is contradictory. Then, not only all the philosophical systems that have tried to explain God have stopped below their ideal, but the ideal itself is a wild chimera. Not only every religious symbol is incomplete and insufficient, but every religious symbol is an extravagance. We may no longer say that human kind makes to itself symbols of God more or less pure; the very idea of a religious symbol is a contradiction; consequently, all religion is false and chimerical. Besides, how are we to estimate the value of these different symbols? There must be a criterion. You say that the symbols of one religion are infinitely richer that those of another—nobler, more expressive, more poetical. Poetical, that is just the word; you make religion an affair of the imagination. But the judge of poetry has his eye fixed on the ideal of the beautiful; you, on the contrary—critics without a criterion—have no fixed rule to measure the beautiful any more than the good; and you are obliged to say at last that truth in matters of religion, as in matters of art, and in every order of thought, is not made for man. Then what means that divine origin, that superior destiny, which you attribute to it? The words divine and heavenly have no sense from your lips. They only call up an illusion, and, if you are right, the best service one could do to humanity would be to cure it of this illusion once for all. What is emptier than an investigation which knows that it is objectless? what more fragile than a love without hope? There is, you say, an exquisite pleasure in the search, and, besides, we need not trouble ourselves, men will be always sufficiently curious to persist in it. Yes, as long as they are believing, as long as they are persuaded that truth and goodness are not illusions. As soon as you shall have persuaded them of this, they will sink into incuriousness and torpor.

Whatever you may say, this refined delight in a useless search can only be attained by a small number of chosen spirits, intoxicated with a superabundant ardour which conceals from them the real consequences of absolute scepticism—I mean indifference. History is there to warn us. It is two thousand years since Heraclitus said with graceful melancholy, "We cannot bathe twice in the same stream; everything becomes, nothing remains." Soon after came Pyrrho, who completed thus the formula of Heraclitus: "There is nothing that is more false than true, more beautiful than ugly, more good than bad." All is relative. No; all is not relative; all is not given up to change. There is one truth which remains, and that living truth is God.

Third Meditation.

Can there be anything but God?

I HAVE set myself free from a harassing difficulty. I have placed my belief in God beyond the shadow of a doubt. My God is not an undetermined something, which thought cannot seize, an empty form without contents, substance without quality, thought without consciousness and without ideas, being without existence, a phantom which only appears to man's bewildered gaze to drag him into a vain pursuit, or to lead him to an unfathomable abyss. The God of my consciousness is the Being who is truly perfect, finished in all the powers of His being, determinate, real, living. His life, as far as I can comprehend it, is the life of intelligence, the full possession of truth, the perfect thought apprehending the perfect being, and apprehending itself without intervention, without effort, with one simple, single, eternal, equal act. And must this thought be solitary, and, so to speak, egotistic, absorbed in itself, solely occupied with itself? That were strange. And yet how can we explain that the Divine thought can come out of itself to conceive anything beyond itself?

How can the Absolute not be all?

Anything, I say, anything but God. For God is the perfect and infinite being, and beyond the perfect being who possesses all the powers of being, nothing is possible, nothing can be conceived. I cannot elude this difficulty. It met me at the moment when scepticism told me that to think about the Absolute was to make myself distinct from Him, and consequently to deny Him as absolute; for how can the Absolute being be anything but the whole of being, and where is there room for anything besides Himself? Here is the great mystery.

From the idea of perfect being it is impossible to deduce the possibility of the imperfect being. It seems indeed strange to be told that God being given, all other beings follow as a matter of course. This is to place oneself at the antipodes of truth, to conceive God as insufficient to Himself, as a dark hidden germ which needs to be developed. But the real difficulty is this. God is a perfect being eternally complete. How can there be anything else than God?

I can conceive that a finite thinking being should imagine something beyond himself; that is to say, finite beings like himself. Or again, I can conceive that such a being, seeing himself incomplete, should imagine an extension, or possible increase of his being. But that the infinite and perfect Being, who lives in Himself with a perfect life, should think of anything but Himself, is what I cannot conceive. There are mysteries everywhere. I hardly know that God exists, and I find myself face to face with the mystery of

His inaccessible essence. I have just satisfied myself, not without labour and trouble, that God is a perfect idea, which embraces all that is and all that can be; and when I seek to understand how God can conceive other beings than Himself, I feel my sight grow dim.

Experience to be consulted as well as pure reason.

Shall I then stop short? And because my reason, in its efforts to conceive the origin and order of things, has met with an insurmountable obstacle, must I despair, and weakly forego the search? No; pure reason is not my whole reason; I can still call experience to my aid; for I am not a celestial being disengaged from earthly ties, and formed to contemplate face to face the Divine essence; I am an intelligence joined to senses, and surely it were not too much to make use of all the collected powers of my nature in order to throw some light on this darkest of all problems.

I feel myself live, and think. I see around me millions of beings who display their activity in space and duration. The earth and the skies, motion and life, my equals and myself, are not vain shadows. Therefore there is not a doubt that the imperfect being exists, and if it has being, I conclude that before being it was a possibility. When I say before being, I do not mean to decide whether it began to exist. That is of little consequence. From the moment that such and such a being is granted as imperfect, it follows that the possibility of that being is logically anterior to its reality. For being imperfect, consequently not having in itself the reason of its existence, it cannot exist without an anterior condition. Even if going backward through all time, I could not find its beginning, its existence would not the less depend upon a condition which is beyond it, and which governs it, and that condition is independent of duration, it is eternal. It is quite evident that the perfect being is the only one that can elude this law. He has in Himself the reason of His own being, therefore it does not depend on an anterior condition, but the contingent being can only exist by finding without itself the reason of its existence; and this is what I call its possibility.

For, granted the existence of a contingent and imperfect being; in order to exist it must have a possibility, it must have beyond and without it a reason for its existence, and that reason must be independent of time. Then since this imperfect being actually exists, whether or not it ever began to exist is of little consequence, for there must have been an eternal possibility of its existence. Now where is the origin of this eternal possibility of imperfect beings—this eternal reason for their existence? Clearly in God—since God, we know, is the reason of existence in all that exists. And since God is intelligent, knowing Himself perfectly, and all that is in Him, how should He not know this eternal possibility of beings? Hence I conclude, not by a direct and immediate intuition of my reason, but in an indirect manner, and with the assistance of all my means of knowledge combined, that there is in the divine intelligence beyond the eternal consciousness of the perfect being, the idea of the eternal possibility of the imperfect being, an idea which embraces all possible existences.

Now by what connection this eternal possibility of the imperfect being is united to the existence of the perfect being, is a secret hidden from every human eye—a mystery buried in the furthest depths of the Divine essence. God alone knows why God exists. God alone knows why anything but God is eternally possible. The reason of the being of God, and the reason of the eternal possibility of the imperfect being, are two enigmas linked one to the other, alike impenetrable. But this hinders me not from knowing three things certainly—that the Perfect Being exists, and contains within Himself the reason of His existence; that imperfect beings are possible; and that the reason of this possibility forms an integral part of the Divine thought. Thus, then, my thought has cast a bridge between God and the world. Still I hesitate as I set my foot upon it, and fear to trust it; for, is it not a flagrant contradiction to suppose that God, the perfect being, should think within Himself of anything but Himself? If this were but a difficulty I would pass on, but a contradiction arrests me.

The imperfect a possible expression of infinite perfection—not a limit or prolongation.

Let me examine it again. This is the point of the question. It seems that the imperfect being can only be conceived in two modes as distinct from the perfect being—as a limit or as a prolongation. But these two suppositions are equally absurd; for the infinite and perfect Being cannot, as infinite, be limited, as perfect, be prolonged or expanded. Still I think I perceive a way to solve the difficulty. Certainly the imperfect being cannot limit or prolong the perfect Being, but it can express Him—manifest Him by His image. Nor is this idea a phantom which arouses and deceives my imagination; it is rather a gleam which enlightens my reason, and dissipates my doubts. The more I reflect the more I think I perceive clearly that the perfect Being thinking Himself, thinks also the imperfect being, not as a prolongation, not as a limit, but as a possible expression of His existence. And why should not the eternal Being be eternally capable of expression? Why, outside eternity, should there not be time which is its image? Why, outside immensity, shall there not be extent to express its grandeur? Why, outside the perfect thought, the eternal reason, the shadowless light that burns eternally—why should there not be imperfect intelligences to reflect some of its rays? I may then, with all safety, cross the bridge that I have constructed between God and the universe. God alone exists eternally, but the universe is eternally possible. God conceives it eternally, conceiving Himself. He conceives it as a possible expression of His infinite perfection.

This is the sum of the whole matter. I do not understand why God exists, nor how the possibility of imperfect being is connected with the existence of the perfect Being, but I am certain that it contains no contradiction, and that is enough, if not to satisfy my insatiable curiosity on divine things, at least to settle the doubts in my mind, and to give a little light and repose to its restless ardour.

Fourth Meditation.

God the Creator.

—o—

I THOUGHT I saw a ray of light amid the obscurity of the problem of creation. Let me turn towards that light, which is still weak and uncertain; I shall see it perhaps grow larger and become more steady.

I know now, without the shadow of a doubt, that God thinks the universe eternally, as a possible manifestation of the communicable powers of His existence; can I suppose that God would remain indifferent, or powerless, in presence of this image of Himself? An indifferent God, a powerless God, would be strange hypotheses; but before discussing them *à priori*, there is one fact that resolves the question. The universe exists. God has not remained powerless or indifferent before the image of the universe eternally impressed on His intelligence. He resolved to realise it—He had power to effect it; and He made use of that power, because He was not indifferent, because He saw that the universe was good, because He is good Himself, and because He loves all that is like Him.

But let me not go too fast in these uncertain and perilous paths. I represent to myself a God

Am I authorised in speaking of will, resolution, and love in God?

who wills, a God who resolves, a God who loves; but is not this to attribute to the perfect Being the imperfect modes of my own being? God has first appeared to me as a father, who desires to produce a living image of Himself, to see a witness of His fecundity grow and increase. But is not this image, which seems to me august and touching, infinitely beneath the ineffable perfection of the absolute Being? Is it not a pious superstition of my heart, or rather an illusion of my pride, and a degradation of the Divine essence? When we look at things with the cool eye of reason, can love be conceived in the perfect Being? The perfect Being is sufficient of Himself, and love is an aspiration towards an object foreign to ourselves—an effort to ennoble and complete our being, by uniting it to another being, equal or superior. Love is then the sign of an imperfect nature, and cannot be conceived in a complete and infinite being.

I perceive the difficulty, but it presents itself in vain; a secret instinct within me protests, and tells me that love as well as intelligence is something divine. I can see but dimly, yet I feel with an irresistible force, that there must be in love, along with its terrestrial and human part, a celestial and divine part; and I seek now, as before, to divide its pure essence from its separable accidents.

The love of God.

From the moment that I feel my existence, I feel that I love; I love to live—I love to think—I love to love. All my powers please and delight me, and I am happy to employ them; but every where I meet with obstacles: I feel that I must endure and struggle. My whole life is made up of this. A feeling of power which makes me happy, and a feeling of impotence which weighs me down and torments me—a need of evolving my faculties, and a weary effort to overcome the obstacles that I meet—such is my own actual condition. And this is an epitome of the drama of the universe, where there are everywhere powers which limit each other and strive together, which have here the joy of triumph, there the weakness and the torments of impotence and defeat.

It is a universal law that every being loves to be, and seeks to maintain and develope its being; but if the love of being is inherent in being, is it possible to conceive that the perfect Being could be indifferent to be or not to be? God is, He thinks Himself, He knows Himself to be perfect, how should He not love to be and to think? Whence comes the law that unites everywhere love and being, if it does not reside in the very first principle of all love and of all being? And is there anything in love and joy repugnant to this Divine essence? He knows Himself, He possesses Himself, He loves Himself, He enjoys His thought and His perfection: from thence springs a felicity which is sublime, incomparable, the complete type of all felicity.

Imperfection of human love.

Love in the imperfect being is accompanied by desire, by the need of developing and completing its being—so its joy is mingled with sadness, its hope with fear, its possession with dissatisfaction. Its power of loving can never be fully satisfied, obstacles are constantly rising, and when there are none the beloved object fails to yield what it sought, and it wanders from object to object, always seeking, and after a hundred vanished

Divine love.

illusions, always hoping for the peace and the satisfaction which always eludes its grasp.

In the perfect Being on the contrary there is one sole love which finds eternally its object, and possesses it without effort, a love accompanied by an eternal joy. Nor is there in these ideas of love and joy and possession anything involuntarily profane, or which my reason should mistrust, for reason tells me that the essence of love is divine, that the first principle of love is in God, and my heart supporting my reason tells me that there is nothing purer or more divine than joy in the possession of the perfect life.

And now new lights appear, and I see a little clearer into the mysterious depths of the origin of things. If God is love, if God loves His being, if He loves thought, love, joy, felicity, how should He remain indifferent, before those beings, infinite in number, whose idea made a part of the consciousness that He had of Himself, of those beings which, each according to its nature, according to the form and degree of its power, reflects and expresses in different manners the perfections of the Creator? And if God loves these beings before they exist, because loving Himself He loves all that resembles Him, if God loves these beings, why should he refuse them reality? for this God must be impotent, the most absurd of all suppositions, belied both by the idea of the all-perfect Being, and by the existence of the universe, that undeniable witness of the fecundity of God. Thus, little by little, a kind of idea of the creation forms itself in my mind—a very imperfect idea of mingled light and shade, where I must be content to let dark mysteries lie beside shining truths, aiming only at putting away contradictions, and overstepping the limits of invincible ignorance.

Thus, then, the world, eternally thought as a possible manifestation of the Perfect Being, is in some sort the ideal and divine matter of creation. The agent is the absolute power of God, and love is the motive which inspired Him, and the reason which determined Him to come forth out of Himself. Therefore this universe is a work of power, of intelligence, and of love. Intelligence has eternally conceived its germ, love has brooded upon it, power has given it expansion.

OBJECTIONS OF A PANTHEIST.

The state of mind among Pantheists.

As long as I keep it to myself the idea that I have formed of the creative act is perfectly satisfactory. I congratulate myself on having regained by an effort of reflection the gift and the happiness of faith. But as soon as I permit my thoughts to venture forth and plunge again into the troubled atmosphere, where one breathes only doubt, contradiction, and sarcasm, in spite of myself I fall anew into uncertainty. I see one of my friends long enslaved by the doctrines of Plotinus, Spinoza, and Hegel, smiling at the very name of God the Creator.

A Personal God—as conceived by modern Religious Philosophy—accused of being an old superstition dressed up.

"It is rather late," says he, "to go back to the old Theodicea. He must be a bold man who expects to succeed where Leibnitz has failed. We have done with all that: you must leave in the abysses of the past, the personal God, the God who creates by chance or through benevolence, the solitary and capricious artist who wakens up now and then from his sleep, and takes pleasure in his work. These are pious creeds, I grant, touching symbols, but to speak the truth, pure superstitions. Now, when we come to superstitions, the simplest are the best, and you by your refinements, only despoil popular superstitions of their fascination and their poetry, by trying in vain to clothe them in the severe forms of science.

The universe *is* God.

"Look at what has been passing in the world for two centuries. Science has destroyed for ever the distinction between God and the universe. God is the universe united to its eternal first principle, the universe is the living God, the infinite evolution of divine life. This is what science tells us, all the rest is imagination and sentiment."

Pantheistic dilemma.

"Let us discuss the matter seriously. I propose to you this alternative;—your God is conceived as *either* creating the universe out of Himself, and this hypothesis is big with a thousand contradictions; *or* your God creates the universe in Himself, and therefore the universe is Himself, is His life, and so far you agree with us.

Or to view it in another light—If you conceive God as living in Himself, and wholly sufficient to Himself, you are driven to admit that the work of creation is an accident, or a thoughtless caprice; or, if you acknowledge that such a manner of conceiving things is puerile and absurd, you must unite the creation again to the Creator, you must confess that God conceives and loves the world eternally, therefore the creation is eternal, therefore it is part of God, being His necessary manifestation; and here again you agree with us. You must take your choice, for between the God of superstition and the God of science there is no medium.

"We need not argue formally to prove that your idea of a personal God, coming out of the sphere of His being to manifest Himself beyond it, creating for any reason a world that He need not have created, is an anti-scientific idea; for if there is anything evident in the world it is that a being who acts out of Himself is a finite being, for if He were really infinite there would be nothing real or possible beyond Him. Action exercised out of oneself, or, as the schools say, transitive action, is the effect of a cause that oversteps the boundaries of its own being to act upon an exterior term, as a sculptor hews a block of marble. You would not make of your God an artist fashioning chaotic matter at His will. You are too much of a philosopher not to leave chaos to mythology. But take care. The Nous of Anaxagoras lending regular motion to the inert mass of similar parts; the Demiurgos of Plato setting on the bosom of matter the luminous impression of the ideas of the good and the beautiful; even the profounder and more scientific doctrine of Aristotle, I mean that of an eternal world which moves by virtue of its secret aspirations toward a solitary happy God, who attracts all beings and knows them not;—all these things are as much behind the age as the theogony of Hesiod.

Creation would make God finite.

"Transitive action."

"But you will say, God has no need of matter

to form the world; that ideal matter, which is only the world conceived eternally in His thought, is sufficient. Granted; but you only put off the difficulty, you do not destroy it. You set it aside for a while to fall on you again with all its weight. God, you say, thinks the world eternally; but what is the world? Is it anything beside God? This is just the difficulty; your fatal stumbling-block. It is no more possible for God to think than to do anything out of Himself, for out of Himself there is nothing.

Theistic God is man idealised.

The individualised God is not infinite.

"You must in honesty acknowledge that your personal God is a determined separate being, more powerful and more intelligent than man, but of the same species; in fact, an idealised man. He has consciousness; He says I; and these things attest a separate existence, which is distinct from that which it is not, which is concentrated in itself, and possesses its own individuality. Your God is an individual. He is some one, or some thing. He is not the Being, the infinite, universal, absolute Being, He who is, He in whom we all have being, life, and motion. You make to yourself a superb idol which inhabits the heights of heaven, but by that very idea you limit Him to a place. In vain you load Him with brilliant gifts and magnificent attributes. He is but a poor child's toy beside the Infinite Being who has no place but immensity, no duration but eternity; who, far from being contained, contains in Himself space and time, who is comparable to nothing, resembles nothing, is distinct from nothing; for He holds and envelopes all. This is God; the

God of manly reason, and of free enlarged science."

"We are willing to say that He is a Creator, a cause; not a transitive, but an absolute and immanent cause. He creates the world within Himself, and thenceforth there is no separation of the Creator and the creature; for the creature is still the Creator considered in His eternal and necessary action. Take away the world there only remains an abstraction, the being in itself, the potential being. But as it is, the potential passes into actual being, the universal Being becomes successively all particular beings, which are only the *momenta* of His life, the inexhaustible forms of His essence. Nothing is separated, all beings are the acts of one and the same principle, and compose one and the same harmonious tissue which is Divine life."

God immanent, not transitive cause.

"But how will you pass from your idea of a personal God to that of the universe? Will you be satisfied with the infantine thought that God bethought Himself one day that He would create the world? But if God is complete without the world, if He lives in Himself a perfect happy life, needing nothing beyond Himself, why should He go out of Himself? You will have to acknowledge that the creative act in God is something fortuitous and miraculous. If you do not say that God is indifferent to the creation, that the being or non-being of creatures is identical to Him, that creation adds nothing to His happiness or to His perfection; if you do not say this, if, pressed by the laws of science, you try to join effect to cause by some intelligible relation, you

God infinite and absolute.

must say that God creates from love or from duty. Now, without noticing what is palpably human in these images, cannot you see that if God loves He cannot be without what He loves; if to create is better than not to create, God cannot but obey His wisdom which shows Him the best, His holiness which forbids the wrong? And thus the world is necessary to God either as an object of love or duty, and thus God without the world is an incomplete God, a God to whom something essential is wanting, a power without effect, a cause without activity, a wisdom without object, a love without effusion; and thus the world is as necessary to God as God is to the world. Without God no world, without the world no God. God and the world are mutually complementary, and realize each other. Let us hear no more of a personal God, living in Himself, distinct from the universe. Instead of this phantom let us recognize the true God, the God who is neither a thing nor a person, but the impersonal and universal principle of every person and every thing, the God who inhabits not the heavens, but whom the earth and the heavens inhabit—the Immense, the Eternal, the Infinite, the Absolute, the Being of beings."

Who are they that speak thus? not only one or two Hegelians of my acquaintance; to-day it is one of my friends, to-morrow another; for these opinions are too common. Issuing from the German schools, they have made their way to France, England, Italy, through all Europe. I find them alike in serious books and frivolous ones, with learned men and critics, with poets and romancers, even in after-dinner talk. Rejected under this

Prevalence of these views.

or that particular form, they still make their way, as a general tendency, seeking to substitute a vague religiosity for the little dogmatic faith that still exists.

Of this flood of Pantheistic ideas I can only say, that it is as impossible for me to deny their existence, as to share in their attraction. I grant to my friends the Spinozists and Hegelians, that they excel in bringing out the difficulty of a God distinct from the world. I will go further; I will acknowledge that Pantheism is a seductive conception, and, as it were, an eternal temptation to the metaphysical mind. In fact, it satisfies that need of finding unity which is felt by speculative reason. It charms our reason to find a first principle, from which all things are deduced as a necessary consequence. But the search of truth is no intellectual play, no mere satisfaction in the regular movement of ideas, but an earnest seeking for the truth with all the powers of our being.

Pantheism seductive to speculative reason.

Its primary dilemma.

The more I think over the problem of creation and the Pantheistic idea, the more I am satisfied that the difficulties about the creation only arise from the diversity and defectiveness of our means of knowledge, while the Pantheistic idea contains in itself such absolute contradictions that no logical mind could hold it. The *fort* of Pantheists, the grand argument on which they build their thesis of immanence, so popular beyond the Rhine, is reduced to this: To be the cause of the universe, God must be the transitive or immanent cause of it. There is no middle course, for to say that God does not form the universe out of Himself is to say that He forms it within Himself. Now, God does not form the universe out of Himself, for out of God, out of the Absolute and Infinite, nothing can exist, or be conceived to exist: the very words *out of God* are a contradiction. God then forms the world within Himself; He produces it of His own substance; He animates it with His own life; in a word, He is its cause, eternally and necessarily acting—a cause not separated from its effect—but realizing itself by its effects, the immanent cause: *Deus omnium rerum causa immanens non vero transiens.*

Pantheism anthropomorphic also.

This is their decisive, victorious, triumphant reasoning. Yet, I tell those who are satisfied with it that they are the dupes of a strange illusion. What do they do? They consider the things of this world, the things of time and space, and amongst the different modes of action that they find, they choose out one and want to impose it on the Creator of the universe. As if absolute activity could be subject to the conditions of finite activity—as if the relations of finite things, one with the other, could be compared to the relation of the finite with the infinite. Strange to say, these Pantheists who accuse their adversaries of humanizing God, fall themselves into anthropomorphism, and the philosophers of the absolute are caught in the very act of superstition.

Transitive cause—must have matter.

To prove this, it is sufficient to show how the spectacle of the imperfection of relative causes raises us to the idea of the absolute and creative cause. Chained by our senses to this material world, reason at first only grasps causes in their grossest and most common action—the action of a power on an external object. The river flows; it bears away my load with it. The branch of a tree crosses my path; I break it or turn it aside. I can do more. Here is a piece of clay; I mould it and give it the form that I choose. All human industry is in this. James Watt, with some coal and some water, produces a new and inexhaustible source of motion. Michael Angelo draws his Moses from a block of granite; here is the transitive cause.

Immanent cause.

But a cause of this kind, however powerful it be, can only act with the help of matter foreign to itself. Without marble and without chisel where were Michael Angelo? But there are causes whose energy has something more intimate and more profound. They are productive without coming out of themselves. A grain of corn germinates; an oak spreads out its roots; a flower unfolds. This is a beautiful sight, yet these are but a gross and material development. I can conceive evolutions of a much higher order; the thought of genius germinates and expands in a superior intellect: Newton conceives the system of the world. Here is the immanent cause; and unquestionably this spiritual fecundity of an intellect that seems to owe all to itself is the sublimest type of activity that man and the universe can produce.

Both imperfect as needing materials, and do not exhaust causes.

Does it follow that we have exhausted all possible forms of activity, and that we must attribute one of these to the Infinite Being? Evidently not. Immanent activity, producing its work within itself, is certainly superior to transitive activity, and I admit that to conceive God as a power reduced to impress movement on independent and eternal corpuscles, is to go back to the days of Anaxagoras;

also, to represent God as a skilful architect, as a great artist embellishing matter by the imprint of His ideas, is a symbol infinitely defective. But even the forms of immanent activity, though of a higher order, are imperfect forms which cannot be transported into the absolute, eternal Being. A grain of corn is a marvel—granted; but it needs light, and air, and water. It developes itself—true; but in virtue of a power which is not its own, and on condition of finding around it conditions favourable to its development. Newton himself is subject to a thousand external conditions; he must have the world to contemplate, and an instrument to make his calculations with. Imagine even a pure spirit, an angel, speculating on abstract ideas, his ideas must come from a higher source; without them he can do nothing.

To assimilate God to an "immanent cause" is to degrade Him.

Immanent activity, then, such as we find it in the universe, is not independent of external conditions. Let us look at the thing closer. There is nothing more opposed to the idea of perfection than the idea of a being who developes himself, a germ that struggles for expansion. This is where the Pantheists deceive themselves; they cannot see that to assimilate God to the immanent activities of the universe is to make of Him a being who developes himself, consequently an imperfect being,—is to fall infinitely below God. To act within oneself or without oneself are forms of finite activity. The language here is singularly expressive. Without—within; these words suppose finite beings, limited in space and time, much more in the radical conditions of their existence. But God is the Infinite, Eternal, Perfect, Complete

Being. Nothing finite is then properly without or within God; the imperfect being and the Perfect Being cannot bear any relation of this kind to each other. God is the complete Being; the world is being in the way of development; God is in eternity, the world is in time. Can one conceive that time is without or within eternity? it were a manifest absurdity. Such a century is outside such another century, precedes or continues it; such a day contains within itself a certain number of hours, which compose its total duration; but time is not a sequel to eternity; the moments of time do not make up eternity. Time is, then, neither within nor without eternity, and yet there is a reason for its existence.

Imperfect being properly neither "within" nor "without" perfect.

In the same way, the imperfect being, the being who developes himself, is properly neither without nor within the perfect being eternally developed. He does not continue him, nor is his eternal development, and yet he has his reason for his existence—a most mysterious and incomparable, but, at the same time, certain and demonstrable relation.

Illustration from time and space.

Here the Pantheists meet me. Explain this relation, they say; "you call it mysterious that you may not be driven to confess that it is unintelligible and contradictory." I deny the contradiction—the unintelligibility is another question. Where, I ask, is the contradiction? It consists, according to you, in setting down God as a Perfect Being, embracing all the powers of existence, and admitting that there can be anything beside God. I reply that there would be a contradiction if the imperfect being was set down as a prolongation of the Perfect Being. But this is not the case; time is not a prolongation of eternity, nor space of immensity. The finite thought which developes itself is not a prolongation of the infinite thought eternally developed.

This will help us, if not to understand, at least to perceive, the relation of these two terms, for I can clearly conceive that time manifests and expresses eternity. Plato has said that time is the mobile image of eternity, and this profound thought, passing from philosophy to poetry, has become accessible to common sense. And this is not to be wondered at; for if nothing is more sublime, nothing at the same time is more familiar, than this opposition, and this harmony of time and eternity. It is the opposition and the harmony of heaven and earth—of things human and things divine. Every one perceives that time is a different thing from eternity, and that time is not, and cannot be, a prolongation of infinite eternity, nor a development of motionless eternity. And yet time exists outside of eternity. Time has the reason of its being in eternity, and eternity has its image in time. In the same manner, extension, with its infinite variety of forms and movements, expresses the immensity of the motionless and invisible Creator. In general, the life of nature and that of man—I mean the endeavour of being to feel, to think, to enjoy, to rise incessantly towards a larger and purer form of existence—expresses and manifests the divine life—I mean the full possession of being in the bosom of thought, of love, of joy, and of felicity.

"You are the dupe of a metaphor," say the Pantheists; you substitute for the unintelligible word creation the words expression and manifestation, which seem to you clearer, but they are only clear as applied to man. Man expresses his thought—he speaks; he speaks to make himself understood. Speech, then, supposes two persons at least conversing, and between them a material means of expression. I reply that there is, besides material and sensible speech, an internal speech, of which we find some trace in our thoughts. It is this spiritual language that I imagine in God. Eternally He sees time and space and the universe. He sees in time the expression of His eternity; in space, the expression of His immensity; in the universe, the expression of all the communicable forms of His Infinite Being, and He takes pleasure in this image, and He realises it by an act of love, enlightened by wisdom and wrought out by almighty power. He realises it; how, pray? I humbly confess that I do not know, and, to speak the truth, I have no difficulty in confessing my ignorance on the *how* of creation, when I think that so many other, so much nearer to me, *hows*—the *how* of the union of soul and body, the *how* of the communication of the simplest motion, leave me in invincible ignorance.

Here, then, is a fresh mystery, a new blank to fill up in the human science of things divine; to the mystery of the inaccessible essence of God, to the mystery of the eternal possibility of imperfect being, is added the mystery of the how of creation. Three mysteries bound the one to the other, three mysteries as impenetrable the one as the other: three mysteries, I say, but not one contradiction.

Three mysteries.

After this honest discussion on the capital point of the question, I shall not stop long at a secondary difficulty. "Is your creator God," ask the Pantheists, "a creator by accident, or by nature, by caprice, or by necessity?" You reject a fortuitous and accidental creation; you deny that freedom of indifference which makes of the divine will, the capricious arbiter of good and evil, of beauty and deformity, and which is forced to deify chance under the name of divine liberty. That is well enough, but then the creative act has its reason in the nature of God; it is as necessary as God Himself; one cannot conceive activity without the creative act, nor the creative act without its effect, the creature. Creative activity—the creative act, creation—these form an indivisible whole, and you must come to the conclusion that there is no real distinction between God and the universe, between the infinite and the finite—the universe being only God considered in his life, as God is only the universe considered in its unity.

The universe is the *manifestation*, not the *development* of God.

My reply shall be very simple: If even the universe were the natural and necessary manifestation of God, that would not signify that it was His development. Superficial eyes will only see a shade between the two words, but the difference of the two conceptions is immeasurable. On one side, a perfect, complete, personal God who is sufficient to Himself, who does but express His perfection by creating the world, but who without the world would be equally perfect. On the other side, a God who is altogether in power, and nothing in act; a germ which developes itself, and which is only realised by development; a God who, minus the world, is reduced to a pure potentiality and an abstract possibility. This is the first capital distinction between the true God and the chimera of the Pantheist. More than that, when I say that the creative act is a natural and necessary expression of the divine life, I do not speak of a blind necessity, of an absolute necessity, of that Pantheistic necessity which insists that the primitive germ of things must develope itself without will or knowledge to be realised in nature and humanity; I speak of a suitable moral necessity, a necessity based upon wisdom and love, the holy necessity of an Infallible Impeccable Being, who cannot do wrong, and who moreover does necessarily all that He does.

And now, he were no philosopher who should deny that there must be a difficulty in understanding how, in the bosom of the creative act, there exists love without want, and liberty without the moral possibility of doing otherwise. But this granted, I turn again upon the Pantheists, and tell them that I am about to show in their system not only difficulties, confusion, and defects, but impossibilities, absurdities, and contradictions.

True view of Pantheism, as distinguished from Atheism and Mysticism.

I shall state in the first place plainly, the leading idea of Pantheism. Pantheism has been sometimes understood as the absorption of the infinite into the finite, at other times, on the contrary, as the absorption of the finite into the infinite; both these ideas are false. The absorption of the infinite into the finite, of God into nature, is an attempt to deny the infinite, to reduce everything to the universe, it is Atheism. The absorption of the finite into the infinite is an effort to deny the finite, to reduce everything to God; it is Mysticism. Pantheism is a more profound system, it is an attempt to keep at an equal distance from mysticism and atheism.

That this attempt should be in vain, that Pantheism should necessarily fall into one of these alternatives is, in my mind, its condition, its necessary law, and its condemnation. But if Pantheism ends there, it does not begin there. It begins by wanting to bring God and nature, the finite and the Infinite, to the unity of one single, identical existence.

According to Pantheism, nature without God is but an effect without a cause, a mode without substance, a shadow without reality; and God without nature is but a cause without effect, a substance without mode, a power without life; from the bosom of motionless eternity, of infinite immensity, of the almighty cause, of the being without limits, there break unceasingly an infinite variety of contingent and imperfect beings, which succeed either in time, which are in juxtaposition in space, ever coming from God, ever aspiring to return to Him. God and nature are not two beings, but the single being under a double aspect. Here unity multiplied, there multiplicity which unites itself again to unity. On the one side is the *natura naturans*, on the other, the *natura naturata*. The true being is not in the finite or the infinite, he is their eternal, necessary, and indivisible co-existence.

Various formulæ of Pantheism, with an underlying identity.

This is Pantheism. You may vary the formulas *ad infinitum*, as you take them from the East, or from Greece, or from modern Europe. You may say with one philosopher, that nature is an overflow of the absolute unity; with another, that God is the eternal coincidence of contraries; with a third, that nature is a collection of modes of which God is the substance; or, again, that the finite and the infinite, and contradictories, in general, are identical; but under every variety of formula, through all the changes and progressions of Pantheism, analysis finds one single conception always the same, and that conception is, the necessary and eternal co-existence of the finite and the infinite.

Pantheism in history.

History teaches us what is the necessary development and the inevitable result of this idea; and she only declares, in strong characters, the laws of the human mind, and the real nature of things. History shows that everywhere, and at all times, in the East, and in Greece, at Athens, as at Alexandria, in the modern world, and in the ancient, Pantheism has always been led either to deny the proper reality and individuality of finite beings, and to concentre all life and existence in God, which is the mysticism of the Oriental religions, and of Plotinus and Jacob Boehme; or to give their individuality to the world and to man, and to reduce God to an abstraction, which is the atheism of Epicurus, of Hobbes, and of their contemporaneous disciples. There is nothing in this which does not find its reason in the constitution of the human mind. In fact, a metaphysical system only exists on one condition, that is, to give a reason for the nature of beings, for their most essential conditions, for their most intimate relations. You have hardly done anything when you have set down, in a general way, God, nature, and humanity. You must determine all these conceptions. You must say what God is, whether or not He has attributes, what is His manner of being. You must explain yourself on finite things, on the precise degree of their existence. It is useless to view with complacency the logical arrangement of notions, you must pay your tax to experience, you must give a reason for the realities of this world. Not only the visible universe strikes our senses, but the human consciousness, always present, makes its imperious language heard. The mind has its laws, the heart has its needs; the soul has its inspirations, its impulses, its mysterious presentiments. Every system of philosophy must collect these facts, and make allowance for them.

Radical vice of Pantheism.

Here Pantheism meets with insurmountable difficulties. It recognises the existence of the finite and the infinite, and so far it is in harmony with the laws of the human mind and the aspirations of universal consciousness. But the human race is not satisfied with asserting nature and God; it believes in a nature which is not peopled with phantoms but with effective things, with living powers; it believes in a God who is not an abstraction or a sign in algebra, but a living, active, productive God. Such is the faith of the human race, and, whether it will or no, Pantheism must account for it. All its most celebrated partisans have tried to do so. But if Pantheism is obliged to come into contact with real life, it is not less imperiously obliged to remain faithful to the conditions of its essence. Now, the essence of Pantheism is the reduction of the finite and the infinite, of nature and God, into one absolute unity. According to us the difficulty is insoluble, or rather the contradiction is radical. On the one hand, the human mind and universal consciousness demand a real God and a real nature; on the other, Pantheism requires the reduction of all beings to unity. If God is not to be merely abstract and indeterminate, He must have attributes, and these attributes must have motion and life; but then these modes, these attributes, these determinations of God, being only God himself, nature is absorbed in Him; there is no longer any nature, there is nothing but the life of God. On the other side, if nature is to have its proper reality, and it be admitted that the beings of this world have a certain consistency and a certain individuality, what becomes, then, of the reality of God? God is henceforth only a name, a sign. He disappears—he vanishes. In one word, Pantheism is condemned to this alternative, to diminish and impoverish the divine existence in order to give reality to the universe, or to annihilate the existence of visible things in order to concentrate all actual existence in God.

Fundamental difficulty.

I insist on this fundamental point, and, to show it in a stronger light, I shall choose narrower ground and concentrate the difficulty on a precise problem.

Reality of *minds*.

Among the attributes which the human race recognises in God, there is none more striking or more august than intelligence; among the beings which people this universe, there is no existence more certain or better known than that of intellectual beings. There is then an infinite intelligence, and there are imperfect limited intelligences which conceive and adore in God the plenitude and the perfection of intellect. Pantheism is obliged to recognise these two sorts of intellect, and at first it does not seek to deny them. But it is not enough to recognise them, we must conceive their co-existence and determine their relation. The problem is difficult and formidable to any system, but Pantheism finds in it a special difficulty. In fact, while laying down as real the infinite intelligence and the variety of finite minds, it must bring these two species of intellect to an absolute unity.

Some Pantheistic schemes absorb all particular intelligences into modes of the absolute intelligence.

This is the shoal on which the Pantheistic systems make shipwreck; so far they have gone on vigorously in a straight and simple path, but stumbling at this difficulty, they divide and diverge in two contrary directions. A philosopher penetrated with a profound sentiment of the Divinity, with that perfect and finished thought Which knows no bound, in Whom are concentrated all the rays of absolute truth, Who embraces with a single and eternal glance the plenitude of being, the real and the possible, the past and the future: such a philosopher will never be satisfied to make an undetermined thought of the Divine intelligence—a thought void of ideas, without consciousness; in a word, the abstraction of thought instead of real living thought. He will admit then a rich and fertile intelligence, full of life, containing in itself all the forms of thought. But then, what will he make of our finite intellects? Are they to be outside of the absolute intelligence? Are their ideas to be distinct from His ideas, their life from His life? Thus we deny at once the fundamental principle of pantheism—the law of absolute unity; and we must either renounce all logic and desert our principles, or else submit to this consequence—that what we call a finite intelligence is but a part of infinite Intelligence, a fugitive moment of His eternal life, that our feeble intellects lose all distinct reality, all individual consistence, and are resolved into pure modes into particular ideas of the absolute intelligence.

Others make finite intelligences the only real ones.

But there are minds which cannot renounce the consciousness of their own reality. There are robust idiosyncracies, determined not to sacrifice themselves, not to be absorbed into the bosom of an extraneous existence. Spirits of this kind, strongly attached to the data of consciousness, undertake to reconcile them with their fundamental principle, which is the absolute unity of beings. There is only one way to do that, that is to refuse all distinct life to the Infinite intelligence, to reduce Him to a pure thought, to an indeterminate thought—to the bond of all thought, and of all finite intelligences. Then, in the place of a sole intelligence, who alone lives, who alone thinks, who alone is real, you have an infinite variety of distinct and determinate intelligences, joined by a general character and a common sign. In the first case God alone is real, and creatures are but the series of His actions; in the second, creatures only have reality, and God is the sign that unites them.

Such is the inevitable law imposed upon Pantheism by logic, and by the nature of things. It sees before it two realities, which no reasonable mind can deny, and it undertakes to reduce them to the absolute unity of a single existence. And it finds itself reduced, if it wants a real and living God, to absorb in Him all creatures, and so to fall into mysticism; or if it wants a real and effective universe, to make of God a pure abstraction, a mere name, and so to be in danger of Atheism.

Of two contrary tendencies of Pantheism, that towards Atheism prevails.

This terrible alternative weighs upon the Pantheism of the present day, as it weighed upon Malebranche and Spinoza, and before them on the schools of Athens and Alexandria. Which side will our Pantheists take? There is in a certain number of the schools of our time, chiefly among the disciples of Schelling, some tendency towards mysticism, but it is quite evident that the strength and the danger are not on that side. These germs are abortions, and they must perish in an age like ours, when the sentiment of things celestial is weakened, when the love of life, the ardour of enjoyment, the exaggerated notions of the power of man, form a torrent which carries away the firmest characters and the noblest intellects. What follows? That the mystic Pantheism of Baader and Gœrres, which sacrifices man to God, has vanished, and that the opposite tendency of Pantheism universally prevails. The Hegelian school has decided resolutely to sacrifice the Divine personality, and to know no other God but that which it calls the impersonal God.

God is nothing more to the Pantheists of our day than the abstraction of being. He only arrives at consciousness after having passed through all the degrees of life, and it is man who is at last the really perfect being. There is in the idea of being a necessary dialectic, which urges it to develope itself, and from progress to progress, from evolution to evolution, the idea becomes man. Then only God has consciousness of Himself. In other terms, God instead of being the first principle and the Creator, is but the last consequence.

The Absolute.

We must examine more closely this conception, which is given us as the last effort of a new science, of some unheard of dialectic, armed with its theses and its antitheses, and which, setting out from the abstraction of being, fancies that it arrives at the complete being, by passing through all possible forms of existence. The common aim of French and German Hegelians, when they set out from the principle which they call the Absolute, and which in their system plays the part of God, is to take their stand on the highest idea of reason. I ask what they mean by the Absolute. The difference of definitions and formulæ is of very little consequence here, for they all agree in acknowledging that this Absolute, taken in itself, is not a living and determinate principle. As soon as it is determined, as soon as it lives, it is no longer the pure absolute, it is no longer itself, it becomes another, it becomes nature and humanity.

Not the highest principle of reason.

Now, so far from such an Absolute being the highest principle of reason, in my opinion it is denying reason altogether to give it this rank and character; for properly speaking it is confounding reason, intuitive reason, with those secondary faculties of analysis and abstraction, which preside over the operations of discursive reason; or, in other words, it is substituting for the idea of the perfect Being—that primitive, natural, spontaneous idea full of reality and life—the abstract and dead conception of the indeterminate being. Certainly, to conceive the Perfect and Absolute Being, is the proper function of reason; and there is not a thought of the mind, an emotion of the heart, an impulse of the imagination, not even a perception of the senses, which does not contain this notion. But what is its real character? Far from being an abstract idea representing an indeterminate object, it is of all ideas the most determinate and the most concrete. I cannot contemplate being and life under their changeable and imperfect forms; I cannot see some gleams of intelligence shine around me and in me; I cannot catch some impressions of strength, of beauty, of justice, of joy, of happiness, without conceiving beyond the beings of visible nature, a First Existence, where plenitude of intelligence, perfect beauty, and the possession of Almighty Power, compose in their harmonious unity the eternity of a perfect life.

The idea of the Perfect Being concrete.

Dissensions of the Pantheistic school.

Collect these partial acts of a sole and identical intellectual function, these divided members of an idea always present in the depths of thought, and you have the idea of the Perfect Being. And this is not an abstract idea, nor an idea which represents an indeterminate object; it is emphatically the concrete idea, since it represents the most real being, not potential, but actual being, the plenitude of perfection, the accomplishment of all the forms of being, and of all the attributes of life. Here is the real Absolute, here is true perfection, but a determinate living perfection. It is easy to conceive that such an Absolute should be a true principle, really first and really productive, for it is an evident fact that the imperfect has its reason in the perfect, the finite in the infinite, the relative in the absolute. But what follows from the Pantheistic system? They take for their principle a false Absolute, an indeterminate being, a being in potentiality. I say that this principle is radically sterile. In fact, it is inconceivable that this indeterminate being should become determinate, that this being in potentiality should pass into actuality. It is absolutely impossible, and we must here exhibit the spectacle of the internal discord of the Pantheistic school, in face of the impossibility of making one step beyond their sterile absolute, which is common to all its masters.

Schelling and Hegel.

It is well-known that Schelling lays down as the origin of things a principle which he calls the identical absolute, or the subject-object. This principle determines itself, makes itself objective by its nature, and thus gives to itself a primary form, which it immediately destroys to take up another till it has exhausted its power of objectivity, and has come into full possession of its being. Here Hegel stops his master, and says, You are unfaithful to the conditions of science. Science must explain and demonstrate everything. Now you set out with an hypothesis and enigma. You say the absolute can divide itself, the identical can differentiate itself. What is the absolute? What is the identical? Why and how should it divide itself or differentiate itself? The first principle of the system should be particularly clear, since it is to give light to the whole. Your first principle is unintelligible, and it dims the rest of the system with its darkness. Then how will you describe the evolution of the absolute in nature and in man?

You do not define the essence of the Absolute and the internal laws of its development. How can you see the Absolute in other things, if you cannot see it in itself? You must have recourse to experience, you leave the region of absolute science.

We really cannot see what Schelling has to answer to these objections. It is impossible to put him more effectually at variance with his own principles, and to point out the two things in his system which ought never to be found in a philosophy *à priori*—unexplained mysteries, and helps drawn from experience.

But if Hegel triumphs over Schelling, the master is equally strong against the disciple. It is amusing to hear Schelling following up with his lively dialectic the boastful theories, whose greatest fault is, that they have eclipsed his own. "It has been said," he exclaims, "that in metaphysics one must not suppose anything. I am blamed for making hypotheses: how does my opponent begin? With a hypothesis, the strangest of all, that of the logical notion, or the idea to which he attributes the faculty of transforming itself by its nature into its contrary, and then of turning back and becoming itself again, a thing that may be imagined of a living real being, but that cannot be said of the simple logical notion, without the most absurd of fictions."

Here, according to Schelling, is a perfectly gratuitous first supposition. Nevertheless the system maintains itself well enough, as long as we remain in the sphere of pure logic, which has to do with the combination of abstractions; but how to pass from the idea to the being is both inconceivable and impossible; and then follows necessarily a new hypothesis, and a new absurdity, which Schelling shows up with the sharpest irony. "The idea," says he, "Hegel's idea, one cannot tell why, but probably tired of its purely logical existence, takes it into its head to resolve itself into its momenta, in order to explain creation." It could not have been better said, and Schelling revenges himself admirably on his proud and faithless pupil. But what must every disinterested friend of truth think, listening to these two adversaries, who are so clever in attack, so weak in defence? He will say that the passage so much desired from the abstract to the real is manifestly not to be found by the Pantheists.

The *prozess* a fall from the absolute.

And I ask them if this passage from power to act, from indifference to difference, from the indeterminate to the determinate, is to the Absolute a progress or a decadence. They may hesitate between these two alternatives, but they must choose. All the Pantheists of Germany, celebrate with one voice the idea of the necessary and internal progress of being (prozess) as the most original idea of modern metaphysics. On the other side, Schelling has often appeared to lean towards the idea of a primitive decadence; borrowing from the latter Pantheists of the Athenian school, particularly from Proclus, their strange doctrine, he has said that the production of the world was *a fall of the Absolute.*

We must confess that the choice is rather dangerous between two such strange alternatives. What! the perfect being degenerates! its essence is perfection, and it ceases to be perfect! The contradiction is palpable. But on the other side, how shall we conceive that the perfect being should grow more perfect; that the complete being should receive an increase of reality? There is but one idea equal in absurdity to the idea of the decadence of God, and that is the idea of His progress.

Absurdities in the Absolute.

It may be thought that I reason from settled prejudices, and that I am substituting the old notion of God, the all Perfect Being, for the transcendental new idea of the Absolute. Not at all. I demand whether the Absolute of the Pantheist is in itself perfect or imperfect. If it is perfect in itself, it is evident that its perfection can neither be added to nor diminished. They must then acknowledge that their absolute is imperfect; and then they fall into an abyss of absurdities. According to this hypothesis, the last which has been put out by the Pantheists of the present day, everything begins with imperfection, and perfection is at the term. But if the Absolute be imperfect in itself, it has not its reason of existence in itself, it has no reason for its existence. Supposing it to exist, why should it develope itself?—this is also inexplicable and impossible.

The expedient of the Pantheists is to say that it developes itself necessarily; but this is no answer. For whence this necessity? They will tell us that as a fact the world exists. But this fact is only a fact, which cannot establish an absolute necessity, so that the necessity is purely gratuitous. Not only one cannot conceive that the absolute should be developed, but one can conceive very clearly that it should not be developed, because it is impossible that imperfection should be a first principle, that the perfect should proceed from the imperfect. We are forced then to say with Hegel, that it is necessary that the contradictory should take place, that nothing should become being, and zero should become the origin of the unit and of numbers. Nothing producing everything, that which is absurd in itself become necessary, and entrusted with the task of explaining and throwing light upon all the mysteries of existence—such is the last limit that Pantheism has been destined to reach.

Refutation of Pantheism from the Practical Reason.

I think I have proved, by placing myself with the Pantheists in the region of speculative reason, that their Absolute is a false Absolute, that their impersonal God is a false God, a sterile chimera of abstraction. Can the Pantheists defend themselves better upon the platform of practical reason and experimental facts? Have they compensated themselves for having sacrificed divine personality by establishing human personality in the plenitude of its rights? On this point one would sometimes say that the Pantheists deceive themselves less than on all the rest. They feel so strongly that the authority of experience is not on their side, that they hasten at once to reject it. Hear the Pantheists of all ages. Parmenides, Plotinus, Bruno, Spinoza, Hegel, will tell you that the senses are deceitful, that the vulgar, taking them for guides, feed their intellect with pure delusions, that it belongs to true philosophy to get rid of the senses, and to regard everything with the eye of reason. Has not experience always deceived us, they cry, and after all what does she give us? Phenomena and not causes, existences and not essences, what happens, what is, and not what ought to be, what cannot fail to be. But philosophy is essentially the knowledge of causes and of essences, the science of the how and the why of every thing, the contemplation of the necessary and the absolute. Let pure reason then be a torch to lead the philosopher through the profound mystery of the origin of things far from the vulgar crowds and the commerce of the senses.

Pantheists despise experience. Yet must avail themselves of it.

Such is the haughty language of the Pantheists, and it is natural enough that they should despise experience, but whether they will or not, a moment comes when the proudest will have to reckon with her. I only know one man who has held for an instant this kind of wager against impossibility, that man is Parmenides. This daring genius alone dared to maintain to the end that philosophy must confine itself to pure reason, to the idea of being, and hold all the rest for nothing.[1] The rigorous consequence is, that motion and nature are not, and that there is only the Absolute being, without attributes, without difference, without life. Had they been strictly true to their principles, Plotinus, Spinoza, and Hegel, should have ended in the same result, at once logical and absurd. I defy Plotinus to get out of his absolute unity, Spinoza to make one step beyond the affirmation of substance, Hegel to break the narrow circle of the absolutely indeterminate idea, if they do not borrow one of her data from experience, if they do not bow to consciousness and the senses. Plotinus sees in his unity the principle of an eternal emanation; Spinoza deduces from substance attribute, and from attribute mode; Hegel explains all the developments of the idea, by a certain internal processus, by a necessary motion obedient to a very simple and uniform law. This is all

[1] *Οὐδὲ ποτ' εκ τοῦ ἐόντος ἐφήσει πίστιος ἰσχὺς . . γιγνεσθαι τι παρ' αὐτό*—Parmenidis *Fragmenta*, Ed. Karsten, vers. 67, 68.

very good; but where did these philosophers find the ideas of emanation, of attribute, of mode, of progress, of motion? Was it not really experience that furnished them with the type of these notions? And what advantage can it be to any sincere and serious philosopher, after having made use of these indispensable notions, to conceal their origin? Pantheism, then, must take its choice; not more than other systems can it dispense with experience, and it does not, in fact, dispense with it. Pantheism cannot be accepted as repudiating the data of the senses. To deny facts from the vantage-ground of an *à priori* principle, would be not only to attempt the impossible, and to convict oneself of extravagance, it would be to contradict oneself miserably, to make use of experience when she is useful and necessary, and to proscribe her as soon as she becomes troublesome. Such a position is not tenable, and I consider it as demonstrated that to reason against Pantheism in the name of experience, is to make use of a right incontestable in itself, and, what is more, incontestable to every honest Pantheist.

What makes man a person? The moral law.

Also, the acknowledged aim of the Hegelians is to give a satisfactory explanation of human personality, and even to be in close communion with the moral and religious traditions of humanity. Now let us see what constitutes human personality. How it is that man is not a thing but a person—that he takes a place apart from the other beings of creation—that he pursues an infinite ideal, and aspires to immortality? It is because man feels himself a free agent, and responsible for his destiny. He bows before order, as before a sacred law; he acknowledges absolute obligations and inviolable rights. Whilst the other beings of the universe develope themselves, fatally following laws which they know not and cannot modify, man beholds universal order, and puts himself freely in harmony or in strife with it. Fact rules nature, man inhabits a higher world where right reigns. Responsible for his destiny, man beholds his judge in God. Subject to the trial of labour and of pain, he seeks a consoler and a support. Filled with an immense love for truth, beauty, and perfection of every kind, and unable to satisfy it perfectly in his earthly condition, he looks towards heaven—he desires, he hopes for a life to come. His thought flies from earth, flings itself into the infinite, and enjoys there a foretaste of celestial felicity. It is thus that man raises himself from the region of fatality to that of liberty and justice, and that morality leads him to religion.

Pantheistic profession of religion not perhaps insincere.

There are no truths more simple, none more closely bound together. If there be no liberty, there is no right, no justice, no future life, no hope in God, no religion.

Let us do justice to the Pantheists. They do not carelessly repudiate these holy truths; they make sincere efforts to bring them into their system. But if thereby they deserve our respect, they lay themselves open to that pitiless logic which does not give credit for intentions. First let us hear what they say. Spinoza subscribes on his book the sacred name—*morality;* the final end of his philosophy is, he assures us, the liberty of man. He affirms, or I should say, he demonstrates geometrically, the immortality of the soul, and finishes his system with a theory of divine love.

Hegel's intentions are not less exalted, nor his language less specious. Thus he speaks of religion: "It is the region where the enigmas of life, and all the contradictions of thought, find their solution, where all the pains of sentiment are appeased: the region of eternal truth and eternal peace. There flows the stream of Lethe, there the soul drinks oblivion of all its ills; there all the clouds of time are dissipated in the brightness of the infinite."[1]

But most inconsistent.

Hegel flatters himself that he has explained the true sense of Christianity, and reconciled for ever religion and philosophy. In fact, according to him, the common foundation of all philosophy and of all religion is the idea of the Word made flesh, of the man God; in other words, it is the identity of the human mind and the universal mind; or again, it is the universal mind taking consciousness of itself in the human mind. This is, according to Hegel, the real title of human personality; this is the living source of morality and religion. I doubt not of the sincerity and high-mindedness of Hegel, any more than of his genius; but I have a right to tell him, that these words, liberty, responsibility, duty, right, immortality, adoration, religion, have no sense in his system, and that to give them any meaning he must employ miraculous subtilty and prodigious refinement.

The leading idea of Pantheism is the idea of an indeterminate principle, which determines itself after a necessary law, to become successively everything. Absolute necessity is at the beginning, the middle, and the end of it. Brute nature, living

[1] Hegel, *Lessons on the Philosophy of Religion*, vol. xi.

Necessity in the Pantheistic scheme.

nature, intellectual nature, individuals, and society, laws, creeds, manners, and institutions, are ruled and swayed by her. With Spinoza this necessity is clothed in a geometrical form. He believes that the bending of a blade of grass, or the fall of an empire, is as necessary as the proposition, that the three angles of a triangle are equal to two right angles. Hegel has imagined another necessity, which he calls dialectical. Everything is subject, according to him, to the law of the absolute identity of contradictories. Being and nothing, the infinite and the finite, beauty and deformity, good and evil, life and death, are at first wrapped confusedly together in a primary term, they separate in the second, to come together again in the third. This is the uniform rhythm of the idea, the sovereign law of creation.

Inconsistent with religion.

It matters little whether this theory is more or less original. It is enough to know that for Hegel, as for Spinoza, the evolution of man is subject, as well as that of the stone, to an absolute necessity; and certainly he must possess a rare power of self-deception who does not see that such a system strikes at the root of the moral and religious life. What, the actions of my life are to be unrolled like the rings of an iron chain, and I am to think myself responsible! What is called God is nothing but the dialectic law, and I am to adore that law even when it crushes and destroys me! I am only a necessary form of being destined to be replaced by another, and I am to hope for a life to come! And then they tell me that God is myself, and that I should find my happiness in feeling myself to be God. What!

I feel pain, I must die, and I am God—a strange sort of God! Shall I not cry out with Pascal, *O ridicolosissimo eroe!*

But let us treat this theory seriously, if possible. God, you say, takes consciousness of Himself in man. So God in Himself has no consciousness of Himself, but He takes consciousness of Himself in another. This is strange, especially when this other is not one individual, but millions of individuals, some dead, some living, others to be born, who do not know each other, and are separated by spaces and ages. Where is the unity of such a consciousness? What is the meaning of a consciousness which divides itself, and breaks itself into a thousand pieces? What is the meaning of a consciousness which is made in time, and which is never made—which is always seeking for itself, and never finds itself? Then I who speak am not God, I am only a fragment of that indefinite existence. This is to tell me, in a strange dark language, a very simple thing, most easily known, namely, that man is but a necessary form of being, like that tree, or that pebble, or that stream; with this small difference, that man believes himself to be a free agent, without being so in reality; that he sees before him death, with the full certainty of dying, and that in this excess of misery, he has only to persuade himself for a moment that he is God to be consoled for all.

Position that God assumes self-consciousness in man.

The great Pantheists have intellects which are too acute not to have perceived these contradictions. So what do they do? they take away with one hand what they have given with the other. Spinoza recognises liberty, but he calls it a free necessity;

Hegel's and Spinoza's "free necessity."

and this is also the sentiment of Hegel. "The moral man," says he, "has consciousness of his action, as of something necessary, and thereby only is he truly free."[1]

Ultimate results of Pantheism.

There is the same strange agreement between Spinoza and Hegel on the distinction of good and evil; they begin by acknowledging it, and a short time after they deny it. Both of them tell us that the soul is immortal, and then they proceed to reduce this immortality to the consciousness that we have, of being an eternally necessary form of the absolute being. Liberty without responsibility, morality without duties, immortality without consciousness, mad idolatry of self—these are the practical conclusions of Pantheism, this is what it makes of human personality.

In a word, contemporary Pantheism, forced to choose between an extravagant mysticism which is rejected by all the instincts good and bad of our day, and the contrary tendency, decides for the latter, and sacrifices resolutely the personality of God, in hopes of making more of man. What is the result? It destroys human personality. So true is this profound saying of a contemporary spiritualist:[2] "There are two poles of all human science—the personal I, with whom all begins, and the personal God, in whom all ends." Yes, man without God is an enigma,—I know not what,—an inexplicable monster. He has no mission upon earth, and no hope in heaven. Losing his divine ideal, trying to take himself for his ideal, he falls below himself, and his punishment for desiring to be God is, that he ceases to be man.

[1] Hegel, *Encyclopédie*, add. an. § 35.

[2] Maine de Biran.

Fifth Meditation.

Is the World Eternal and Infinite?

THERE is no more room for hesitation, since I have declared open war against Pantheism; nor is my adversary a phantom; assuredly not; for I have long meditated on those high thoughts with which Hegel and Spinoza have allowed themselves to be intoxicated—those ideas of absolute unity, and of the eternal evolution of beings. I know their seductiveness; I would not willingly weaken them; nor would I conceal the terrible difficulties which rise against the idea of a God distinct from the universe. Yet they have been overcome. Yes! the God of science, as well as the God of our hearts and of common sense, is a God distinct from the world, a God living by His own life, an adorable God, God the Creator. He was before the world, He was fully sufficient to Himself; not from necessity, but from love, He became the Creator; the universe is the work of His goodness. But what am I saying? God, the eternal Being, *was* before His creatures; God, the immutable Being, *became* a Creator. Is not that a difficulty which I have not resolved, and which the very laws of language make palpable—Misery of human speech, or rather, of human reason! I have mastered a truth of inestimable value; and when I want to confess it, when a word of adoration would exhale from my lips, my language seems to impeach my thought; I impose on the Eternal the condition of time, I lend Him the vicissitudes of change.

How should God be before creatures if He has not a relation with them? If time, and if time only, exists as a relation between creatures, what sense is there in the words *before creatures?* For what is the meaning of an empty time which neither measures the life of God, since it is superior to time, nor the life of creatures, since it does not yet exist? And then, how can God become the Creator? He must change His condition; He must pass from fecundity in potentiality to fecundity in action; He must come out of rest to set Himself to work, and He must return again to rest; and all this apparently through caprice, or from being tired of His long inaction.

Is the world eternal?

Away from me, vain phantoms of the imagination! God is eternally all that He is. If He is the Creator, He creates eternally; if He creates the world, it is not from chance or from caprice, but for reasons worthy of Himself; and these reasons are eternal. Nothing new, nothing fortuitous can arise in the counsels of eternity. If the world be a work where wisdom and love concur with Almighty power, all that is eternal, and the creative act, is equally so. What more simple and more luminous than these principles? But here is the difficulty. If the creative act be eternal, why is not the effect of that act also eternal? and then we have the world, without beginning or end, partaking of an essential attribute of the Creator.

It may be said that this difficulty is not serious —that we are played upon here by the laws of human language, which, using its means of expression in sensible things, transports, by a necessary and innocent artifice, the forms of time and space into the things of eternity. In God nothing begins; all is eternal, the creative act as well as the motives of creation; but in the creature everything is subject to time, everything must begin to have being—this is the solution of the difficulty. God did not begin to create, but the creature began to exist, and with the creature, time, which is but the relation and the measure of its changes.

But does this solve the difficulty? I could wish it, but reason is not so easily satisfied; and I understand too well with what perplexities the Christian soul of St. Augustine was agitated when he raised this question: Has God always been the Lord? or again—Has God always been adored? It would be very easy to reduce all metaphysical questions to questions of words. Some one even pointed out to St. Augustine a still more expeditious mode of cutting short the difficulty; namely, to reply to those who ask what God was doing before He created the world, that He was preparing punishment for people who asked indiscreet questions. I know not if the question be indiscreet, but I know that the difficulty is inevitable.

Nor does it resolve the difficulty to say—God alone is without beginning or end; the world had a beginning, and time with the world, since the world and time are inseparable. But to speak in this way is to overlook the fact that even if a commencement of the world be conceivable and possible, yet as soon as our mind proceeds to assign to the world a definite origin, however remote, it necessarily conceives the possibility of a more remote origin, and so on, *ad infinitum.* In the same way I may possibly assign limits to the extension of the world; but scarcely has my mind fixed these limits before it displaces them, and conceives beyond them the possibility of a vaster world, and this without end and cessation. But, if these ages, extensions, and worlds, are not necessary, they are at least possible. So far is certain. But if it be once granted to me that they are possible, must I not, when I consider them in reference to God, conceive them as necessarily realized by His will? Admit an universe which began to exist some ages ago—say a hundred ages or a million; admit that this same universe is limited to a certain extent—it matters not whether great or little in relation to man—admit all this if you can—I ask you what relation, what proportion, is there between such a creation and the Creator? The universe is the image of God, the expression of His all-perfect being; it is by this right that the universe exists; it is the reason of its being; and can I picture to myself a finite universe—that is to say, an universe like an atom made to last an instant? Could such as that be the image of the eternal and the immense? Could God be eternally recognised in

There is no proportion between a finite creature and the Creator.

this phantom of His thought, and would He will to see as existent, not I will say this image, but this irony on His omnipotence? Is God, then, a master grudging existence and life? else why these empty ages before the world; why these empty spaces beyond the universe? I am told that empty ages are not ages, that empty spaces are not spaces, that all this has no effectual existence, since without bodies and without changing realities it is all reduced to abstraction. Be it so; but these ages are possible, these spaces can be realised, and, to go to the bottom of the matter, there are millions of possible beings to fill all spaces and all ages.

The universe, in a certain sense, infinite

Any number of beings, however large, any number of years, any number of spaces, is not a true expression of the infinity of the Creator. We must, then, whether we will or no, come to the conclusion that the work of the creation is not only an eternal, immutable, infinite act, as regards the Creator, but that even as regards the creature if we would not make it an accidental and capricious effort of infinite omnipotence, but a work worthy of the Creator, fit to express His eternity, His immensity, His fecundity, all His infinite perfections —the universe must extend indefinitely in time, in space, in the infinite greatness, and in the infinite littleness of its parts, in the infinite variety of its species, of its forms, and of its degrees of existence. The finite cannot express the infinite, but by being multiplied infinitely. The finite, so far as it is finite, is not in a reasonable relation or an intelligible proportion to the infinite. But the finite multiplied infinitely, ages upon ages, spaces beyond spaces, stars beyond stars, worlds beyond worlds, is a true expression of the Infinite Being.

This view not necessarily Pantheistic.

How sublime is this thought of the infinity of worlds! I could yield myself to it without the least scruple, if I did not happen to remember that it was introduced into the modern world by a Pantheist, the bold and unfortunate Bruno. Must I then fall again into the clutches of Pantheism, at the very moment when I thought I had escaped from it for ever? Does it follow, because the universe has no limits, either in time or space, or in the number and kind and degree of its parts, that the universe must therefore be eternal, immense, infinite, as God Himself? No; that is but a vain scruple, which springs from the imagination, and not from the reason. The imagination is always confounding what reason should ever distinguish, eternity and time, immensity and space, relative infinity and absolute infinity. The Creator alone is eternal, immense, absolutely infinite. The creation is scattered over space and time, subject to division and to limits. Time, in the inexhaustible flux of its moments, endeavours, so to speak, to imitate eternity, as much as its nature will permit. Space, by the infinite development of its extension, tries also to express immensity. In general, the inexhaustible evolution of finite things represents, as far as the nature of the finite allows, the internal evolution of the divine life. And yet there remains always between the model and the image, between the cause and the effect, together with a certain proportion, an infinite difference, not only in the degree of perfection but in the essence. Ages, spaces, stars, plants, intellectual beings, earth and heaven, each is variable, incomplete,

Relative and absolute infinity.

contingent, incapable of being or of subsisting in itself. Each is then contained in an ineffable manner in the depths of the self-existent being, who wraps round ages with His eternity, space with His immensity, changeable beings with His immutable being, who alone is really infinite, alone complete, alone in full possession of absolute existence.

So I consider myself saved at once from Pantheism and superstition. I feared the abstract God of Spinoza and Hegel, but I feared also a humanised God, and an accidental, arbitrary, or capricious creation. My fears are dispersed. I conceive a God who is not potential being, a sterile germ, but being in action, the perfect being, possessing perfect life, the life of thought and love; and then as the expression of this God, a universe which imitates, as far as may be, infinity, which is not the ephemeral production of caprice, or chance, but the work of an infinite omnipotence, directed by wisdom and inspired by goodness.

I am, then, in possession of an idea which can stand the test of reflection and doubt, and which at the same time answers to the deepest and sublimest instincts of the human heart. The God that my reason and my heart adore is at once a complete ideal of perfection, and an inexhaustible source of life. From His bosom, eternally fertile, across innumerable ages, and immeasurable spaces, life gushes forth and expands in forms ever new; and He the absolute being, He remains complete in Himself, in His incommunicable essence, in His blessed personality and His consciousness.

DISCUSSION OF AN ANTINOMY.

I should desire to go on and make fresh progress in the knowledge of divine things, but in vain I try to proceed; a scruple stops me; I turn back on one of the antinomies of Kant, that which has for its object the infinity of the universe. If Kant is right, if the human intellect is so framed that the ideas of a finite world and an infinite world are perpetually at war within it, so that the thesis and the anti-thesis can, in turn, be demonstrated and refuted with equal rigour, what have I done by representing to myself a universe whose illimitable greatness expresses, as I think, the infinity of the Creator? I have but taken up an old claim of pure reason, without showing the least regard to insoluble objections, and as if the dialectic of Kant did not exist.

Famous Antinomy.

I must then look this famous antinomy in the face—what does it say? It lays down first a world which has a beginning in time and limits in space. Here is the thesis, and this is how Kant proves it. To suppose that the world had no beginning, is to admit that at any given moment, say the moment in which I speak, an infinite series of successive states of the world have passed away. Now, that is absurd, for the property of an infinite series is, that in enumerating successively the terms that compose it you can never find an end. An eternity actually past away is then a contradiction. Similarly, if you suppose a world which has no limits in space, you admit an infinite whole, which is contradictory, for in order that a whole actually given should be composed of an infinite number of parts, you must be able to count them successively; an impossible operation, since it would require an eternity. Therefore the world is not infinite, therefore it must have a beginning in time, and limits in space.

But on the other side, if you suppose a world which did begin, the very idea supposes a time anterior to the world, an empty time. Now in an empty time nothing can begin, for why should it begin at such a moment, rather than at another? And in the same way, if you suppose a world limited in space, you suppose a space beyond the world, an infinite empty space. But then you admit a necessary relation between the world and something which yet is nothing. This relation is absurd. Therefore the world is not more limited in space than in time, and therefore it is infinite. This is the anti-thesis.

What conclusion does Kant draw from this antinomy? Does he pretend that human reason is here taken in the fact of necessary self-contradiction? This consequence would be very serious, for evidently it would bring in its train absolute scepticism.

Kant recoils from this extreme, which goes very far beyond the end that he had proposed to himself. He did not intend to make war with human reason, but with the dogmatism of the schools. He certainly wanted to kill metaphysics, but without hurting reason. What does he do in this perplexity? After having stated the antinomy, he refutes it, but in a very singular way.

Kant's solution.

There is one point, he says, common to the

thesis and the anti-thesis. When we reason on the dimensions of the universe, whether we hold a finite world, or an infinite world, in both cases we consider the universe as a real thing, we attribute to it an absolute existence independent of our senses. We believe then that the universe is something more than a collection of phenomena, we make of it a *noumenon*—a being in itself. In the same way we look upon time and space as objective and absolute realities, and when all this is postulated, the thesis and the anti-thesis come into collision and produce an antinomy. Should human reason be moved at this and despair of herself? Not at all, for this antinomy only warns her that she was about to take the wrong road, and fall into an abyss of illusions. Instead of giving to the universe, to space, and to time, an objective and absolute reality, to which they have not reasonable right, let her conceive the universe as a collection of phenomena, let her reduce space and time to simple forms of thought—to purely subjective conditions of experience, then the thesis and the anti-thesis fall together, and with them the antinomy.

We need not inquire any further, if the world be finite or infinite. For the world is nothing but the series of our sensations. Consequently it is not infinite because we are finite beings, neither is it finite because as we go on living, new impressions are added to the old, and that indefinitely.

Not satisfactory.

This is Kant's ingenious system, but he weaves it in vain. If this world, in the bosom of which I am plunged, if these extensions, these motions, these colours, this universal life, if all this is nothing beyond my own sensations, my reason deceives me, I can no longer trust her, and absolute doubt is inevitable. In vain Kant and his disciples would make a stand against scepticism; and after having sacrificed to it the objective, would maintain, as they say, the subjective. From the moment that the universe, God, and the soul itself are resolved into pure forms of thought, I ask where is the link of these empty forms deprived of all real contents, where is their centre, their unity, their support? Evidently they have none; they are all separated, disconcerted, scattered like smoke, and thought after having denied its objects destroys itself.

Let us leave this artificial world where the mind is consumed in mortal subtleties. The difficulties which disturbed the strong spirit of Kant are such as speculative reason must meet at every step. He took these difficulties for contradictions, and applying to them his subtle dialectic, composed the specious and regular system of his antinomies. Only to speak of the one which we have mentioned, I venture to say that the thesis and the anti-thesis are very weakly established. It would have been easy for Kant to invoke in favour of his idea of an infinite world, twenty arguments stronger than the only one which it suited him to borrow from Leibnitz. But what ought especially to be remarked is, that the thesis of a finite world, which ought to be rigorously proved, is based upon very insufficient proofs. If the world had not a beginning, says Kant, an eternity would have flowed away at the moment when I speak. This language is not correct. Eternity is a different thing from time, it does not flow away, it does not become, it is. Time only becomes and flows as the world changes and is modified. I admit that it is difficult to conceive the infinite flow of time, but this difficulty only exists in the imagination. Reason conceives distinctly that all duration supposes a before and an after. It may be great or little, millions of ages, or a quarter of a minute, still whoever speaks of duration speaks of past, present, and future. We must then give up the idea of time altogether, or else acknowledge that every moment that flows away, supposes, before it, an infinite series of moments past, and after it an infinite series of moments to come. All duration is comprised between these two series. Added one to another, they form, not eternity, but time. To man assuredly the difference is great. He sees one of these series, and he is willing to believe it infinite. The other is behind him, and he can hardly conceive it at all. But for God, who has neither past nor future, who exists outside and above time, the two series exist by the same name, and He surrounds them both with his immutable eternity. This astonishes the imagination, but reason conceives it with clear geometrical precision.

In the same way, all finite extension supposes a larger extension. If you pass a line through any point of space, this line divides space into two halves, which are each in its way infinite. Taken together, they constitute unlimited space. Here is no serious difficulty to reason. Kant says, that if the world had not limits in space it would be an infinite whole; and that a whole must have parts that can be counted. Yes, the totals that man can master; but the world is only an infinite whole in the eyes of God. To count the parts of an infinite world, you must have, says Kant, an infinite time. Granted: and man is incapable of embracing the world; he can only conceive it, and he conceives it, not as a real, eternal, absolute, immutable infinite, but as an expression of the infinite, that is to say, as unlimited in space, in time, and in every order of existence.

There is no opposition between the real world of science, and the ideal world of Metaphysics.

Moreover, is there really any opposition between the senses which explore the world, and reason which would impose upon it, *à priori*, its conditions and its laws: between the real world, such as science represents it, and the ideal world, such as Metaphysics dares to affirm it? None; this opposition is only apparent. It belongs to the weakness of our senses, and the progress of science dispels it every day.

The world of modern science.

See what a revolution has been wrought in the mind of man since the great discoveries of the three last centuries. When the system of Copernicus appeared, it was like the passage from a dream to the awaking. Man had gone to sleep with the idea of a little world made to his own measure; the earth was its centre, and around it revolved a circumscribed heaven. All at once, at the voice of Copernicus, the human mind awoke. Earth is but one planet, the sun is the centre of one little world; but in space, millions of suns form so many luminous centres, round which move other planets, and other satellites. This idea appeared a vision. But when the discoveries of Galileo, and the laws of Kepler, came to be widely known and to be believed, prejudice felt itself conquered, and prepared to withdraw. In the meantime, a new philosophy had set aside the philosophy of the schools. Its founder, Descartes, an able physical philosopher, and as great a geometer as he was a metaphysician, got possession of the idea of the infinity of the universe, and communicated it to his numerous disciples. One only, Malebranche, hesitates at the boldness of this conception; and soon the strength of his own mind, and the logic of his own system, led him to an idea infinitely more audacious, that of a necessary incarnation of God in the universe.

Descartes holds infinity of Universe, so Malebranche after some scruples.

Malebranche, who adores a wise and good God—a God who never could do anything but according to that which He is; Malebranche wants to have a universe worthy of God, and this imperfect universe would never express the infinite perfection of its Author, if God Himself were not joined to it, to give it a supernatural value, and an infinite preciousness. Thus the modern idea of the infinity of the world is set side by side with the faith of Jesus Christ in the soul of the pious Cartesian of the Oratory. We see in another eminent Christian, the same compromise between science and faith.

So Pascal.

"Let man, then," says Pascal, "contemplate entire nature in her high and full majesty. Let him put out of sight the low objects which surround him. Let him behold this shining light, set like an eternal lamp to enlighten the universe. Let earth appear to him as a point in comparison of the vast circle that this orb describes; and let him be further amazed that this vast circle itself is but a very delicate point compared with that embraced by the stars which roll in the firmament. But if our sight must stop here, let imagination pass on, it will sooner be weary of conceiving, than nature of furnishing. All the visible world is but an imperceptible line in the ample bosom of nature. No idea can approach it. We may inflate our conceptions beyond imaginable spaces, we only produce atoms, compared to the reality of things. It is an infinite sphere, of which the centre is everywhere, and the circumference no where."[1]

Here is the infinity of the universe, conceived as to the extent of its dimensions. Here it is again as to the infinite number of its parts:—

"What is man in the infinite? Let him search into what he knows of the minutest things, to find a prodigy as startling. Let him see in the littleness of the maggot's body parts incomparably smaller, legs with joints, veins in these legs, blood in these veins, humours in this blood, drops in these humours, vapours in these drops. Let him, dividing again these last, exhaust his strength in these conceptions, and let the last object that he reaches be the subject of our discourse; he will think perhaps that this must be the extreme littleness of nature. But I can show him within it a new abyss. I can show him not only the visible universe, but all that can be conceived of immensity in nature, contained in this small atom. Let him see in it an infinity of universes of which each has its firmament, its planets, its earth, in the same proportion as in the visible world, in this earth, animals, even maggots, in

[1] Pascal. *Pensées*, p. 1. M. Havet's edition.

which he finds all that the first have given, and finding still in others the same thing without end and without rest, let him be lost in these marvels, as astonishing in their littleness as the others in their extension. For is it not worthy of admiration that our body, which lately was not perceptible in the universe, itself imperceptible in the bosom of the whole, should be now a colossus, a world, or rather a whole, with respect to the nothing which cannot be reached."[1]

Pascal's answer to objections of the religious mind.

Pascal was not a man to ignore the objections that can be raised against an infinite world, either on the side of an imagination disturbed by all that is beyond it, or of a jealous religion, which scruples at giving infinity to aught but God. But far from recoiling from these difficulties, he resolves them as a Christian philosopher and a geometrician. He asks himself if the world, from the moment it ceases to have limits in space or time, does not form a kind of infinite and eternal. "No," he answers, "nothing of that kind can be infinite and eternal; but these finite beings are multiplied infinitely." Thus, it appears, it is only the number that multiplies them that is infinite.

To the objection that an infinite universe is incomprehensible.

Then there is another objection; an infinite universe is something incomprehensible to man. True, replies Pascal, but this incomprehensibility has its reason. For what is man in nature? a nothing with regard to Infinity, à whole with regard to nothing, a medium between a nothing and all. Infinitely far from comprehending extremes, the end of things and their beginning are

[1] Pascal. *Pensées*, Art. xxv., p. 9. M. Havet's edition. This pensée is one of those which were not published before 1843.

to him invincibly hidden in an impenetrable secrecy. He is equally incapable of discerning the nothing from whence he is taken, and the infinite where he is swallowed up. What must he do, then, but observe some shadow of the middle of things in an eternal despair of knowing either their beginning or their end? All things have come out of nothing, and are carried on to infinity. Who shall follow this astounding progress? The Author of these marvels understands them; none other can." Objectors will perhaps insist that the idea of infinite number implies a contradiction. By no means. "It is false," says Pascal, "that numbers are finite; then it is true that there is an infinite in numbers; but we know not what it is. It is false that it is even, it is false that it is odd; yet it is a number, and every number must be either odd or even. It is true that that is understood of every finite number."[1]

Leading idea which solves all objections.

But here is the leading idea which, in Pascal's eyes, overrules all objections more or less subtle and embarrassing—namely, that nature being the image of God, must bear the impress of the Infinity of the Creator in the greatness as well as in the number of its parts.[2] "A thoughtful man understands that nature, having graven its image and that of its Creator on all things, they almost all partake of its double infinity. Thus we perceive that all sciences are infinite in the extension of their researches; for who doubts that geometry, for example, has an infinitely infinite order of proportions to propose. They are equally infinite in

[1] *Pensées*, Art. x., p. 1.
[2] *Pensées*, Art. i., p. 9. M. Havet's edition.

the multitude and the delicacy of their principles; for who does not see that those which are considered the last do not sustain themselves, but that they are supported upon others, which, having others for their support, never allow of a last. But we do with those which appear to our reason to be final, as we do in material things, where we consider that an indivisible point, beyond which our senses can perceive nothing, although it be infinitely divisible by its nature. Of these two infinites of science, that of greatness is much the most sensible. We think ourselves naturally much more capable of reaching the centre of things than of embracing their circumference. The visible extension of the world visibly surpasses us; but as it is ourselves who surpass little things, we believe ourselves more capable of possessing them; and yet it requires as great a capacity to reach the nothing as to reach the whole. Infinity is needed for the one as for the other; and it seems to me that he who understands the last principle of things, might go on to know the Infinite. One depends upon the other, and one leads to the other. The extremities touch each other, and are joined by their very distance, and are found again in God and in God only."

Newton opposed to the infinity of the universe.

One only philosopher, Newton, in the seventeenth century, wrote against the infinity of the universe. Carried away by his reactionary movement against the philosophy of Descartes, he reserves for God infinity in space and duration, and conceives the universe as formed of a number of particles, vast but finite, which the Divine hand has collected for a time in various masses in the bosom of an infinite void. In vain he tries later to correct the vice of this conception, by the hypothesis of an infinite and imponderable ether, destined to explain the communication of motion across celestial spaces. Leibnitz raises his voice and denounces the Newtonian metaphysics to all Europe, as lowering at once the idea of the Cosmos and the idea of God. What! would you say that space is unlimited, and that in these immense extensions filled by the ever present being of God, float some inert molecules out of all proportion with the infinite void which surrounds them? And even this union of lifeless atoms is only transitory, and the laws of nature are not sufficient to guard them against inevitable perturbations; so that the Divinity, like a clumsy artist, must retouch His work. That cannot be; the world is well made; it is made to last, and God will not change its laws, because that would be to change His own designs. He has commanded once—He obeys always; or, to speak better, His command is immutable, because it is perfect and eternal.

Leibnitz, on the contrary, asserts that all in nature "va à l'infini."

But whilst he is making this protest against a finite and perishable world, which the researches of Lagrange and Laplace will one day confirm, Leibnitz praises the discoveries of Swammerdam, of Leuwenhœck, and of Malpighi, and preludes the great hypotheses of modern geology. He knows that a law of gradation links all the beings of the universe, that nature does not go by leaps and bounds, but by an insensible succession of progress.[1] Wherever a link of the chain is wanting, Leibnitz affirms that science will discover it,

[1] ["*Continuo*, non vero *per saltum*."]

and the fine discoveries of polypes by Tremblay bear him out. He insists that every thing in the universe tends to the Infinite, the succession of years, the number of species, the series of their metamorphoses, the progress of their evolution. He is told that the actual Infinite cannot be found in nature. He replies, "I am so much in favour of an actual Infinite, that instead of admitting that nature abhors it, as is vulgarly said, I hold that she affects it everywhere, the better to mark the perfections of her author."[1] The eighteenth century and our own have received these great views of Leibnitz as the vivifying principles of science. Astronomy, armed with its gigantic telescopes, conspires with physiology and its powerful microscopes to show forth the infinite greatness of the Cosmos. Herschell counts twenty millions of stars in the milky way. Ehrenberg forty millions of animalculæ in a cubic inch of Tripoli. The sun is no longer motionless; Argelander proves that it has a translative motion, and actually directs itself towards a point in the constellation of Hercules. Bessel calculates the swiftness of this progressive motion, and reckons it at more than six hundred thousand myriamètres a day. We know twenty-eight thousand stars which have planets circulating round a common centre of gravity in elliptic orbits, and according to the laws of universal gravitation; and surely Pascal was right to say that our imagination would sooner be tired of conceiving than nature of furnishing. How can imagination represent to itself the distance of a star, whose light requires two millions of years to reach us!

[1] *Lettre à l'Abbe Foucher.* Erdmann, p. 118.

All limits recede, those of time as well as those of space. Comparative anatomy finds out and recomposes organic systems which have preceded the actual system, and which themselves have had ancestors. The face of the earth has changed more than once, and geology has discovered in its entrails the certain trace of vanished ages. Heaven itself has its epochs, and every star its story and its life. Before being what it is, it has passed through a thousand metamorphoses. An ingenious astronomer observes, that "as we remark in our forests trees of the same species that have reached all possible degrees of growth, so we may observe in the immensity of the celestial plains the different phases of the gradual formation of stars." A particular form of existence may be recent, a certain manifestation of life may have its date, but the world itself has none, at least its first origin flies before the eyes of man when he observes it best, and so do the barriers of extension and the hidden principles of life.

Modern science confirms Leibnitz.

Thus for three centuries, experience and pure reason, each beholding the universe from its own point of view, far from contradicting each other, as Kant says, have always inclined to agree. The ideal speculations of the metaphysician, the positive researches of the observer, the calculations of the geometrician, the conjectures of the historian, all form an irresistible current which undermines every day the old prejudice of a finite world, and substitutes for it the modern idea of the infinity of the universe. And think not that there is anything in this to discourage philosophical observers. Nothing, on the contrary, excites and spurs on

Thus Metaphysical speculation and science meet.

This view encourages science.

scientific curiosity like the idea of the infinite greatness of worlds. I appeal to that illustrious and venerable man, who so grandly united in one magnificent whole the discoveries of modern science. I appeal to the author of the Cosmos, to M. de Humboldt. "In the midst of the riches of nature, and of observations ever increasing, man becomes penetrated with a profound conviction, that on the surface and in the bowels of the earth, in the depths of the seas and in those of the skies, even after millions of years, space will never be wanting to the scientific conqueror. The regret of Alexander can never be addressed to the progress of observation and of intellect."[1]

[1] [The view maintained by M. Saisset in this chapter is, that the universe expresses the absolute infinity of God by its relative infinity, that is, by illimitable extension in time and space. M. Henri Martin has accused M. Saisset's thesis, or rather his arguments:—(1) of a Pantheistic tendency; and (2) of associating two contradictory ideas, created matter and the Infinite. I have said something on this question at the close of this volume. For my own part, though M. Saisset has elsewhere declared his conviction of the accordance of this theory with the Bible doctrine of the creation, and though he cites St. Augustine and Aquinas as partially, and Descartes, Pascal, and Leibnitz, as altogether agreeing with him, I cannot but regret that he should have given such prominence to a speculation based chiefly upon a hypothetical view of the Divine character.]

Sixth Meditation.

Providence in the Universe.

I CONTEMPLATE with joy the idea of a universe without limits, unfolding itself through space and time, and expressing, by an inexhaustible multitude of created beings, the omnipotence of the immense and eternal Creator. But hitherto I have proceeded in company with Pantheism, and its nearness affrights me. Spinoza and Bruno have each of them a most profound sentiment of the infinity of worlds, and yet their universe cannot be mine, because their God is not my God. They only see in nature and man various forms with which an impersonal activity successively clothes himself beneath the law of a blind destiny. To my eyes, on the contrary, according to the idea that I have formed of the All-perfect Being, this world, which is His image, must everywhere show traces of an intelligent will, on the side of the good and the beautiful, who has freely chosen, formed, and disposed all things for the best end. It must be referred to the universe itself, and to man's observation, whether my idea of it or the Pantheist's is the most right and true.

But the problem which overwhelms and makes

Three worlds of Gravitation, Life, Humanity—which is their law, Providence or Necessity?

me feel most strongly the extent of my ignorance is this. One must be a Humboldt to embrace the Cosmos; nor is this enough; for not only must one know the heaven and the earth, the world of gravity, and the world of life, but also that invisible world, more changeable and unapproachable than the two others—the world of humanity. Thus we must question these three universes, and ask of each if its last word be necessity, or Providence.

The first glance gives the idea of ordering Thought in the starry world.

When I begin to contemplate nature in simplicity and truth, I find her beautiful, and full of harmonies. The sight of the starry heavens throws me into a sort of ecstasy. These stars, these worlds without number, the splendour of their fires, the prodigy of their greatness and of their distances, that infinite multitude of luminous globes, in their constant and varied groups, ordered in space to accomplish with the same motion their majestic revolution, like an immense concert, where one feels that a superior harmony runs through the different notes of the instruments and the voices—in presence of these beautiful objects, beneath the charm of their grand impressions, I feel my whole mind penetrated and subdued by the idea of an ordaining thought.

So does the inner world.

And when my thought leaves the vault of heaven to enter into itself, if it find within a soul at peace with itself and with its equals, whose every feeling, insensibly softened by contemplation, has borrowed from the beautiful night something of its serenity, I begin to understand that harmony of visible nature and of internal consciousness which made a philosopher[1] say, "Two ob-

[1] [Kant.]

jects fill my soul with an ever-increasing admiration and respect—above us the starry heaven, within us the moral law." At such moments I believe in God, King of Heaven and Ruler of man. I believe in Him with a faith without reserve, with that spontaneous faith, which is prompter and sweeter than the faith which reflects. But soon reflection has its way, and I ask myself if I am not the dupe of an illusion.

I have just admired the vault of heaven, and I have seen in it worlds without number gravitating through space under the same law of equilibrium and of harmony.

Does this faith come from Modern Science?

Am I sure that my eyes have seen it, or was it perchance my reason, delivered from its native ignorance, that guessed by a miracle of intuition, the order and the structure of the Heavens? It was modern science that fed me with such thoughts as immense globes, infinite worlds, gravitation, eternal equilibrium. If I had been born among the aborigines of Australia, or if I had lived three thousand years ago, I should have seen in the starry Heaven, only a dark vault, sprinkled with some brilliant vapours. Do what I can, I cannot seize again the first simple impressions of nature. On all sides acquired prejudices enwrap me; and the echoes, more or less distant, of modern science, resound in my spirit in spite of myself.

Reference to Copernicus, Kepler, and Newton.

What is to be done in this impossibility of hearing clearly the voice of nature? Let us try to find out exactly what science says or thinks. In the first place let us refer to those extraordinary men, who are considered to have discovered the laws of creation—Copernicus, Kepler, and Newton. One, say the learned, has marked the true place of our earth and our sky in the vast economy of the celestial globes. The other has defined the precise curve that the earth and the other planets describe around their luminous centre. And the last, drawing from the laws of Kepler the consequences that they contain, has succeeded, by the matchless power of his calculation, in determining the certain number which subjects all the stars of our world, and moreover all stars and all bodies, in all spaces, and in all time, to one and the same law.

Theism of Copernicus.

There is a marvellous succession in this series of discoveries, but it is hard to be understood. I am incapable of reading the book of Copernicus, *De revolutionibus orbium cælestium*, or the *Harmonice mundi* of Kepler. The calculations, the numbers, the figures, the algebra are all beyond me and perplex me. But after all, what I want is to know what these great observers have thought of the plan of the universe, and having reduced it to this single point, I think I may find an end to my labours. If it were true that an eternal and blind necessity presides over the movements of the universe, surely the inventors of astronomy must have known it better than any one. But, on the contrary, I find that the more these great minds succeeded in laying bare the general economy of the world, they recognised in more glowing characters the free and wise hand of the Creator. Copernicus had deeply studied, not only the systems of Ptolemy, but those of Philolaus, of Ecphante, of Hicetas, of Heraclides.

The first doubts that came into his mind as to the truth of the old systems, arose from his observing one common fault in all, that of imposing on the universe a plan destitute of simplicity and of symmetry: and he was led to the first idea of his own system, by seeking out the simplest and the most beautiful plan, that which is most conformable to the idea of a wise and foreseeing Ordainer. It was not necessary in itself that the earth should turn round the sun, but reason told Copernicus that this arrangement was the best, because it was the most simple, and experience and calculation confirmed the inspiration of his reason. Let us hear his own words. "By no other combination," he exclaims, "have I been able to find so admirable a symmetry in the diverse parts of this great whole, as by placing the torch of the world, the sun which governs the whole family of stars, upon a royal throne, in the centre of Nature's temple."

This earth forms a part of a collection of planets which revolve round the sun. Each of these has its own proper orbit, one a circle, another an ellipsis, a third a different curve, or rather we may presume that they describe similar curves ruled by the same laws. **Kepler.**

Kepler employed more than twenty years in observations, in calculations, in unwearied researches, to verify this sublime presentiment. He reached the goal, at last; he discovered the three laws which immortalize his name, and he exclaimed—"Now what is it to me that my book be read by the present age, or by a future age! my book can wait for readers. Has not God waited six thousand years contemplating His work?" I cannot exactly tell by what means Kepler reached these three laws. I know not how much we are to attribute to experiment, how much to calculation, how much again to all sorts of strange mystical, symbolical, Pythagorean ideas; but that which is the dominant idea of all his calculations, all his observations, all his hypotheses, all his reveries, is his profound conviction that the world is beautiful, that it has been made on an ideal model by an Artist of infinite skill and knowledge.

Newton. But there is one who has penetrated further than Copernicus and Kepler; further than any man before him, into the secrets of celestial things; one who bringing back the laws of Kepler to their generative principle, has demonstrated mathematically the system that Copernicus had merely discovered, and made likely: and has fixed finally the sole and supreme condition, whence results the eternal equilibrium of worlds. What would Newton have said if he had been told that the law of universal gravitation, and the magnificent system that it governs, are but a necessary consequence of the nature of bodies, that they contain neither order, nor wisdom, nor suitableness, nor beauty, nor harmony, but pure and simple necessity? He would surely have answered, "I know not how you have made yourselves acquainted with the essence of matter and the movements and laws which necessarily result from it. I do not pretend to be so skilful, I profess my ignorance of the essence of bodies. I only know matter by its sensible properties. I have made some experiments, and some new calculations, which have taught me that all the motions of the universe may be referred to a single law, which I have called, for want of a better name, the law of attraction. Now as a fact and a law I can take hold of this attraction and demonstrate it; as a cause I know nothing about it; I cannot even tell its mode of action, whether it acts from a distance, or by the intermediary of an invisible fluid called ether, or otherwise. Upon this point I dare not pronounce, for want of observations, and sufficient proofs; but what I do know is, that all these regular movements suppose a first cause which is not a mechanical cause (*Et hi omnes motus regulares originem non habent ex causis mechanicis*): that this admirable arrangement of the sun, the planets, and the comets cannot be explained but by the design and government of an intelligent and powerful Cause. (*Elegantissima hæcce solis, planetarum et cometarum, compages non nisi consilio et dominio entis intelligentis et potentis oriri potuit.*) That a blind necessity does not explain anything, for that necessity being the same at all times and in all places, a variety of things cannot proceed from it. (*A cæcâ necessitate metaphysicâ quæ utique eadem est semper et ubique, nulla oritur rerum variatio.*) And consequently, the universe, with the order of its parts appropriated to a variety of times and places, can only have originated from a Primitive Being, having ideas and a will. (*Tota rerum conditarum pro locis ac temporibus diversitas ab ideis et voluntate entis necessario existentis solum modo oriri potuit.*)

"God must neither be represented as a soul of

the world, dispersed in the variety of things, nor as a Being, dead and abstract. He is the Creator, distinct from the world and acting upon it. It is not enough to contemplate Him as an eternal, infinite, absolute Being, not even enough to admire Him as the infinitely wise Architect of the universe. He must be venerated as our Lord and Sovereign. We do not say, my Eternal, my Infinite; we say, my God, that is, my Master. God is no longer God, He is but nature and fate, without a Providence. (*Deus sine dominio, providentiâ et causis finalibus nihil aliud est quàm fatum et natura.*) The true God is then an intelligent living God, who moves, orders, and governs the universe. Thus natural philosophy teaches us the origin of things, for it belongs to that science, supported by the observation of phenomena, to raise us up to God. (*Et hoc de Deo de quo utique ex phænominis disserere ad philosophiam naturalem pertinet.*)"

Objection—"These great men were prejudiced."

Lagrange and Laplace not Theistic.

We cannot fail to be touched with a faith so strong, exhaling from the lips of Newton in such grand and simple words. I know it will be said that Copernicus, Kepler, and Newton speak like Christians rather than philosophers, that having breathed from infancy the air of Christianity, and fed upon her milk, they beheld the universe with prejudiced eyes. It will be remarked how much astronomers must have changed their point of sight, when an age of doubt and negation has succeeded to an age of faith. Nature, in the days of Copernicus, apparently was just the same as in the days of d'Alembert. The laws of Kepler, and the attraction of Newton, far from having received the slightest refutation from the progress of observation and calculation, on the contrary, have shone out with an ever-increasing splendour. Yet in the eighteenth century, new astronomers, new geometricians, those even who have verified, extended, and completed the Newtonian system—a Lagrange, the inventor of the calculus of variations, a Laplace, author of the "Celestial Mechanism," have not found in the heavens a trace of God. The only divinity before which astronomy will henceforth bow, is mathematical science; the ideas of propriety, of beauty, of free choice, and arrangement have neither sense nor meaning since numbers must govern the universe; for in geometry and mechanics everything must be demonstrated rigorously, everything is in a chain, and must be deduced by immutable relations, every thing is what it needs must be—it is the empire of necessity.

I confess these arguments make no impression upon me; I can see without difficulty that the essential character of mathematical truths is to be absolutely necessary; but this necessity, be it understood, is purely ideal, for this simple reason—that the object of mathematics is also ideal. Numbers, circles, and curves are not real and effective things; by no means, they only express abstract possibilities which may have an eternally real basis in the intellect of the eternal geometrician; but which, taken in themselves, have no force and no virtue, and cannot explain the existence of a grain of sand.

You say that it is absolutely necessary that the

Necessity does not solve the *phenomena* so well as intelligence.

radii of a circle should be equal; that may be, but it is not necessary that there should be a certain circular body, say the sun. Granted a universe with stars and worlds, governed by the mathematical law of attraction, undoubtedly several things must necessarily follow: for instance, it will be necessary that planets should describe elliptic curves round the sun; but it is evident that of itself there is nothing necessary in this motion. If the ellipsis were the curve necessary for stars which have a translative motion other stars would not describe different curves. If you tell me that all celestial motions are the necessary consequences of the law of attraction, which is necessary in itself, I ask how you prove it? Is the necessity of this law evident? Then it would not have needed the labour of ages and the genius of a Newton to discover it. Do you call it a consequence of the essence of bodies? then you must have the kindness to explain what the essence of bodies is, and what attraction is in itself, and what is its mode of action; and, further, you will have to prove that bodies themselves exist necessarily. Away with these childish speculations! Let us only reason on what modern science has established—with the help of observation, analogy, and calculation. One thing only is established, that there is a grand, universal, sole, sovereign law, which gives an incomparable beauty, solidity, and harmony to the universe. Everywhere in the heavens there is order, simplicity, and arrangement; therefore everywhere intelligence and choice; therefore no where blind necessity.

Leaving those immense worlds which human

science only perceives afar, and in the aggregate of their masses and their movements, I turn to the things of earth, which can be taken up and handled. Here the absolute empire of mathematics ceases. There succeeds to the inflexible regularity of the heavenly bodies a harmony more varied, more delicate, more simple. I see around me life. Here I find a flower hidden in the grass; it rears bravely its frail and flexible stem to seek the sunbeam, which helps it to expand, to tint its leaves with thin, delicate hues, to exhale its sweet perfume. Close beside it I see a little insect, which spreads its wings, flutters from flower to flower, sucks out their odorous sweets, and, laden with its spoil, bears it to the hive, where tribes of winged reapers follow. If some one should come and tell me that that flower and that bee are the work of an absolute necessity, without any thought of suitableness, or free and harmonious arrangement, I should find it difficult to understand him, and unpleasant to listen to him. I understand and appreciate much more that observer (Leibnitz, I think) who, having one day taken a grub from a bush to admire it more closely, was suddenly seized with an involuntary emotion, and hastened to replace the insect on its leaf with a sort of respect, fearing to profane or tarnish one of those living mirrors where the wisdom of the Creator is reflected.

The world of flowers and insects. Purpose there.

Before allowing myself to mistrust the inspirations of nature, or those acquired prejudices which may unconsciously influence me, I will consult again those naturalists, those learned men of genius, Harvey, Linneus, or better still, those last

Naturalists.

great creators, Cuvier and Geoffroy Saint-Hilaire, and those whom they have initiated into their researches. I am told, indeed, that these eminent men could not agree—that if the ideas of Cuvier are conformable to a Providential system, those of Geoffroy Saint-Hilaire favour that of necessity. I am not prepared to enter into the infinite complications of this illustrious controversy, but I may succeed in seizing its great features and their most certain results.

Cuvier and Saint Hilaire.

Cuvier was convinced that the innumerable multitude of individuals which compose the organized world, may be referred to a certain number of essentially different plans and types. In the animal kingdom especially, whatever may be the analogies which are found between different groups, anatomy lays down four plans of organisation which it is impossible to confound, and which divide animals for ever into four orders. Geoffroy Saint Hilaire only beheld a factitious work in this great classification, which has overthrown that of Linneus, and which has been succeeded by no other. According to him nature works on a single type. The differences which seem to divide living beings, are purely exterior; and the philosophical observer finds everywhere the same essential organs.

A learner, like myself, cannot decide between Cuvier and his antagonist; but I ask both, and Cuvier first, what the principles are that have presided over their respective labours. Cuvier answers thus:—

"Every organized being forms a whole; a single united system, the parts of which mutually correspond, and concur to the same definitive action, by a reciprocal reaction. None of these parts can change, without the others changing also; and consequently each of them taken separately indicates and gives all the others. If the intestines of an animal are so organized that they will only digest flesh, and that newly killed; it follows that his jaws will be constructed to devour his prey, his claws to lay hold of and tear it, his teeth to cut and divide it, the whole system of his organs of motion to follow and to seize it, his organs of sense to perceive it afar; nature even must have placed in his brain the necessary instinct to know how to hide himself and lay snares for his victims. Such are the general conditions of the carnivorous species. An animal intended to be of this species must infallibly unite them all, for his race could not exist without them."[1]

Cuvier's principle of correlation of organs.

Had Cuvier been told that there has been found, on some old Egyptian monument, the figure of an animal, whose strange organisation would confute the principle of the correlation of organs, how boldly his reserved and positive spirit would have repulsed *à priori* the authenticity of such a testimony. He would say, you have mistaken the pictures of fantastic animals for descriptions of real animals. "In some such design on one of these monuments, Agatharchides must have seen his carnivorous bull, whose jaws reaching from ear to ear spared no other animal, but which assuredly would be disowned by naturalists, since nature never combines cloven feet and horns with sharp teeth." And mixing gracefully

[1] Cuvier. *Discours sur les Revolutions du Globe*, p. 96.

the serious playfulness of the man of wit with the higher views of the Philosopher, Cuvier thus goes on,—Now-a-days any one who only sees the trace of a cloven foot may conclude that the animal who made it was a ruminating animal; and this conclusion is as certain as any other in physics or in moral science. This single track, then, gives to him who observes it, both the form of the teeth, and the form of the jaws, and the form of the vertebra, and the form of all the bones of the leg, of the thighs, of the shoulders, and of the stomach of the animal that has just passed by. It is a surer mark than all those of Zadig.[1]

These great principles of the subordination and correlation of organs, in the hands of Cuvier, have reconstituted, with the help of a few fossil bones, whole races of extinct animals, and have recalled to existence worlds that seemed lost for ever in oblivion. And any one may see that all these labours, all these discoveries, all these miraculous resurrections, are inspired by the thought that nature, in her operations, obeys, not blind mathematics, but laws of convenience, harmony, and proportion.

Saint Hilaire's principle of analogy.

I next inquire of the disciples of Geoffroy Saint-Hilaire if they have a principle. They have one, and they call it analogy. To distinguish and to classify animals, to divide them again into species, genera, orders, classes, ramifications; all this is but the beginning of their science. They must still analyze each of these groups, and grasp analogy under difference, and unity under variety. From one species to another species, from one

[1] Cuvier. *Discours sur les Revolutions du Globe*, p. 103.

kind to another kind, philosophical anatomy discovers or fancies the same elements of organisation. One species, the fish for example, has a skull composed of twenty-six bones; another, such as the bird, has but eight or ten. Here, then, is a marked difference, a line of demarcation. So you think, because you have only examined the bird in its adult state. Examine it in its fœtal state, and you will find in it all the primitive bones, which, later, will melt together and deceive the artificial observers. At other times you let yourself be deceived by the numerous metamorphoses that an organ is subject to, when you observe it in the whole course of the animal series. Its visible forms vary, its dimensions change, its structure becomes complicated or simplified, its functions, even may differ; for different organs serve sometimes for the same function, as the lungs and the branchiæ, and it happens too that the same organ sometimes fulfils different functions, as the organ of locomotion, and the organ of respiration; but the relative position and the mutual dependence of organs never vary. Hence that principle which is the torch of anatomical philosophy; An organ may be maimed or destroyed, it can never be transposed.

Nor is it only in one of the ramifications of the animal kingdom that this law is verified. Vertebrated or unvertebrated, whatever artificial barriers are raised between animal and animal, still the unity of their organic composition prevails; and thus science verifies every day, that sublime conception of the Timeus which Buffon has expressed in language worthy of Plato; "It seems as if the Supreme Being would make use but of one idea, and at the same time vary it in every possible manner, in order that man might equally admire the magnificence of the execution and the simplicity of the design."

Monsters. But we have still to explain an immense series of phenomena which have remained till the present time an enigma and a scandal, I allude to the existence of monsters. But that which is called by this name is not a denial given to the general laws of nature. It may all be explained by an arrest of development, ruled by two very simple laws, that of the balance of organs, and that of the attraction of similar parts. Every time that you meet with an organ developed in an exorbitant fashion, instead of believing it a miracle, try if you cannot find in a corresponding organ a defect of its normal development. If on the one side there is hypertrophy, there is atrophy on the other side. As Goethe has ingeniously remarked, Nature has a fixed budget, and too great an expenditure in one department exacts economy in another.

Really governed by two laws under the principle of the "arrest of development." Thus the law of the balance of organs accounts for simple monstrosities—those which are called double are explained by the attraction of similar parts, which so act that if two germs, if two fœtuses, should happen to join, it is always the heart which will be joined to the heart, the brain to the brain, and so on. We must not then speak of the freaks of nature, of disorder, or of chance.[1]

[1] [*τὰ γὰρ παρὰ φύσιν οὐδὲν δεῖ ἀκριβολογεῖσθαι πότερον κατὰ φύσιν τινὰ ἢ ἄλλην αἰτίαν γίγνεται.—Arist. Rhetor.* I., c. xi. 13. Modern philosophy proves that monstrosities are *κατὰ φύσιν τινὰ*.]

Monsters are not a disorder, but an accident subject to laws—a transient deflection, always contained, corrected, and ruled by the superior laws of order, which are above all.

These are the great discoveries which give to Geoffroy Saint-Hilaire an immortal place beside Cuvier. Where is now the necessary contradiction between these two men of genius?—From the point of sight of religious philosophy, it does not exist at all. To Geoffroy, as to Cuvier, the world has a plan, it is governed by laws—not laws of necessity, but laws of convenience and harmony. One, led by the stern genius of analysis, sees best the differences of beings; the other, carried away by the audacious inspirations of synthesis, can only see their analogies. Both make me understand that faith in Providence is independent of the diversity and the contradiction of systems. Systems change and clash, because they represent the unequal efforts of man to grasp the often mysterious economy of the divine plan; but in proportion as some of the great lines of this plan are more clearly discovered, the world appears to us more harmonious, vaster, more simple, and more beautiful, and the eye of man beholds in more visible characters the free and intelligent Principle which it reflects.

These two great naturalists really bring out one truth.

Seventh Meditation.

Providence in Man.

The other world (besides *Gravitation* and *Life*)—*Humanity.*

I HASTEN to return to the internal world, and to hide myself from that torrent of sensible phenomena, where I am always in fear of making shipwreck of my ignorance. There is one being in the universe that I not only see without, but whom I can observe within, and that being is myself. Little as I am, I form a part of the universe, I am mingled in its motion, and I have my part to play in the drama of universal life. Now the question is, to know if I am but a wheel bound by destiny to a blind inflexible mechanical power, or if I find in myself the sure signs of a plan, of order, of a law of fitness and love. There is no further conjecture here. Were being and life absolutely unknown to me everywhere else, I grasp them at least in my own consciousness; and my view of them must be true, for this fragment of universal existence is myself. I may be ignorant of everything, but I must know him who is ignorant and who confesses his ignorance. Life and being are there; I can question them at leisure.

Make answer, my soul! Art thou a predestined force, which is developed by necessary acts, at the will of an irresistible destiny? All the powers of my soul protest against such an idea. I feel myself free—I know that my destiny is in my own hands. Not that I can always develope my faculties according to my desires, but I can always make an effort to do so, and I succeed in a certain measure, more or less. Whether my intellect be sterile or fertile, whether my organs, supple or rebellious, serve me with more or less docility, my will remains always master of itself. Load my body with chains, place a seal upon my lips, you can hinder me from speaking, from writing, from exercising my material rights, you cannot hinder me from affirming them in my conscience, and from protesting against violence with all the energy of that moral liberty which is inaccessible to your blows. These are simple facts, immediate, and not depending upon systems or conjectures upon the unknown. Let us now put these facts face to face with systems. If the universe is the necessary development of a sole principle which, under all its forms, in such a time and place, or under such relations, is always what it can be, and can never be anything but what it is, it is clear that a free being is the most chimerical and impossible thing in the world. For how can I feel myself free, how can I have even the idea of liberty, if I am only a necessary form of life?

Liberty, not necessity, its law.

Pantheists tell me that I do not see all the secret springs which make me act, and that feeling my action, and only feeling the causes of it partly, I cover this ignorance with the flattering chimera of an unlimited independence. But this

Pantheistic Objection Answered.

cannot be the case; for if it were, the less I knew of myself, the more frivolously I lived, the more I should see this phantom of liberty increase. But quite the contrary happens. When the stream of my being seems to flow by chance, when I give myself up to the current of external things, I feel the consciousness of my personality grow weaker, I feel that my moral liberty is departing, and that I am falling under the yoke of passing objects. I become like a drunken man or a somnambulist, who acts with his eyes shut, without directing himself, or knowing what he is about. But on the other hand, when I tear myself by a manly effort from the empire of external objects, when I enter into myself to grasp my life, to seize with a firm hand the government of my sensations and my ideas, then I feel in the strongest manner my personality and my independence; I feel them with a marvellous lucidity, strength, and vivacity; I see then that I can lose everything except this self-government, and that I can resist all the powers allied against me, when I am protected by that impenetrable intrenchment, liberty of the heart.

Liberty—yet law.

I am then a free agent, but that does not mean that my activity is subject to no law; far from it,—while I feel my liberty, I feel it made to be conformable to a law. An absolute liberty, that is, a liberty which should find in itself no principle of determination, no motive for doing this thing, rather than that, would not be liberty, but caprice—nor even caprice, for to act by caprice is still to act with an intention and an end: it would be chance, that is to say, an effect without a cause, or rather a pure phantom, and an impossibility. Then again, if my liberty allows itself to be subject to law, this law of a free agent cannot evidently be a law of necessity, excluding the possibility of any infraction, but a law of order and fitness, the law of duty.

As liberty supposes an overruling duty, so duty supposes liberty. The two ideas imply each other, and both are the basis of the idea of right. If I did not feel that I myself have liberty, I should not recognise it in my equals; and believing them subject to the law of necessity, I should not impose upon them a law of order and of fitness, the law of duty. And if it were true that my equals have no duties, either towards themselves or towards me, what would avail the right that I claim of developing my faculties without hindrance, of expressing my thoughts freely, of preserving my field and my house? As soon as that necessity which governs man should impel irresistibly some individual to take possession of what I call mine, I may oppose him with force, but not with right. Duty.

In the system of necessity there are beings, some of them more intelligent, more acute, more violent, more timid, more to be feared than others, but a free being submitting to duty, a society of moral beings governed by a law of order and fitness, on which rests a system of duties and of rights, must be a chimera, a contradiction, and an absurdity. Thus all my moral nature, all the principles of sociability that are naturally engraven in my soul, in a word, all the humanity in me, protests against the system of necessity. Therefore Right.

there is a Providence. Being free, I must emanate from a free Creator. It is from Him that I hold this law of duty, which I recognise as inviolable and holy, and He imposes it upon me because Himself has made it the eternal rule of His will. And this law has nothing in it peculiar to man; it is the law of order, and by this title it is universal, and absolute, and obligatory upon every being capable of understanding and fulfilling it. God, who has engraven this law in me, is conformed to it Himself. God, who has willed that justice, and order, and good should be things sacred and respected of every intelligent being, cannot be indifferent to justice, to order, and to right. From the idea of the lowest of my duties reason rises to a supreme law, which governs the whole creation, and the creative will itself. Is it too daring to endeavour to comprehend this law?

I feel myself obliged to do right, and to avoid the contrary. Now, what is right? I set aside for a moment the universe and my equals. I consider myself alone, and what right is in that which concerns myself. I conceive it is this, to develope my faculties harmoniously, that is to develope each of them according to the degree of excellence that belongs to it, due regard had to all the others. I find in my mind a certain number of natural powers, which lead me each in its way to the knowledge of truth. I have senses to explore material things, memory to recall the past, induction to conjecture the future, imagination to represent absent things, to lend a body to invisible objects, to embellish real objects; judgment interweaves idea, reasoning orders judgment, reason goes back to first principles, triumphs over extension and duration, beholds eternal truths.

Evidently all these powers are good, their natural object is what is or may be, in a word truth. They only fail in their object when they exceed their own limits, if one is substituted for the others, lives at their expense, changes or destroys them. Thus, memory may extinguish judgment, reasoning may contradict the senses, imagination may deceive us, and reason itself like imagination may become the "fool of the house."

Right of being unhindered in moral development.

In the heart of man there is the same need for subordination, for measure, and for harmony. I have within me the germ of all the loves, and there is not one that does not respond to some perfection, and does not lead to some good. Naturally I love order, proportion, grace, beauty, and intelligence. The love that I have for myself is not an ill-regulated affection, for I love in myself existence and life, strength, health, and all good things belonging to the body; thought, liberty, and all good things belonging to the soul; and that inferior love which makes me seek my own well-being for itself, without regard to any other good, is a perfectly legitimate principle of preservation which only becomes evil by growing beyond bounds, and compressing or extinguishing better feelings. All the powers of my heart and mind, such as God has made them, are then legitimate and good. Evil only begins when I interpose to modify the divine work, when, instead of developing it in the sense of equilibrium and harmony, I introduce into it disproportion, excess, disorder, and wrong. And if I go out of myself to consult my equals, I find that good and evil are to them what they are to me; and my duty being to develope my faculties with harmony, their duty is the same. They have then, in relation to me, the right of being respected in the development of their faculties, and I have the same right in regard to them.

Sympathy. Yet surely to be good it is not enough to do no injury to others; that solitary and negative virtue would leave man very incomplete. I find in my heart a whole treasury of sympathetic yearnings. I have need of men as men have need of me. In them as in me the object of love is first existence and life in their harmonious beauty, but especially the human person. I cannot remain imprisoned in my solitary self. I must enter into the souls of others, live in them, draw them towards me, and feel them live with my life. A sweet and irresistible sympathy makes me feel what they feel, makes me sad with their sadness. happy in their happiness, doubly joyful when they are associated in my joy—almost insensible to sorrow when I feel it is shared, wanting to extend to them all the good that I have, to give them my strength, my thought, my whole soul: feeling myself richer, freer, stronger, and completer the more I strip myself and impoverish myself for them. This sympathy for man extends itself to everything in nature more or less resembling humanity. I love in animals the faint lines of human personality, I look for signs of will, of intelligence, of love, even in the most infinitessimal created beings, and when I cannot find them, imagination comes to my aid, gives a soul to the flower, and something to be respected and loved to all that lives.

This, then, is my law, to love right and order, to love the harmonious development of beings. And it is also the universal law of creation, the law of order and fitness which God proposes to free agents, and which He maintains among the beings which are not free. This world, then, has a plan, a plan of incomparable beauty, where every part is joined, sometimes by visible knots, sometimes by mysterious bonds, to a simple, universal, eternal law of development and harmony. All beings concur to the Divine designs, some according to inflexible, mathematical, uniform, absolute laws, which govern them without their seeming to know it, sonorous but insensible echoes of the Divine harmonies: others, according to laws of another character, more diverse, more supple, giving freer play to life which begins to feel and to master itself: others, finally, and they are beings like myself, participate in the accomplishment of the views of Providence, in virtue of a free and intelligent activity.

And my place in the bosom of the vast universe is this: Lost in a corner of its spaces, made to stay there but one swift moment, a drop of water in that river of human generations which flows on engulphing individuals and bearing the whole race through a thousand storms to unknown destinies, I know not the particular designs of the Divinity for myself, or for any other; but during my short pilgrimage I need only cast a glance upon the world to perceive in it the certain trace of a Divine government. I see Providence shine amid the marvels of Heaven; I feel Him in the secret depths of myself, and, delighted with that radiant intuition, I proceed on my journey with a calmed spirit and a strengthened heart.

Eighth Meditation.

The Mystery of Suffering.

INTERNAL observation has led me further into the secrets of universal order than my senses could have done. The sight of this immense moving universe had confounded my thought. In the human soul I have seen more clearly; I have felt God to be nearer there; yet how wretched is the condition of my intellect. In proportion as I discover new horizons new mysteries appear, and if the lights are brighter the clouds, too, seem to darken. I am free; I acknowledge a law of fitness and harmony, to which I must be conformable. This is a certain fact, but even from it there springs up a formidable objection against Divine Providence, for how can the consequences of human actions enter into the plan of His government? If that which I shall will to-morrow, with all its consequences, great and little, depends on my free determination, it follows that before existing in act it is absolutely undetermined, and therefore escapes from all prevision.[1] Whether divine pre-

[1] [A full and interesting discussion on God's prescience of man's free actions will be found in St. August. De Civit.: Dei. lib. v. c. ix. x., where he criticises Cicero De Divin., lib. II., c. v. vi. vii. Cicero denied

vision or human prevision, whether perfect or imperfect, finite or infinite, it is all the same—it is of the essence of that which is free that it cannot be foreseen. I should form a strange idea of the sovereign being, if I were to suppose that God knew beforehand what I should do to-morrow, and that He had arranged in consequence the general conduct of His designs, for God then would be subordinating His designs to my will, or caprices, or folly. Perhaps these difficulties only spring from an excess of presumption and curiosity. I try to enter into the counsels of God, and I form a human idea of His foreseeing wisdom, forgetting that Divine thought is not subject to the condition

this prescience. If all things were the objects of this prescience, they would come in the order in which they were foreseen: if there is a certain order of things, there is a certain order of causes; if there is a certain order of causes, all things are done by *fate*. But if all things are done by *fate*, there is no such thing as free-will, and our moral nature is a delusion. Upon these grounds Cicero (like Socinus after him), denied the prescience of free actions. The alternative presented it to himself in this shape—either postulate God's prescience, and take away free-will, or postulate free-will, and take away God's prescience—and he chose the latter. But to Augustine God's prescience and man's free-will form an *antinomy*, both capable of proof, both to be believed. He denies that the process from a certain order of causes to the impotence of the human will is valid. The human will is the effective cause of human works. Our wills, therefore, are in that order of causes, which is certain to God and comprised by His prescience. But if God foreknew all causes, among those He knew our wills, which He foreknew as the causes of our works. His conclusion is admirable: "Nullo modo cogimur, aut retentâ præscientiâ Dei tollere voluntatis arbitrium, aut retento voluntatis arbitrio Deum (quod nefas est) negare præscium futurorum: sed utrumque amplectimur, utrumque confitemur. Illud ut benè credamus; hoc, ut bene vivamus." Cardinal Cajetan concludes a passage, of which Sir W. Hamilton has said that is "the ablest and truest criticism" on the subject, with these words: "Optimum autem est in hâc re inchoare ab his quæ certò scimus et experimur in nobis, scilicet quòd omnia quæ sub arbitrio nostro continentur, evitabilia à nobis sunt . . . . . quomodo autem, hoc salvo, divina salvetur Providentia ac prædestinatio credere quod ecclesia credit; Scriptum est enim, Altiora te ne quæsieris."—*Summa T. D. T. Aquinatis cum Commentariis Caietani*, Art. I. quæst. xxiii., vol. I., p. 93.]

of time,[1] that it has consequently no relation before or after with events of the world, and that it embraces everything in its eternal act in an incomprehensible and ineffable manner. Be it so; I will be silent and prostrate before the difficulty; but there is another mystery that I cannot pierce which is terrible in a different manner. My condition in this world is one of suffering; it is the condition of all men; nay, more, of all sentient beings. Pain is not an accident, it is law of universal life. O mystery which disconcerts and troubles me! The other enigmas of nature only tormented my intellect—this oppresses my whole being. I cannot understand how, under the government of a God of justice and of love, a kind of curse reigns upon the noblest beings in the universe. Nature is a field of battle and slaughter, where the law of the strongest reigns in all its brutal ferocity.[2] I cannot advance a step without crushing living beings. I am preserved at their expense. That I may live they must die. Nor is the empire that I claim over other beings of much use

Suffering a law of existence.

[1] ["The transference of the idea of time to the Divine intuition is anthropopathic," says Kant. Scaliger says, with that matchless happiness of style which was not always employed so well:—"Ne verbum quidem illut *prævidere* Dei convenit omnipotentiæ, nisi quoad nostrâ mutilâ intellectione metimur infinitatem. Nobis quidem, quibus est futurum, *prævisio* illa est: Deus, cui nihil futurum est, non prœvidet, sed videt simplicissimè quod est prœsens."—*De Subtil:* Exerc. ccclxv. 8. So Boethius: "Itaque si præscientiam pensare velis, quâ cuncta dignoscit, non esse præscientiam, quasi futuri, sed scientiam nunquam deficientis instantiæ, rectius æstimabis."—*De Consol.*, Phil. v. 6. These authorities will be satisfactory or not, according as we consider Time merely a psychological condition of thought or otherwise.]

[2] [This "law of destruction" is constantly referred to by Tennyson. Joseph de Maistre views it as part of a great law of expiation by blood, of which war is an instance. See *Soirées de Saint Petersbourg*, ii., 2-39, especially the sections, "Comment s'accomplit la destruction violente des êtres vivants," and "La Guenes est Divine, une loi du Monde."]

to me. Of all living creatures it is I that suffer the most. The animal at least knows not its own sadness. Its needs are limited. Feed it and it is calm—it appears happy. But man, to all the ills that he endures, adds those that he dreads—distress, sickness, loneliness, old age, and death.

Dreams of amelioration.

Some sages will tell me, all these evils are accidental and transitory; they arise from imperfections in science or in the social condition. Study the history of man's condition, especially for the last half century. Every discovery in physics has given an impulse to industry, and every advance in industry has been a relief to man. In the same way, in proportion as lights increase manners are softened and laws improved. Every day some prejudice disappears, some natural injustice is repaired, some inequality is rubbed off. Human society is approaching rapidly to a state of universal justice, of reciprocal benevolence, and of peace.

Mere dreams.

When I was younger I listened to words like these, but the experience of life soon taught me that there is no chimera in the world more absurd than that of the abolition of suffering. No science, no industry, no political combination can free my body from its miseries, or my soul from its weakness and its passions; and then what is the end? However amusing the play, the last act is always bloody; two or three shovelfulls of earth will be thrown over me, and all is over.

Shall I here bow my head and say that pain, having its indestructible root in the nature of things, that proves that the nature of things is neither good nor bad, just nor unjust, and that, consequently, pleasure and pain, joy and sadness, life and death, spring equally from a blind and indifferent necessity? I confess this is a thought which has crossed my mind at times of bitter pain and extreme dejection; but when the spring of my soul, suspended for an instant by some violent blow, resumes its natural strength, when I escape from the blind impression of the present moment, and contemplate with the eye of my reason, once more ascendant, my condition on earth and that of my equals, and the laws of universal life, then other thoughts come to soften and strengthen my soul, and it is restored by degrees to the sentiment of order, to serenity and peace.

I must have strength to detach myself for a while from my individual being to consider things collectively. On the lowest steps of this immense ladder, I find beings who seem plunged in a complete inertia. Yet they have motion; for even in the repose of equilibrium, there is a strife of forces—a life; but it is a diffuse, external life, which is not concentrated. In the midst of these insensible masses, I meet with other beings whose life is evident; I see organs more and more diverse, rich, and complicated, which all conspire to one common end. But life does not seem to me complete till the organised being is aware that his activity, instead of displaying itself with ease, has met with an obstacle, for then it reacts, it sets aside this, it attracts that; it interferes in its own destiny, it shows discernment and choice, and a beginning of reason and of will.

Now, it is pain that warns the animal that his short life is in danger of being shortened; pain, then, is nothing but the feeling of an alteration of life, of a diminution of being, in the same way that pleasure is the animal's feeling of an increase operating within us. If it be so, pain appears to me under a new light. It is no longer an arbitrary state, it is the natural condition of a being who has limits, and who feels himself live. Besides being a useful warning to him, and hindering him from falling asleep in deceitful security, it also spurs him on, and urges him to defend himself from death, and to extend continually the sphere of his activity. Would it be better to feel nothing? Should the animal regret that it is not a plant, the plant that it is not a stone, the stone that it has any existence whatever?

Man has more exquisite joys and keener sufferings than other creatures.

Man forming a part of animal nature, for that reason is subject to the general law of pain. Now, it is certain that I suffer more evils than other animals, but the reason of this is plain. I also taste a thousand blessings and enjoyments that they have not. In proportion as the life of a being is more complex and ample; so, the more obstacles it meets, the more favourable opportunities of development it will meet also. It has more room for pleasure and pain, it has joys more varied and more exquisite,[1] it has also more

[1] [Even in pleasures, vulgarly considered as merely animal, man's complex and subtle associations give him a vast superiority in gratification. This is, perhaps, more evident in the sense of smell than in any other. Beasts have a delicacy in that sense wonderfully superior to ours. Yet, as Aristotle has remarked, they only experience gratification from odours *accidentally*. The dog is not pleased with the smell of the hare, but with eating it, of which the scent brings a perception before him (Ethica Nic. III. 13). "Hunc sensum valdè imperfectum habemus; ideòque vocabulis utimur *saporum* ad explicandes nonnullas odorum differentias, dicimusque odorem suavem, etc. Duo sunt odorum genera, quorum alterum per se alimentum sequitur, ut nidor qui famelicis gratissimus est, saturis ingratus. Alterum genus per se non sequitur alimentum, ut odor ex floribus. Utrumque genus percipiunt tam

and deeper sufferings. But this is not all. There is in me something better than an animal, completer and more perfect than aught else: there is man, the free and reasonable person. I conceive truth, justice, beauty, order, and right. I am capable of science and virtue; but science and virtue have one common condition, namely, effort,[1] and the consequence of effort is pain.

Capable of knowledge and virtue; but these come by effort, and effort is pain.

I sometimes imagine that my condition would be infinitely better if all my natural faculties, instead of being discordant and at strife, could attain their object spontaneously, and enjoy them without obstacle in the bosom of a perfect harmony and a sweet felicity. Chiefly in the hard labour of some difficult quest, or in the painful

bestiæ quam homines; sed bestiæ tamen ex hoc posteriori genere nec luptatem nec dolorem capiunt, sicut homines. Hi odores habent materiam subtiliorem, magisque *aeream*."—*Burgersdyk Coll. Phys. Disp.* XVIII. Scaliger investigates the question whether other animals besides men delight in scents, and rakes together curious instances of aversion and attraction. Most brutes like the scent of the panther. Serpents hate galbanum, and mice burnt mule's hoof. Bees are attracted by some flowers and hate others. I have heard that a cat is fond of mint. Of this superiority of pleasure even in the sensual enjoyment of a creature like man, Young finely says:—

> "Our *senses* as our *reason* are divine;
> Objects are but the occasion, ours the exploit:
> Ours is the cloth, the pencil, and the paint
> Which nature's admirable picture draws,
> And beautifies creation's ample dome.
> Like Milton's Eve, when gazing on the lake,
> Man makes the matchless image man admires.
> Our *senses* which inherit earth and heaven,
> Enjoy the various riches nature yields—
> *Far nobler! give the riches they enjoy.*"
>
> *Night, VI.* 420.

Of these riches given by the senses, the rarest come from *analogies*, sometimes very subtle. The quivering of moonlight upon the waters perhaps affects us with more exquisite pleasure from an analogy with the palpitating flutter of dying music.]

[1] [Τὸ γὰρ χαλεπὸν ὁρίζεται ἢ λύπῃ ἢ πλήθει χρόνου. *Arist. Rhetor.* I. VII. 27.]

strife of passions one against the other, and all against reason, in these moments of anguish I find myself exclaiming, O how sweet it would be to know truth without an effort, and to do right without a struggle! but this is a vain wish, a chimerical desire, the dream of a weak heart that knows not virtue or science, nor what it is that gives to human life its real greatness. Knowest thou, O my soul, what must happen if thy propensions were naturally harmonious and attained their objects without obstacle? Thou wouldest remain eternally in infancy, or rather not even that, for there are already in the infant struggle and effort, the noble seeds of manhood: thou wouldest have nothing of personality, thou wouldest be a *thing!* That which awakens personality in us is just the jar and strife of discordant propensions, the necessity for intervention in the government of our powers and for substituting rule, measure, and subordination in place of their natural anarchy and insubordination. The condition and the dignity of thy moral being is to cause harmony to reign in thy inclinations, thy loves, thy actions, in all the parts of thy nature. True, thou must purchase knowledge and virtue at the cost of pain, but when thou hast learned their divine charm thou wilt never complain of having bought them at too high a price.

Death. To look now beyond this visible world. Among the evils which weigh most upon man is the idea of death; and doubtless death is an object of terror to the imagination, but is imagination or reason to be the rule of our life? What are life and death to reason? They are accidents which

Annihilation would be a miracle.

do but touch the surface of existence. Beings are transformed; none perishes. And if death is only a transformation for the plant and the beast, how shall it scathe man? Nature loses none of its individuals; shall God lose one of his persons? Try to conceive the absolute annihilation of a grain of sand; you cannot attain to it. As well might you try to understand that the smallest atom, if it did not exist a minute before, should begin to exist all of a sudden. It is not impossible to conceive that invisible parcels of matter should conglomerate, and form a palpable body; nor that they should separate again, and be scattered in dust; but it is impossible to conceive that they should cease to exist, at least unless we suppose the intervention of Infinite Omnipotence. Unquestionably the God who is capable of creating can also annihilate all. But let us reflect upon it; as soon as we ascend to the creative cause, we pass from one order of facts and ideas to an order entirely different. We leave the things of time and nature, to transport ourselves into the realm of the supernatural and the eternal. When we suppose that creative power interferes at a given moment to annihilate a being, we are supposing a supernatural event—a miracle—who shall measure the absurdity of such a supposition, especially when it concerns not merely a mass of matter, but a person, a moral being. Is there anything in the world whose value does not fade away when compared with the priceless value of a being capable of virtue, devotion, and sacrifice? In the eyes of God the humblest of moral creatures is worth more than all the stars of the firmament. It was not for no end that, after having united in man all the marvels scattered through the worlds, God added above all the purest ray of His divine essence, a moral nature. Thereby He has raised us infinitely above sensible nature. We only belong to earth by the roots of our being; by our moral life we are raised to the celestial regions. The great care of the animal is to seek pleasure, to avoid pain, above all to put off death. This fear of death is not even reasoned out; it is but an instinct, a blind but beneficent counsellor who prolongs for the animal the joy of living while sparing it the painful care of death. But what my soul fears above all things in its moments of recollection is not suffering but doing evil. Man only in the universe thinks of death, because it is his honour to brave it, and his destiny to conquer it. No, we cannot perish, for it is not possible for any natural power to prevail over what is better than it and comes from the Most High. The God who has made alone can annihilate. But to do so, we must suppose Him to will something that is not just, and wise, and good. Would it be just if He were to engulph all souls together, the pure as well as the impure, in the same nothing? Would it be wise and good if, after having brought us into communication through reason and liberty with things divine, He were to shut against us the gates of futurity, half open to our hopes and our wishes? Away with these fearful thoughts. To want faith in God is to fail in reverence to ourselves. All in us is allied to infinity: our pain like our pleasure, our ignorance like our knowledge, our virtue and beauty like our vice and deformity. Our sufferings upon earth have no limit. But let us not complain. This means that our power of knowing, of willing, of feeling, and loving has for its career the course of illimitable ages, and for its object the Infinite God.

Ninth Meditation.

Religion.

Religion, as such, good.

THUS convinced in the depths of my consciousness, and all my doubts slowly overcome by a determined and persevering reflection, when I consider all these great truths I understand what religion is, I can explain to myself why it is universal and imperishable. I recognise it as legitimate and holy under every form that it has ever worn, and I feel myself united with my whole soul to every human creature who has ever raised to God a word of faith, an impulse of love, a sigh of hope, or a hymn of adoration. For the diversity of symbols does not matter so much here. Religion consists not in the formulas pronounced by our lips, but in the feelings of our hearts: it is not by external practices, but by internal and effective acts that it proclaims its power. Whosoever adores and prays is my brother in God.

There is a best.

Does this mean that all religions have the same sense and the same moral value? Certainly not. The religious symbols that have surrounded and guarded my infancy, have impressed my soul too deeply with their singular purity, and their incomparable sublimity, to permit me for one moment to compare them with those of any other time or country. But since every religion expresses the idea that some people, race, or family of nations has made to itself of the origin and the sum total of things, it must be, that the symbols which make this idea sensible to the imagination and the heart, will change with time and place, with laws, with the manners and minds of men; it must be that the revolutions of empires, the exchange of ideas between different people, the insensible transformation of souls, the discoveries of science will leave their impress on it. But amid these differences and variations, above those religious forms which are produced and organised, and mixed, which degenerate and die, there are a certain number of truths which never die. I find them scattered every where, at least their germs, even in the least spiritual creeds. They go on increasing, growing purer and stronger from age to age, ever young, ever living, and in their progressive evolution they maintain and consecrate the religious fraternity of nations. And the first of all these truths, that which contains all the others, is that there exists beyond the visible world, a first principle altogether distinct from what is transitory; a divine and celestial city, wherein is the origin, the model, and the end of the city here below.

Here is the essence of religion, herein lies its strength and its immortal truth, that it tears us from the thoughts of earth, and gives us the sentiment of the things of heaven. Through it, man triumphs over the tyranny of selfish thoughts, and the miserable cares of his daily needs and interests. He conceives a universal order, a harmony, a perfection, a stainless beauty that nothing can change or tarnish. This is why religion is to simple souls both poetry and philosophy. It does more than show them, on high, the incorruptible Judge of the living and the dead, the supreme refuge against oppression and violence, the unfailing support of the weak, the witness to their secret tears, and the consoler of their griefs. It makes them forget their very griefs, by pouring into their hearts a disinterested joy, and initiating them into purer contemplations. Strengthened, consoled, overjoyed, the religious soul becomes aware that it is worth more than all the fragile gifts of earth, and that its destiny calls it to enjoy eternal blessings.

Universal principles of religion. Existence of principles distinct from all; besides, this religion gives joy and poetry.

Now, if the essence of religion is to conceive God as anterior and superior to the world, as the first principle, the perfect model and last end of existence here below, I conclude that religion is essentially reasonable and true. Have I not descended to the depths of my consciousness, and there amid the silence of passions and senses, seeking truth and seeking only her, have I not consulted reason, have I not listened to the voice of the Master within, and what has it said?

Essentially reasonable.

Beauty of God.

It has told me that before the imperfect changeable finite being, there is the eternal unchangeable Infinite Being—God. It has told me that God is the complete being, not an abstract, undetermined being, a dark germ of existence, but the most real of all beings, the being in whom all the powers of life are expanded and displayed. It has told me that the Perfect Being, living in Himself a perfect life, is fully sufficient to Himself, and that if He has made the world, it is not from a necessity inherent in His nature, but by a free act of His omnipotence, by a counsel of His wisdom, by an effusion of His goodness; and thenceforth this world, the work of liberty, of intelligence, and of love, becomes the living expression of its first principle. Through all the immensity of space and time there rules a law of fitness and harmony, a divine law, a sovereign law, which rules the relations of all beings, conquers all resistance, effaces all accidental discord, and leads every being through its appropriate transformation to all the beauty, perfection, and happiness which are conformable to its particular nature and to universal order.

And must not the heart beat and the soul be moved when they glance over and embrace this solid succession of sublime thoughts? Can I think of the Perfect Being without adoration? I, who seek eagerly in the beings which surround me for the weakest rays of intelligence and beauty, who ask of every scene of nature and every work of art its invisible thought and its poetry; I who am enchanted by proportion, by measure, by the harmony of colours and of sound, and, better still, by those holy harmonies which are called wisdom, justice, and truth; when I say to myself that all these perfections which delight, and these harmonies which charm me, these truths, whose sweet light rejoices my heart and mind, are but the reflections of divine truth and beauty, the eternal concord of all the powers of being, shall I not fall down and worship?

And as I taste more and more of the sweets of this worship, I feel all the powers of my soul in-

Duty towards our neighbours.

crase, and there runs through my veins a new current of youth, and sap, and energy. I feel an insatiable need of union with God. How? God is good, productive, creative good. He has produced the world His eternal work; and wherefore? because the world is good, because it expresses truth, beauty, harmony, and divine happiness. I would then imitate God; I would love truth beauty, order, and harmony; I would tend to the highest happiness; I would love all the creatures of God, and I would love them more the better they expressed His perfections. What is sweeter than love, and how easy for man to love other men! I would love them as my brothers, as the trial companions that God has given me in my earthly voyage; I would respect them as privileged beings on whom God has laid the sacred sign of personality.

Function of power.

A marvellous gift, but an awful trust of which I shall have to give account. Who can think on Divine justice without an inward shudder? God has given me liberty—how have I used it? I who could even in my lowly condition do so much good, and who have done so little, mingling with it oftentimes so much ill, how humbled I feel when I think that I shall have to give account of all the ill that I have done, and of all the good that I might have done. Do I rebel against suffering which has often been my own work, often too my punishment, and which, perhaps, has purified me and lightened part of my burden, by expiating beforehand a part of my sin?[1] Do I say that I have not deserved it, that were no reason to rebel,

[1] [I must protest against this view, as unsanctioned alike by natural and revealed religion, however prevalent in many Christian lands.]

for every limited being must pay his tax to suffering, the inseparable companion of pleasure; and if my portion of the trial appears too large, reason tells me that it is not I but God who must regulate it.

Religion not only a thought or a sentiment.

I am humiliated at the feeling of my own ignorance, I confess it; and overcoming pain, misery, murmurs, doubts, despair, I cast myself on the good and adorable God, and all my sentiments of humility and resignation, of hope and fear, are found, and met, and harmonised in one supreme act of confidence and love. This is the religious sentiment.

Principle of action.

Religion, then, is true as a thought and as a sentiment. It remains to be proved that religion is also true as a proper principle of action. To be religious, to perform an act of religion, is not only to conceive God or to love God, it is also to pray to God. But to pray to God is to ask Him for some benefit, some help, some favour. Here all my perplexities begin again. Just as I thought myself at the end of them, a new abyss yawns at my feet. Does not prayer like revelation, grace, a miracle, suppose a particular local temporary intervention of the Divinity in terrestrial matters and the things of time? God is immutable, eternal, immense; there is no succession in Him; all that He does He does by a single act, which embraces all times, and spaces, and beings. If, then, I conceive God as acting in such a place or time by such a particular act, I assimilate God to a secondary cause; I submit Him to the conditions of space and time; I degrade Him, I make of Him an idol or a Jupiter.

Prayer does

Can it be, then, that prayer as a request is

not degrade God, nor is it irreconcilable with the immutability of the Divine law.

utterly irreconcileable with the immutability of the Divine laws? This difficulty did not stop great mathematicians, such as Malebranche and Leibnitz. God, say they, does not act by particular will. It is true; He acts by a general will; but consider all that is comprehended in that will. God, from all eternity, has embraced the course of ages; all is bound together in His designs. He knows all causes and all their effects. He has co-ordained them in His plan. God knows that such a creature, at such a minute on such a globe, will seek a help necessary to his weakness. He has prepared it for him beforehand. Our prayers, our wants, our sighs, and our tears are eternally before His eyes, and He takes note of them as He deems best.

Solution of Malebranche and Leibnitz.

Their proof does not perfectly satisfy.

Here is certainly a deep and subtle metaphysical theory. Yet it does not persuade me, it leaves me still in uncertainty. When I feel an ardent desire of seeing some event accomplished which does not depend on my will, an irresistible impulse impels me to raise my hands to God, and to cry, "Lord! help me;" but at such moments, God is to me the Sovereign arbiter of all things. I suppress the thought of every secondary cause, I forget that nature has laws according to which life and death, health and sickness, joy and sorrow, are distributed to all beings. Losing sight of all this, I only think of the power of God. This is the impulse of the heart, this is prayer in itssublime spontaneousness and familiarity. All is carried on between the soul and God, between the servant and the master, the subject and the sovereign, between the subordinate and suppliant, and the omnipotent and infinite will. But when reason resumes its empire, I say to myself that my prayer is vain and indiscreet, that there is a divine plan in the universe, and at that thought of the immutable laws of nature, my heart freezes, and prayer dies upon my lips.

Seek the ideal of prayer as a solution of the difficulty.

Shall I suffer my soul to be overcome by this difficulty? Is it evident that if it responds in fact to a particular internal condition, it is a condition of weakness and languor, not of moral strength and health. Let me examine better what prayer is, and amid the imperfect forms which it wears in hearts of men, let me seek its real essence, its sacred ideal. There are two degrees in prayer—the first has no value but as a means to reach the second. He who stops at the first step of prayer knows not its greatness or its value. At its outset prayer is born of want. Like its parent it is egotistical, and self-interested, it asks a favour. It is the prayer of the imagination, the prayer of the child, and there is always something childish in the most manly being. It asks a miracle, nothing less, but it asks it ignorantly. For the idea of a miracle supposes the laws of nature, and the soul which prays on the spur of an imperious necessity knows not whether nature has any laws. It only knows one thing, that it wants a certain assistance, and it asks it of the omnipotent will.

Two degrees of prayer.

1. First, More egotism.

2\. But the religious soul does not stop there. It knows that the events of the world are not given over to caprice or chance; that the hairs of our head are all numbered; that everything in the universe is ruled by universal eternal laws, full

2. Second and higher, "Thy will be done."

of wisdom, of foresight, of mercy, and love. Thus disappear selfish wishes and indiscreet claims. The soul, raised above itself, above its restless wishes and its transitory ills, cries out, My Father, thy will be done. It is no longer an arbitrary, capricious, tyrannical will. It is a will inspired by love, and regulated by wisdom. Why ask this or that from Him who knows better than we, what is our real good? Prayer far from perishing when it is disentangled from all particular solicitation, is raised and transformed. There is no local presence of the Divinity, no egotistical coming back upon ourselves,[1] nothing but a lively sentiment of the universal presence of God, an overpowering impression of His infallible wisdom and His helpful omnipotence, an intimate adhesion to His will, an unreserved submission to His designs, heart, will, intellect, soul, given up wholly to Him. The human person concentrating all its powers into one act of love, is associated and subordinated to the Divine Person. The great mystery of existence, the distinction and union of the two personalities—this mystery where pure reason is lost, where reasoning so often goes astray—this mystery does not exist to the soul that has prayed.

[1] [I must here confess myself dissatisfied, more, perhaps, with the language than with the meaning of M. Saisset, who seems to me to have been unconsciously influenced in this passage by his recollections of Malebranche. The "*first* degree" of prayer is a *revealed condition* of *all* prayer. "Give us this day our daily bread," *follows* "Thy will be done." What is that but a particular solicitation? The Deist, Chubb, asserted that "God's end in requiring prayer is *wholly and solely* that it may be a means to work in the petitioner a suitable frame of mind." Isaac Barrow had well said before: "It is both a means by impetration acquiring, and an effectual instrument, working all true good in us." See this question discussed in King's *Origin of Evil*, Chapter V., Subject IV., *Concerning th efficacy of Prayer;* in Leland's *Deistical Writers*, Letter XIII., p. 160; and in Woollaston's *Religion of Nature Delineated*, pp. 125, 126.]

Essay by the Translator.

Essay: By the Translator.

Most educated men have for some time been aware of the presence, in our contemporary literature, of a certain Pantheistic element, which perhaps they have felt rather than been able to analyse. Twenty years ago, a learned and pious divine of the Church of England wrote these warning words: "We hear much of laudable efforts to bring the saving truths of Christianity within the reach of the votaries of Brahmanism; but few amongst us are aware that the very esoteric doctrine of Brahmanism, and of all Pagan theology, is now in the course of propagation to cultivated minds from the centre of Christian Europe."[1] The warning has been fulfilled. The snow has melted in Germany, and we have had a flood in England.

The selection of the subject of Mr. Mansel's Bampton Lectures may be taken as a proof that the ambitious constructions of German Pantheism are viewed with admiration by too many thinkers among ourselves. The strong and subtle author of the *Limits of Religious Thought Examined*, would never have woven his strait-waistcoat of the Con-

[1] Dr. Mill on the *Mythical Interpretation of the Gospel*, p. 6.

ditioned for speculators in delirium, had he not known that such patients existed.

Pantheism is pre-eminently the metaphysical heresy. Few men are metaphysicians: many men have an interest in the refutation of Pantheism. Hence the need of something in the shape of a philosophical manual to modern Pantheism. Such a manual I had not been able to find until I met with M. Saisset's *Essai de Philosophie Religieuse*.

The volume, whose translation I have finished in the midst of many interruptions, appears to me to supply this *desideratum*. M. Saisset is an athletic thinker, who possesses that indescribable air of nobility, which tells us that he has kept the best company which the human intellect can afford. On Pantheism he has a right to be heard which cannot be urged by any other living philosopher. The claims of modern Pantheism to originality are loud and exultant. Philosophy, according to it, has had two epochs, the Greek and the Germanic. The genealogy, in truth, is longer, less august, and less heaven-born than such assertions would imply. It runs something in this way: Hegel, which was the son of Schelling, which was the son of Fichte, which was the son of Kant. As we trace up the older names on the tree, we find that the German has a dash of Leibnitz, his countryman, a good deal more of Plotinus, the Alexandrian, but most of Spinoza, the Jew. Convinced of this fact, M. Saisset spent several years in the study of Spinoza, tracing out the lines of filiation between him and modern Germany downward, between him and Descartes upward. Most volumes of philosophy are but meagre analyses of jarring systems. In the present book every line tends to one centre. In an exquisite passage of his poem, Lucretius observes, that confused as a battle may seem with its glare and noise, there is yet an elevation upon the mountains, from which the contest seems to come to a stand, and all the glitter of the war to remain stationary upon the field.[1] Such a superior point of view M. Saisset has attained. His work, in its first and most important portion, is not an analysis of modern philosophy, but of modern philosophy in relation to Pantheism. How are we to account for the scepticism of Kant and the Pantheism of Hegel, after Descartes, Newton, and Leibnitz? In presence of the hideous phenomenon of Pantheism, the weakness and the strength of the great schools of Theistic philosophy should be rigorously tested. The task is performed in the first or critical portion of the preceding work, with a learning and acuteness which leave nothing to desire. The constructive is seldom equal to the critical portion of metaphysical performances. Every able metaphysician seems to dwell for a while in a shrine, of which he is

> "The priest who slays the slayer,
> And must himself be slain."

With all the beauty and eloquence of the second part, it seems to me less completely satisfactory to a Christian than its predecessor, for reasons which I shall presently endeavour to state.

[1] "Et tamen est quidam locus altis montibus unde
Stare videntur, et in campis consistere fulgur."
Lucret. ii. 331.

The First Part of this work has been translated by myself—the Second by a friendly hand under my supervision. I have placed on the margin a running analysis, which may facilitate the progress of younger students, and have added some notes. The original draft of the Essay obtained the prize offered by the Academy of Moral and Political Sciences on the following subject: *Examen critique, des Principaux Systèmes Modernes de Theodicée.* The second edition carried off the first of the great Monthyon Prizes of the French Academy. A third edition succeeded while the sheets of this translation were passing through the press, with an Appendix, containing three important "*Eclaircissements,*"—the first, a historical sketch of the various proofs of the existence of God; the second, a defence of the author's general view of Pantheism; the third, in support of the peculiar (and rather questionable) view of the infinity of creation, which he has inherited from Descartes, Pascal, and Leibnitz. These additions reached me too late for translation, but the substance of the two first is incorporated in the present Essay, and the sheets have been corrected by the third edition.

To traverse, however rapidly, the critical portion of M. Saisset's work, would be to write a book vastly inferior to its original. I shall, however, make some remarks upon the second, or what I have called the constructive portion of M. Saisset's argument. I shall place together, as clearly as I can, those general features of the book which are most worthy of observation, and I shall, finally, venture to interpose with a few words, which may be taken as the *cautè legendum* placed by the caution of an inferior thinker upon the page that has been written by a master's hand.

I. I proceed with a rapid sketch of the second or constructive portion of M. Saisset's work.

In answer to the question, "Is there a God?" M. Saisset prefers to the Anselmian, Cartesian, and Leibnitian forms of proof, that argument for the affirmative which makes the existence of the Perfect Being a direct intuition of consciousness, and not the conclusion of a syllogism.

Is the God thus revealed to me accessible to my reason? To know perfectly what God is I must of course be God. But if God is inconceivable in His essence, He is not absolutely incommunicable.[1] The Hamiltonian scepticism is represented in language which occasionally reads like a translation of Mr. Mansel. The true portion of this memorable philosophy is that Theology has its mysteries. Beyond God's attributes there is a somewhat ineffable as their foundation, which offers an eternal barrier against the construction *à priori* of a proof of the Divine existence. But the true conclusion from man's incapacity of conceiving God is not, that we are to turn for ever from the object to the ethics of theology, that we are to annihilate theology in every form, from the Nicene Creed to the Savoyard vicar's Confession of Faith. Theology presents neither unclouded brightness nor undi-

[1] The conclusions of profound scholarship on the plural name of God, *Elohim*, in relation to *Jehovah*—the former expressing infinite fulness in its manifestation, the latter unity and infinite Personality—are in perfect accordance with this result of abstract thought.—See Hengstenberg *Genuineness of the Pentateuch*, vol. 1, pp. 213, 393, especially 273. Art: *Names of God in the Pentateuch*.

luted obscurity. God is incommunicable in His essence, communicable in His manifestations.

After answering the interrogations, "Can there be anything but God?" "Can God be the Creator?" M. Saisset grapples with the question of the infinity of the universe. He maintains that in a certain sense it is immense and infinite, though with a relative not an absolute infinity, and he labours to prove that this conclusion is supported by the discoveries of modern science—by the telescope of Herschell and the microscope of Ehrenberg—while it is in accordance with the character and attributes of God, actually accepted by such Christians as Leibnitz and Pascal, and though not received, yet not rejected as absurd or impious by Augustine and Aquinas.

I willingly leave this perilous and insoluble question, in which a resolution of the doubt would involve a process of discovery which is rendered impossible by the very conception of the infinite, and pass on to the more profitable discussion of Providence in the universe and in man. There are three worlds—the worlds of gravitation, life, and human personality. The solemn and awful question arises, Is their law Providence, or blind Necessity? The first simple look gives the idea of order and harmony from the worm to the stars. So does the moral law. Copernicus, Kepler, and Newton, were profoundly Theistic. It may be said that Lagrange and Laplace thought otherwise, but beyond all question, necessity does not solve the phenomena so well as the choice which has adapted means to end, and the order which has blended a rich variety into perfect harmony; and what are choice and purposed order, but intelligence? From the great lines of the architecture of the heavens, we may descend to the bee humming upon the flower, and draw the same conclusion. I may add one other authority to those cited by M. Saisset. If Newton, looking up to the infinite spaces whose silence terrified the spirit of Pascal, perceived the traces of the great Geometer, Linnæus saw His footsteps in the world of animated creatures. He veils his eyes, and exclaims, "I have seen God, the back parts of the Eternal, the Omniscient, the Omnipotent, passing by, and I am mute with amazement.[1] In the works of creation, I have been able to discover some traces of His steps; and in these works, even the smallest, even those which seem as nothing, what power is there, what wisdom, what inconceivable perfection!" Here again it may be urged, that if Cuvier and Linnæus are for Providence, Geoffroy Saint-Hilaire is for necessity. But M. Saisset admirably shows how Saint-Hilaire's principle of analogy leads to the conclusion of Providence even more irresistibly than Cuvier's theory of the correlation of organs. "Monsters," also, are no play of chance; they are really governed by two simple laws, and exist by a "certain kind of nature."[2] Still more is order to be traced in the third world—that of humanity. The irrecusable moral law, the ideas

[1] "Deum sempiternum, omniscium, omnipotentem à tergo transeuntem, vidi, et obstupui," &c.—*Car. Linn. Syst. Natur. Regn. Anim*, 10th edition, p. 9.

[2] Κατὰ φύσιν τινὰ.—Arist. *Rhet*, i. xi. 13.

of duty and right, are there, and point to a moral Governor. In the exquisite chapter on "The Mystery of Suffering," M. Saisset does indeed

"Study the philosophy of tears."

He shows that suffering is an unavoidable law of our nature; that theories of the indefinite amelioration of society are but idle and not innocent dreams. Man has joys which are more exquisite, and sufferings which are much profounder than those of other creatures. He is capable of knowledge and of virtue. But knowledge can only come by effort, and effort is pain. Virtue, too, is a plant which must be watered by tears, and rooted by storms.[1] We have indeed instincts which make us shrink from suffering, but without suffering we should lose the sublimest attributes of personality. "Our grief," is "but our grandeur in disguise." As for death, annihilation would be a miracle, and is not to be hoped or feared. Religion, then, is presented to us as an essentially reasonable thing. It is the deepest fountain of truth and beauty as well as poetry. It is a joy as well as an awe, a consolation no less than a check. It is a principle of social action also; for from the love of God necessarily flows our duty to our neighbour. But this view necessarily leads to prayer. Is prayer not a degradation to God, and irreconcileable with the Divine laws which govern the universe? M. Saisset's answer, I am afraid, is rather unsatisfactory, as it only includes the

[1] "Laissez pleuvoir . . . .
Sous l'orage qui passe, il renaît tant de choses,
Le soleil sans la pluie ouvrirait-il les roses."

Mme. Desbordes Valmore.

prayer of *resignation*, not the prayer of *expectation*. But it closes with words whose depth and grandeur are in every way worthy of a Christian philosopher.

II. I shall now attempt to indicate the strong as well as the weak points of the work which I have so imperfectly analysed.

I. 1. The capital merit of the preceding Essay is, that it draws out in bold and vigorous lines the real character of Pantheism, which appears to be so much misapprehended. Pantheism is constantly falling over into Atheism, as with Hegel and Spinoza, or becoming sublimated into an immoderate Theism, as with Malebranche and Plotinus. Like Scadder, in Mr. Dickens' novel, it has a bright side and a bad side to its face, and he who looks exclusively at one or the other will draw an imperfect representation. Pantheism is as like Atheism as sleep is to death; it resembles mysticism as closely as a drunkard's dream resembles *delirium tremens*. But sleep is not death, though there is a sleep which is soon frozen into death; and a drunken dream is not *delirium tremens*, though such dreams are often its forerunners. Let us trace the origin of this essentially metaphysical heresy, and we shall find light thrown upon this apparently subtle distinction.

There are two ideas which, in one shape or other, are common to us all—the idea of the finite and that of the infinite. It matters not about the order and *genesis*, whether with Descartes we hold the finite to be the negation of the infinite, or with Hobbes, consider the infinite to be the negation of the finite. These two ideas, however acquired, give rise to the earliest and latest problem of metaphysics—to account for the co-existence of the finite and the infinite.

The earliest solution of this problem on which we can rely was in the Eleatic school; and it amounted to this, that there is *nothing but the infinite*. Thales and Heraclitus, on the contrary, taught that *there is nothing but the finite*. All is fleeting and transitory, in continual flux and endless becoming. We cannot bathe twice in the same stream. But it needs few words to show that neither of these opposite systems satisfies the human mind. To teach that there is nothing but the infinite is the sublime of folly. The witness of personality is too consistent and powerful to be overlooked. All the incantations of mysticism cannot lay the mighty ghost of personality. To assert, on the other hand, that there is nothing but the finite, is as absurd, and more degrading. Are these gleams of the infinite nothing but the flashing of the candle of the *Ego* upon the petty window-pane of my consciousness, which I mistake for the lightning shining along the heavens? Do not those mysterious sounds announce to me the infinite as surely as the voices of the sea behind the sand-hills announce to me the existence of its waters, though I cannot catch their glimmerings behind the barrier over which which they murmur? Are my loftiest thoughts a delusion, and my purest sentiments a mockery?

We must take up this problem again. Account for the co-existence of the finite and the infinite. You must not absorb the finite into the infinite, nor shatter the infinite into the finite.

Shall we maintain their *opposition?* The result of this will be a system which is called in religion Manicheism, in philosophy Dualism.

But unity is the most imperious need of our mind. And here is precisely the point at which Pantheism meets our thought. Try the problem again. You must not absorb the finite into the infinite: you must not shatter the infinite into the finite: you must not rigidly oppose the one to the other. What course remains?

The finite and infinite are but two aspects of one and the same existence, called Substance or what you will. They are but one and the same principle, from two different points of view. Nature viewed as attached to its immanent principle is God; God viewed in the course of His evolutions is Nature. This is Pantheism, the system which teaches the eternal and necessary consubstantiality of God and nature, of the infinite and finite.

Such is the luminous account of Pantheism which M. Saisset exhibits. And he proves his account of it by an immense voyage over every sea of human thought. The following *formulæ*, I apprehend, represent his view:—

FINITE AND INFINITE.

Infinite—Finite = Mysticism.
Finite —Infinite = Atheism.
Infinite + Finite = Manicheism.
Finito-infinite, or Infinito-finite = Pantheism.

Pantheism is ever sliding into the first and

second formulæ. This is a subject of importance to the Christian Missionary. In the systems of India, he will find a general Pantheism, in the Vedanta burning into Mysticism, in the Sânkhya freezing into Atheism. So in Greece, Heraclitus represents absolute Naturalism, Parmenides exclusive Theism. The Stoic philosophy, divinizing man with a sort of "heroic materialism," carries on the Heraclitan solution. The Alexandrian school exaggerates the mysticism of Parmenides.

Modern philosophy awoke with a *dualism* in Descartes—*res cogitans* and *res extensa*. Thought would reduce these terms to a unity. Hence, on the one hand, the system of Malebranche. God is the sole agent. Bodies are extension without power of motion. Souls are thinking automata. God's incessant, irresistible motion is the only life. This is mysticism. We have seen the meaning of Spinoza's Substance, Attribute, and Mode. It is Atheism.

Philosophy took a fresh start with Kant. But the result is just the same. The Kantian school had its Malebranche in Schelling, and its Spinoza in Hegel. From Schelling sprang Gœrres and Baader, the mystic school of Munich. And the results of Schelling's philosophy, the "intellectual intuition" in which the soul becomes unified with the Divine Thought, is startlingly like Plotinus and the Alexandrians. From Hegel, on the other hand, issued the fearful Atheism of Oken and Feuerbach, and the still more dreadful anti-Theism of Schopenhauer.

Thus modern Europe and the ancient East,

Alexandria and Athens, France and Germany, point to the same conclusion.[1]

II. 1. 2. Another admirable feature in the present work is the weight which it gives to *every* valid argument for the Personality and Government of God. In a truth which has passed under so many hands, the philosopher finds an almost irresistible temptation to look after new arguments. But new arguments are not to be found, and those which are thought to be so, are but antiquated theories long since weighed and found wanting. Thus, the Cartesian proof was but Anselm's speculation, which had been confuted by Thomas Aquinas.[2]

M. Saisset's view of the whole argument, as stated in the new edition of the present work, is as follows:—

There are truths of *intuition* (νοῦς), and of *reasoning* (διανοία). The existence of God is a truth of *intuition*, like the existence of matter, or the fact of free-will. But as against Berkeley's idealism, or against irreligious fatalism, so against Atheism, *reasoning* is most useful refutatively.

M. Saisset conceives the existence of God to be a truth of intuition. Fichte's principle, when rightly understood, is perfectly valid. "The *Ego* assumes itself in opposing to itself the *Non-Ego*." The finite supposes the infinite. Extension supposes first space, then immensity: duration supposes first time, then eternity. A sudden and irresistible judgment refers this to the necessary,

nave c.osely followed M. Saisset. *Eclaircissement* deuxième. Tome II., Ph. 316-368.

[2] Waterland—*Dissertation upon the Argument a priori.* Chapter 3.

infinite, perfect Being. We may formulate the proof in this proposition, "The imperfect being has its reason in the perfect Being." This is the proper and irrefragable Theistic proof. But the use of reasoning is to refute the Atheist, and bring him to a *reductio ad absurdum;* and in this point of view, the finest exertions of the human intellect have their own proper functions.

To the usual philosophical classifications of the Theistic proofs, M. Saisset prefers the historical order, which he arranges as follows:—

1. *The Socratic proof from Final causes.*—Anaxagoras would seem to have been the first among the Greeks who used it. Socrates, in the Phædo of Plato, says to Cebes—"When I was young, Cebes, it is surprising how earnestly I desired that species of science, which they call physical. For it appeared to me pre-eminently excellent in bringing us to know the causes of each, through what each is produced and destroyed, and exists. But happening to hear some one read in a book, which he said was of Anaxagoras, that it is Intelligence which is the parent of order and cause of all things, I was pleased with this cause, and it seemed to me to be well that Intelligence was the cause of all, and I considered that, were it so, the ordering Intelligence ordered all things, and placed each thing there where it was best."[1] In the *Memorabilia*, Xenophon developes this proof at greater length, in a conversation of Socrates with Aristodemus upon the Divinity. The tone of this passage, in speaking of the corre-

[1] Plato, *Phædo*, CXLV. XLVI.

spondence between our organs and the external world, and of the instances of design in the human frame, reads like part of a chapter of Derham or Paley.[1] In Aristotle, God is the Final Cause (τὸ οὗ ἕνεκα), of all things.[2] In the Middle Ages the argument was abused. Hence Bacon exclaims—"Causarum finalium inquisitio sterilis est, et tanquam virgo Deo consecrata nihil parit." But this condemnation is altogether from a scientific point of view, and does not the least reflect upon the proof from Final causes as a religious argument. De Maistre wastes much indignant eloquence upon the Baconian philosophy from oblivion of this obvious distinction.[3] Descartes went much further, and thought little of the argument as a Theistic proof, most probably from a desire, as Locke said: "to cashier every other argument," out of "overfondness for one darling invention." Leibnitz considers it useful in metaphysics, in Theodicea, in morality, and even in physics. M. Saisset puts the argument into shape in the following syllogism:—

Every effect where we see a choice of means appropriate to an end, supposes an intelligent cause.

But in the universe we see such a choice of means.

Therefore, the universe is the effect of an Intelligent Cause.

[1] Xenophon *Memor*, i. 19.

[2] Mr. Jowett, with his usual vagueness, asserts that "Aristotle was probably the first author" of this argument. St. Paul's Epistles; *Natural Religion*, Vol. II. 4.

[3] *Philosophie De Bacon*, Tom. ii. p. 6 cf. *Bacon De Augm.* Lib. iv. c. 3.

The major, which is only a statement of the principle of causality, will hardly be denied. The minor may be harder to prove from our ignorance. But Harvey's discovery arose from the contemplation of Final Causes. The profound thought of Cuvier and Humboldt is in unison with the instinctive feelings of the human race. Kant attacks the conclusion. He asserts that, taken in its utmost latitude, it would prove Manicheism, as attributing deformities and irregularities to God. Besides, it would not prove an infinite, and infinitely intelligent Cause. A finite cause, a Jupiter, not a Jehovah, would suffice. Even supposing the cosmos to be infinite, we might argue from it, not to God the Creator, but to Νοῦς or Demiurgus, an intelligent ordainer. Still this argument stirs deep chords in the human heart in every age. The Psalmist exclaims, "the heavens declare the glory of God." St. Paul speaks of "the invisible things that are made known by the things that are made."[1] Each successive age has moulded the argument in its own shape, and steeped it in its own colours. St. Augustine does not speak of teleological and cosmological arguments. But he can thrill the heart by reasoning of One who has not left the minutest feather of the birds, or the smallest bud upon the herb, or the lightest leaf upon the tree, without a purpose in its parts, and a certain inexpressible peace. He can paint in hues which seem to anticipate the finest touches

[1] Romans ., 19, 20, may be looked upon as recognising the ntuitional Theistic proof, and that from Final Causes (1.) v. 19. There is a something knowable of God *within* them, ἐν αὐτοῖς. (2.) Ever since the creation, God's invisible attributes, especially of power and wisdom, have been read by men's intellects in His world.

of modern poetry, and which are worthy of Ruskin, the sea clothed in its vesture of many colours, with its green of every tint, sometimes deepening into purple, sometimes lightening into blue,[1] as a witness of the Divine goodness to the unthankful and the evil. Barrow's manly style rises into solemn eloquence, as he asserts the goodness of God from "the rude winds whistling in a tune not unpleasant, and the tossing seas yielding a kind of solemn and graver melody."[2] Paley's "cloud of shrimps," "maggot revelling in carrion," and "prolixity of gut," appeal to common sense; and Chalmers' Astronomical Discourses elevate and delight. Professor Jowett has written a strange paper on "Natural Religion," in which he deals with the argument from Final Causes, as Dr. Newman in a certain notorious Tract dealt with anti-Papal arguments—showing up their weakness, because "we are in no danger of becoming Romanists." Of an argument, which seemed powerful to the Psalmist and to the Apostle—which was solid enough to satisfy Socrates, Plato, Aquinas, Leibnitz, Bossuet, Sir Isaac Newton, Cuvier, Linnæus, Butler, Paley, aad Harvey, Professor Jowett writes with pity, that "it is suited to the faculties of children, rather than of those of full age."[3] M. Saisset appears to me to state the matter accurately in the following passage:—

"These objections are solid, this dialectical process is incapable of refutation, but it does not

[1] *De Civit. Dei.* Lib. v. c. 11. xxii. c. 24.

[2] Barrow, Sermon VI. *The Being of God proved from the Frame of the World.*

[3] *St. Paul's Epistles*, Volume ii., p. 407.

prove that the argument from Final causes is false, but that it is insufficient; not that it should be despised, or rejected, but that it must be restrained to its proper bearing. It does not demonstrate the existence of the Creator, nor even the existence of an Infinite Intelligence, but it helps powerfully to confirm these truths. Hear the last conclusion of Kant. This argument, says he, deserves ever to be remembered with respect. It is the oldest, the clearest, and, at the same time, that which is best adapted to the reason of most men. It vivifies the study of nature, while it draws from her continually new strength. It leads to ends that observation of herself could not have discovered, and it extends our actual knowledge. Therefore, to pretend to take away anything from the authority of this proof, would be not only to deprive ourselves of a consolation, but to attempt an impossibility. Reason, incessantly elevated by such powerful and ever-increasing arguments, cannot be so debased by the uncertainty of a subtle and abstract speculation, that she may not be torn as from a dream, from her irresolute sophistries, at the sight of the marvels of nature, and the majestic structure of the world, so as to rise from greatness to greatness, even to the supreme greatness."

2. There is a *Platonic* argument from *necessary and universal truths*. The ideas of Plato form a proof for those great thinkers who may be considered as forming his immediate family—for Augustine, Anselm, Malebranche, Fenelon, and Bossuet.[1] This argument has perhaps been

[1] The argument is thus stated by Bossuet: "The understanding has

given most fully by Fenelon, in his *Treatise on the Existence of God.* It may be thrown into the following syllogism:—

Absolute modes necessarily belong to an absolute subject.

Universal and necessary truths are absolute modes.

Therefore, universal and necessary truths are referable to an absolute subject (God).

The minor of this syllogism is doubtful, and therefore a proportionate doubt is thrown upon the conclusion. But on the other hand, this proof in its own way, in the world of ideas, is as valid as the proof from final causes, in the world of fact. Universal and necessary truths are inconceivable and impossible in a world where all is contingent and finite. And thus the Platonic proof is most valuable as a *reductio ad absurdum* of Atheism.

3. The special *Peripatetic* proof is that from

eternal truths for its object. The rules of proportion by which we measure all things are eternal and invariable. Everything demonstrative in mathematics, and in every other science, is eternal and immutable, since the effect of demonstration is to make us see that it cannot be otherwise. All such truths subsist independently of all times. In whatever time I place a human intellect, it will know them; in knowing them, it will *find* them, not *make* them true; for it is not our knowledge which makes its objects, it supposes them. Thus all these truths subsist before all ages, and before the existence of a human understanding. Were all that I see in nature destroyed, except myself, these rules would be preserved in my thought; and I can see that they would be always true, were I annihilated. If I now enquire where, and in what subject, these eternal and immutable truths subsist, I am obliged to admit a Being where truth is eternally subsisting: it is from Him that truth is derived in all which is, and is understood out of Him. It is in Him, in some manner incomprehensible by me, that I see these eternal verities; and to see them is to turn myself to Him who is immutably all truth, and to receive His lights. This eternal object is God, eternally subsisting, eternally true, eternally the very truth."—Bossuet, *Traité de la Connaissance de Dieu et de soi meme*, chap. iv., § 5, 6, 7. Cf. Fenelon, *Traité de l'Existence de Dieu*, Part i. chap. iv. § 3.

the *primum mobile*, and amounts to this—that all movement and change supposes an author.[1] It is strongly and clearly put by Aquinas.[2] The Newtonian form of the argument has been given by Rousseau.

"Descartes formed heaven and earth of dice, but he could not give them their first shake, nor put his centrifugal force in play but with the help of a rotatory movement. Newton discovered the law of attraction. But attraction alone would soon reduce the universe to an immoveable mass. To this law he must join a projectile force to cause the heavenly bodies to describe curves. Let Descartes tell us what physical law makes his *vortices* turn: let Newton show us the hand which launched the planets upon the tangent of their orbits."[3]

This argument has a real, but limited use, in reducing Atheism to an infinite retrogression, which is inexplicable, and explains nothing.

4. The argument of St. Anselm, or ontological

[1] Arist. *Physica*, vii. viii., Metaph. xii.

[2] I cite his words, as the *Summa* is not to be found in every library. "Respondeo Deum esse quinque viis probari potest. Prima autem et manifesta via est, quæ sumitur ex parte motûs. Certum est et sensu constat, aliqua moveri in hoc mundo: omne autem quod movetur, ab alio movetur. Nihil enim movetur, nisi secundum quod est in potentiâ ad illud ad quod movetur: movet autem aliquid solum quod est actu. Movere enim nihil aliud est quàm educere aliquid de potentiâ in actum. De potentiâ autem non potest aliquid reduci in actum, nisi per aliquod ens in actu. Non autem est possibile ut idem sit simul in actu et potentiâ secundum idem. Omne ergo quod movetur oportet ab alio moveri. Si ergo id a quo movetur moveatur, oportet et ipsum ab alio moveri, κ. τ. λ. Hic autem non est procedere in infinitum; quia sic non esset aliquod *primum movens*, per consequens nec aliquod aliud movens, quia moventia secunda, non movent nisi per hoc quod sunt mota à primo movente . . . necesse est devenire ad aliquod primum movens, quod à nullo movetur: esse et hoc omnes intelligunt Deum."—*Summa Theol*, Quæst. ii. Art. iii.]

[3] Profession de Foi du Vicaire Savoyard.—*Emile*, tom. iii.

proof, founded upon the supposed necessity that the idea of the perfect Being should imply existence, has already been considered incidentally. Its various fortunes, as revived by Descartes, amended by Leibnitz, and criticised by Kant, would require a separate treatise.—Of all proofs which have been advanced, it seems to be the least satisfactory.

5. The Cartesian proof, derived from the perfect Being, is criticised in the First Treatise of the previous Essay.

6. The Newtonian proof, drawn from the notions of immensity and eternity, and metaphysically elaborated by Clarke, is also amply discussed in the preceding pages. The proof of Clarke is drawn from Newton, and reposes on a fallacious theory of space and time. Space and time are not attributes of God. Leibnitz has shown the insuperable absurdities involved in this. But there are solid points in the Newtonian proof. "The idea of eternal and limitless existence, which is incessantly opposed in our minds to the perception of beings developed and co-ordinated in space and time—our impotence to assign limits to time and space, to reckon time equal to eternity, and space to immensity—would be inexplicable and inconceivable, without admitting the existence of God."

7. The Leibnitian proof, founded upon the principle of "the sufficient reason," had best be given in the words of Leibnitz.[1]

[1] "God is the first reason of things, for those which are limited, like all that we see and of which we have experience, are contingent. We must then seek for the reason of the existence of the world (which is the entire assemblage of contingent things), and that in the substance which carries the reason of its own existence in itself, and which

Here, then, is one of the admirable points in this volume. All the chief proofs are carefully examined.[1] None is contemptuously treated; and while the proof from immediate intuition is most relied upon, the others are regarded as forming a multiple and concordant body of refutative argument.

II. I. 3. M. Saisset's work is also valuable, as affording at least a counterpoise, I will not say to Mr. Mansel's philosophy, but to possible abuses or exaggerations of it. Perhaps there are some disciples of the philosophy of the Conditioned who would cure the fever-fit of Pantheistic pride by superinducing the palsy of scepticism. Let us thank M. Saisset, because after the Zama of the Kantian criticism, he has not despaired of the human reason. Mr. Mansel's book leaves on my mind a certain impression adverse to the Nicene and Athanasian creeds. He

is therefore necessary and eternal. It is also necessary that this cause should be intelligent; for this world which exists being contingent, and an infinity of other worlds being equally possible, and having (so to say) equal pretensions to existence, the cause of the world must have had regard or relation to all these possible worlds to determine any one. And this regard or relation of an existing substance to simple possibilities can be nothing but the *understanding* that has the ideas of it, and to determine upon one can only be the act of the *will* which chooses, and it is the *power* of the substance which renders the will efficacious. Power tends to being, wisdom, or understanding, to truth, and will to good. And this intelligent cause must be infinite in every way, and absolutely perfect in power, wisdom, and goodness, since it tends to all that is possible; and as all is linked together, there is no room for admitting any but one. His understanding is the source of essences, and his will is the origin of existences. Here, in few words, is the proof of one God wlth His perfections, and by Him of the origin of things."—*Essais de Théodicée, ad init.*

[1] I should except the argument from "*universal consent*," which M. Saisset has completely omitted. This argument was at one time much relied upon. In a paper in the *Spectator*, written by Budgell, which speaks with alarm of the growth of atheism, this proof, and that from the theism of such men as Newton, are alone advanced. For a modern form of this argument, see note.—Volume I., Pages 33-34.

cites with approbation a great living thinker, who says:—"We should point out to objectors that what is revealed is *practical* and not speculative; that what the Scriptures are concerned with is, not the philosophy of the human mind in itself, nor yet the philosophy of the divine nature in itself, but (that which is properly *religion*) the *relation* and connection of the two Beings; what God is *to us;* what He has done and will do for us; and what *we* are to be and to do in regard to Him." Now it is very noticeable that the argument implied in the word *religion* falls to the ground, so far as Scripture is concerned, the word being scarcely used in our translation except in a somewhat unfavourable sense, and the Greek term[1] being expressive of a very different shade of meaning. It may be true that what is revealed in the Bible is *practical.* But are there not truths which we are called upon to believe as *speculative*, not as *practical?* Carry out the principle to the utmost, and Christianity had better burn her books of theology, and confine herself to religious psychology and religious ethics. It seems to me that some judicious thinker, using M. Saisset as Mr. Mansel has used Hamilton and Kant, may establish a stronger *Theodicea*, and one more in accordance with the conclusions of the Faith.

II. 1. 4. I should also dwell upon M. Saisset's constant recurrence to *experience*, as the best answer to the Pantheistic systems. These stargazers at the heaven of the Infinite are constantly stumbling over the straw of experience. Thus, Spinoza constructs a hierarchy of knowledge which

[1] θρησκεία. St. James, i. 27.

spurns the *data* supplied by empirical sources. He begins with Substance, and that his system may not come to a dead-lock, gives it the two attributes of thought and extension. But thought and extension both come from experience. *Sense* first reveals particular concrete objects as extended; the *fact* of our inward consciousness gives us the experience of thought.

II. 1. 5. Not less admirable is the calm strength with which he retorts the charge of anthropomorphism and "superstition" upon the Pantheistic schools. It is sport to see "the engineer hoist with his own petard," and hardly less to see a Spinozist or Hegelian caught in *flagrante delicto* of superstition. Let me expand a little one noticeable illustration.

A perpetual formula of the Pantheistic philosophers is that God is a cause, no doubt; but then, say they, He is immanent, and not transitive cause (*causa transiens, non vero immanens*.) Let us prick this bladder of *mots d'enflure*, and see how soon it bursts. The phrases *transitive* and *immanent* cause are easily defined. The transitive cause must be joined with, and yet is dissimilar to, its effect. I push a boat into the stream, and am the transitive cause of that effect. To consider God, *ex. gr.* as the Creator, is, according to Pantheism, to degrade Him, to make Him a *transitive* cause. God, they urge, is *immanent cause*; but what is the *immanent cause?* That which produces the effect within itself. Thus Newton's mind is the immanent cause of the Newtonian system of the world, and Milton's mind of "*Paradise Lost.*" The highest type of the transitive cause is a Michael Angelo shaping out the marble-block into a Moses. The most striking type of the immanent cause is the plant pushing out the flower. But look at the illustration and at the instances. The aloe pushes out its blue and crimson blossoms in a single day. But how? Altogether from external sources; it has stored up a quantity of materials by a lengthened process of assimilation, and, under favourable conditions of moisture and temperature, developes them outwardly. It does not create; it only assimilates, moulds, and colours.[1] Take the poem: we call it a creation. Let us consider. A glance at Johnson's "Life of Milton" will show us certain "very imperfect rudiments" and seminal principles of *Paradise Lost*, pregnant, no doubt, with "latent possibilities of excellence," but rude and almost chaotic. And these very seeds, in all probability, were derived from the withered branches of some old Latin poems. How with those glorious comparisons, that wealth of illustration, that solemn and stately march of musical language? No comparison, no illustration, no word, is the work of an *immanent cause*. "Copious imagery discreetly ordered, and perfectly registered in the memory;"[2] learning sublimated by genius, and thrown off in a spirit unmingled with any grosser particles; materials acquired by sensation, reading, and other sources; these, and the like, are the conditions of *Paradise Lost*. Perhaps, when Shakespeare described so gloriously the bees:

> "Those singing masons, building roofs of gold,"

[1] See Dr. Daubeny on the *Study of Chemistry*.
[2] Hobbes' "*Letter concerning Sir William Davenant's Preface.*"

the thought was suggested by watching the hive some summer-day in Anne Hathaway's garden. At all events, neither Milton nor Shakespeare could create a thought any more than Watt could create the material from which steam is engendered. The *immanent cause* is therefore as unworthy of God as the *transitive cause*.

IV. I desire, with all deference, to suggest some cautions in the study of this volume.

The theory of the *infinity of creation* is at best a very questionable one. M. Saisset's theory of prayer, in his ninth Meditation, is equally unsatisfactory to the philosopher and to the Christian. The philosopher will perceive that it solves the problem of prayer, by quietly eviscerating it of its difficulty. The Christian will have more serious objections. M. Saisset makes two kinds of prayer, a higher and a lower—the lower of impetration, the higher of resignation; and he appears to merge the lower absolutely in the higher. The lower is a pardonable weakness—the higher is the heritage of maturity. I suspect that M. Saisset has been influenced here by his admiration of Malebranche. The Oratorian is bold enough to say that "prayer is only good for Christians who have preserved the Jewish spirit;" "that to seek for eternal goods, and to annihilate the soul in presence of the holiness and greatness of God, is that in which true piety consists," while the imagination of a particular Providence savours of pride. These views are too sublimated to be altogether just. The Lord's Prayer at least contains the lower petition: "Give us this day our daily bread," as well as the higher, "Thy will be done." Without the former, the "sublime familiarity of prayer," as M. Saisset calls it in a phrase which is itself sublime, will cease to exist, and the very idea of Providence be lost.

It is also possible that, against M. Saisset's wish, his work may leave an impression that is unfair to the Gospel Revelation. I suppose most thinkers agree with Aquinas, that "the *existence* of God can be known by natural reason, as is said in the first of Romans, and that this and other truths of the same kind are not properly so much *articles of faith* as *preambles* to those articles, our faith presupposing natural knowledge, as grace presupposes nature."[1] The Christian has reason to thank those who strengthen the *preamble*. Philosophy is incidentally useful to him, negatively and positively. Negatively, she takes Pantheistic and other systems, and shows that they are not invulnerable. Positively, she shows that theistic conclusions are most in accordance with reason as well as feeling. But she is too apt to create a system of natural religion with Kant, Rousseau, and Reid. I need not cite those palmary texts so much "blown upon" (as Addison says), which prove that Plato and Socrates could ascend to the notion of God. I have no reason for supposing—and much for the contrary hypothesis—that M. Saisset would deny the conclusions of Butler and Clarke. He knows much better than I do that, besides many doctrines unknown to reason, Christianity republished authori-

[1] *Summa Theod.*, quæst. II., Art. III.

tatively, in a simple and accessible form, without any intermixture of error, those truths, discoverable indeed and discovered by a few, but unknown generally, which before led a precarious existence, in a scattered and dissipated condition, and were first reduced by the Gospel into one solid sy stem of verity. Joined with each portion of the Revelation, old and new, is a truth of natural religion (so called) which experimentalists are always cutting off, to see it writhe and twist, and to mistake its merely nervous and muscular action for that vitality which it can only permanently have in connection with the head. Take the Commandments. The first teaches the existence and unity of God; the second implies that He is spiritual; the third is based upon His Providence and moral government; the fourth contains a permanent record of God the Creator, and is a standing protest against Pantheism. So God's attribute of Goodness is bound up with the mission and death of Christ. Moral responsibility underlies the article, "from whence He shall come to judge the quick and the dead," and immortality, "the resurrection of the body." What, asks Rousseau, is the soul of religion but to worship God in spirit and in truth? What, indeed! It only needed about four thousand years—the dispensation of the law, the teaching of the Prophets, and the death of the Son of God —to establish this simple and obvious truth—simple and obvious as the fifth proposition of the first book of Euclid is, *i.e., to those who have been taught it;* and when a reasoner against the necessity of revelation parades this principle as an argument, he gives it life, by transfusing into the withered veins of his natural religion drops that have been drawn from the very heart's blood of the revelation which he depreciates. Diderot said that all religions, and Christianity among the rest, were but sects of natural religion: it would be more just to invert the proposition, and to saythat all schemes of natural religion are but wretched sects of Christianity.

> Reveal'd religion first inform'd thy sight,
> And Reason saw not till Faith sprung the light.

Once more, I must repeat my hope and convic-viction that M. Saisset would agree with these sentiments. I am but speaking of the general impression left by the second portion of his work. He seems to present it to us as the method by which he has learned to possess his own soul in peace, and by which he hopes others may attain the same blessing. What is this but to dispense with revelation by a stroke of Occam's razor?

Yet surely one significant, I hope and think intentional omission, on the part of this great intellect, may warn minds inferior to his own of the failure of the method. I read this book. I perceive *one* great *hiatus*. I take it up, and turn it over and over again. I hear much of metaphysical, little of moral, difficulties; much of the agony of the doubting intellect, nothing of the deeper agony of the questioning conscience; much to show truly and powerfully, that God is distinct from His creatures—that they are not absorbed into Him—that I have a right to stand in presence of God, and of the universe, and of other spirits, and to say *I* in presence of each—nothing to indicate how, as one of God's banished ones, I am to be brought back to Him. For, indeed, the delirium of philosophy may teach a handful of dreamers to mutter, "I am God," but the deeper instincts of our misery and sinfulness rather make us shiver on the verge of the black chasm, which yawns between our guilt and God's awful purity. I agree with M. Saisset that philosophy can demonstrate to us the existence of God from the constitution of our own minds and hearts, and from the irrefragable proofs of design in the constitution of the universe. The question has been settled by Socrates and Plato. I admit that he has proved that the arguments against an inconceivable Infinite Personality advanced by Strauss, Schelling, and Fichte, are light indeed compared with the arguments against an absurd infinite non-personality. His pleas for a moral design in suffering, for Providence in the three worlds of gravitation, animal life, and human personality, are strong and convincing. I believe, then, that in some sense Philosophy can find God. I believe that in some sense she can justify me in praying. But M. Saisset has a vast knowledge of philosophic systems. Will he find for us in any record previous to Christianity, or extraneous to its influence, a *single* instance of any child of man so conscious of his being a child of God as to say, not vaguely, "Father Zeus," but, "God, *my* Father!" The Psalms themselves can afford us no such instance. M. Saisset's last section leaves the impression that reason can find the Father. I conceive the juster conclusion to be, that reason can find God, but not the Father.[1] I apprehend the truth to be, that M. Saisset, like many other great writers in France, has been driven by ultramontane exaggeration into an opposite exaggeration of the strength and of the sphere of reason in Divine things. To hear it preached, as it has been by Dr. Newman, that to believe in God is just as hard or just as easy as to believe in the Roman Church: to see a man like M. Bautain exulting in the Kantian categories as the shipwreck of all Theism, short of accepting the creed of Pope Pius, is to make Philosophy feel that she has a vested interest in conquering every possible inch of ground for human reason. Hence M. Saisset's injustice to the "Theological school."

Will the eminent philosopher whom I criticise so freely allow me to go further? I seem to recognise in France a whole school of thinkers, who are eloquent about the beauty of Christianity as a theory, silent upon the incorrigible stubbornness of Christianity as a fact; eloquent upon the Divine eclecticism which has fused all the scattered elements of truth into one mass, silent upon that delicately-balanced evidence, of which it may be said, that if it were more the Gospel would cease to be a faith, and that if it were less the Gospel might become a superstition: that if it were more there would be no probation for the heart, and if less no grappling-point for the reason.

[1] [I owe this thought to a writer who is as *witty* as he is wise, taking the former word in that sense which implies an exquisite sagacity in perceiving delicate lines of resemblance between things apparently dissimilar. It will be found in an original paper on Butler's Analogy, in the *Irish Churchman*, by the author of *New Wine in Old Bottles*, the Rev. J. B. Heard, M.A., of Percy Chapel.]

Reason, on Roman Catholic ground, is like an army stretched along a line with weak points as well as strong points, all of which must be defended. Thus it is that philosophers, who wish to be Christians, refine away many Roman peculiarities into profound symbols, and extending this habit further, the members of the most dogmatic Church in the world become undogmatic to the verge of Socinianism. Rome has a majestic theory of unity; she expresses it in a lath-and-plaster imitation of the heavenly Jerusalem. She has a belief in the dignity of every portion of the corporeal organization of the saints that sleep, as destined to belong to the spiritual body which shall grow in the germ of the flesh; she expresses it in a miserable relic-worship, or disguises it in an enormous hagiology. As she delineates the beautiful ideal of the resurrection of the body in the clay of relic-worship, so she carves out the primitive truth of the redemption of the body in the cherry-stones of fanciful myths. The presence of our Lord in the sacrament is concentrated into the materialism of transubstantiation. Repentance, with its deep sighs and burning tears, is frozen into the sacrament of penance. Thus, the educated mind, which wishes to retain its belief, is perpetually volatilizing into metaphor what its

[1] M. Bautain, in one of the most elegant as well as powerful passages in his writings, is forced to acknowledge how well Pantheism also can find a home in the Roman Catholic ritual: "This religion is made symbolical; if Catholicism is the sublimest of religions, it is chiefly by its *form*. Its cathedrals, with their ogives, lancets, and rose-windows; its worship with its ceremonial, its music and chanting, render it so deeply interesting, and it suits marvellously with that vague religiosity which admits all symbols."—*Philosophie du Christianisme, Supplément à la* 29. *Lettre du Pantheisme*, vol. ii. p. 163.

Church has been congealing into symbols and dogmas. And this habit of mind, once acquired, is exercised at last not only upon the symbol, but upon the dogmatic *truth* which the symbol encases. Thus the sacrament becomes a *mere* beautiful expression of the soul's sustenance, and the Resurrection of our immortality, and the holy Trinity of God's attributes, and the Incarnation of the meeting of the finite and infinite. Thus the Gospel narrative becomes, not indeed absolutely disbelieved, but thin and shadowy under these subtle touches, and the Mosaic account of the creation is rather a majestic symbol of the distinctness of God from the universe than the history of a fact. I am not sure that M. Saisset may not have imbibed something of this spirit.

III. And, now, let me sum up the whole impression which I have attempted to convey in this essay.

I have translated M. Saisset's book with an admiration of his intellectual power, of his learning, and of his masculine eloquence, which makes me wish that my flattery were worth his acceptance. I thank him for a noble testimony of reason to the Personality of God. He has drawn out clearly the central idea of Pantheism. He has analyzed its metaphysics from Spinoza to Hegel, gliding subtilly along its finest threads. He has shown that Pantheism is founded upon deductions from that experience which it condemns; that its vaunted premisses are word-jugglings, false to the verge of madness; that it promises the soul an ocean of light to lead it into an abyss of darkness, without morality, immortality, or God—for its morality is a fancy, its immortality is death, and its God is the negation of God. He has done this not merely by demonstrating the impotence of human reason, which might lead us down another abyss, but with metaphysical good sense as well as subtlety, showing that God is light as well as darkness, and that reason has its strength as well as its weakness. Nor have his services ended there. He has displayed to us all the great proofs for the existence of God, not isolated as in Descartes or Paley, not sneered down with offensive contempt as only suitable for childhood, but ringed together like adamant. The eye that has been bloodshot from gazing upon the blinding snows of Scepticism, or filmed over with looking upon the hot iron of Pantheism, is soothed as by the softness of green fields. I have to thank him too for many lights, thrown upon nature, and upon the mind and condition of man. Even after that matchless sentence in which Paley joins together "at one end of our discoveries, an intelligent power constructing a ring of two hundred thousand miles diameter to surround Saturn's body, and be suspended like a magnificent arch over the heads of his inhabitants—at the other, bending a hooked tooth, concerting and providing an appropriate mechanism, for the clasping and reclasping of the filaments of the feather of the humming birds,"[1] I can turn with pleasure to the Meditation in which M. Saisset binds together the eighteen millions of stars in the Milky Way, and the

[1] *Natural Theology*, Chap. XXVII.

bee upon the flower. Never have I more clearly seen that,

> "Our grief is but our grandeur in disguise."

Never has the prayer of resignation seemed to me more reasonable or more beautiful. Never has my own personality more irresistibly led me to the Personality of God.

These great services have some qualifications. If man, "repelled by intellect, impelled by faith"—as has been so superbly said by Professor Fraser—*will* spring towards the Infinite, it is well that the bars of his cage should be more securely padded than by mere philosophy. I would ask the author of this Essay—Shall I, or any one in a million, ever find peace as you have done? The mer-de-glace of the Infinite is covered with myriads of philosophic insects that have been carried up there and lost. Jacob wrestled one night, and found a blessing at break of day. I must wrestle twenty years, if I am to follow you, and perhaps never say Peniel at the end. I multiply figures because I am in earnest. You have stretched a rope over the river. With mighty muscles and unfailing feet, you have come to shore. But your hair is wet, and your garment saturated with spray, and your face is pale as with the agony of death. I had rather pass over the old bridge by which the Church treads, than on your strong shoulders—and after all your rope *is* fastened to the bridge!

You show me the Personal, Infinite, God, Creator of earth and heaven. But there rises before me the thought of One, without Whom I suspect you would never have told me even that, and He says what draws me towards God, as all the metaphysics on earth, and all the stars in heaven never could. "No man cometh unto *the Father* but by Me."

The last sentence of your book is a noble one. Let me add five words to it. "The great mystery of existence, the distinction and union of two personalities, that mystery where pure reason is confounded, where reasoning has so often gone astray, is no more a mystery for the soul which has prayed." The grand and simple music of the old Collects is echoing in my heart—and I add, "through Jesus Christ our Lord."

Appendix.

I.

On Natural and Revealed Religion.[1]

THE celebrated saying of Diderot, that "all the religions in the world are merely sects of natural religion," characterises with singular exactitude the prevalent opinion of the eighteenth century, upon the nature and value of religious institutions. If we believe the philosophers of that epoch, religions have not been a necessary and fruitful instrument of civilization, but an obstacle. They have corrupted, instead of perfecting natural religion. They have but added to it a mass of errors and superstitions, the product of the credulity of the weak and the policy of the strong.

The history of religions presents us with the wretched spectacle of the aberrations of our ever-credulous and ever-deceived humanity. Religions have no ultimate and solid foundation in the nature of man. They are artificial institutions, which have no intimate connection with the moral destiny of our race. All religions are equally false, if not equally malevolent. Moses and Orpheus, Zoroaster and Confucius, Mahomet and our Lord, are impostors or enthusiasts!

[1] [Translated from M. Saisset's *Essais sur la Philosophie et la Religion, au XIX. Siècle*, pp. 287-304.]

Such is the philosophy of religions conceived by the eighteenth century. Pass from Voltaire and David Hume to Boulanger and Dupuis; sink from the brilliant *Essais sur les Mœurs*, and the ingenious sketch of the *Natural History of Religions*, to the undigested compilation of the *Origine des Cultes*, and the declamatory rhetoric of *Christianisme Dévoilé*, and you will find the same ideas everywhere. Montesquieu and Rousseau perhaps form the only exception to this general law; yet it would not be difficult to find traces of it in the celebrated dialogue, *Le Raissoneur et L'Inspirè*, as well as in more than one *piquant* passage of the *Lettres Persanes*. But what an advance there is from this witty irreverence to the depth and majesty of the *Spirit of Laws!* In that immortal work, the finest monument which the eighteenth century has bequeathed to us, the eminently benevolent and civilizing effect of religions, and above all of Christianity, has been marked in strong and brilliant colours. One feels in each page the genius of a philosophy which rises above the horizon of the eighteenth century, and makes of Montesquieu almost our own contemporary.[1]

At the present time, it is clear enough to every

[1] ["It is bad reasoning against religion to cram together in a great book a long list of the *evils* which it has produced, if we will not do the same by the *benefits* which it has brought with it. Were I to recount all the evils which have been wrought in the world by civil laws, monarchy, republican government, I could say frightful things."—*Esprit des Lois*, xxiv. 2.

"Plutarch tells us, in his life of Numa, that in the time of Saturn there was neither master nor slave. In our lands, Christianity has brought back that age."—*Ibid*, xv. 7.

"Wonderful fact! the Christian religion, which appears to have no other object than felicity in another life, constitutes also our happiness in this."—*Ibid*, xxiv. 3.]

mind of any width, that this theory of the eighteenth century upon religions is radically false. It rests upon one of the strangest hypotheses which have ever been conceived—that of a *perfect religion*, supposed to exist at the cradle of societies, and gradually degraded and obscured under the influence of positive religions. This hypothesis is on a par with that which Rousseau imagined when he painted man in a state of nature, primitively innocent and happy, but corrupted by civilization—a hollow and fantastic theory, which wrote its own condemnation when it formulated the famous paradox, "The man who thinks is a depraved animal." Rousseau and Diderot, like poets who sung an age of gold, imagined in the past of the human race that perfection which is really in its future destinies, thus substituting a barren remembrance and empty regret for holy and fruitful hopes.[1]

The hypothesis of a perfect religion, anterior to civilisation, will not bear close examination. What are the dogmas of that religion? A God, who is spiritual, one, intelligent, free, good, who loves all men equally. But it is clear,

[1] [The first germ of the philosophy of history, the first conception of a true law of progress in human society, is not to be found in Tacitus or Thucydides, in Aristotle, or even in Plato, but in St. Augustine. "Divine providence," says the great theologian, "which conducts all things marvellously, rules the series of human generations from Adam to the end of the world *like one man*, who, from his infancy to his old age, furnishes forth his career in time in passing through all its ages." —*De Questionibus Octoginto tribus*, *quæst.* 58. Again, "The right education of the human race, so far as concerns the people of God, like that of a single man, advanced through certain divisions of time, as that of the individual does through the consecutive ages of human life." "Sicut autem unius hominis, ita humani generis, quod ad Dei populum pertinet, recta eruditio per quondam articulos temporum tanquam œtatum profecit accessibus."—*De Civ. Dei*, lib. x. c. 14.] Does not Bacon imi-

that before Christianity men knew not this God. The Jehovah, worshipped under the Mosaic dispensation itself, is in many respects a national and local God.[1] The idea of the one universal God is essentially and exclusively CHRISTIAN. *Some sages* before Christ had spread it among a few select minds; *Humanity* knew it not. At this very moment, it is utterly unknown to the majority of men. Outside the people of Christendom we shall look in vain for the idea of the one universal God.[2]

tate this in the celebrated aphorism? "The old age and increasing years of the world should, in reality, be considered as antiquity; and this is the character of our own times rather than of the less advanced age of the world in those of the ancients. For the latter, with respect to ourselves, are ancient and elder, with respect to the world, modern and younger. And as we expect a greater knowledge of human affairs, and mature more judgment, from an old man than from a youth, on account of his experience, so we have reason to expect much greater things of our own age than from antiquity, since the world has grown older." (Novum Organ, I. Aph. 24.) This doctrine of progress has been denied by Vico, who would subject human affairs to an invariably recurrent and universal rotation, *corsi e riccorsi*. But more generally it has been misunderstood. Herder compares mankind to one bud perpetually expanding, and has thus prepared the way for a transcendental Pantheism. Turgot and Condorcet dream of a constant perfectibility, and an indefinite prolongation of our animal and terrestrial existence. The doctrine of progress, without that of the Fall, is always a wild dream. St Augustine's doctrine is—

1. That the human race is one, and needs restoration.

2. That this restoration is the object of the law of progress, in which the preventing action of God and the free effort of his creatures are seen.

3. That this progress is not carried out by the immolation of individuals, but consists in the amelioration of individuals in the development of humanity. This moral progress, in comparison with which material progress is nothing, commences in expiation and trial here, and is completed in another existence.

The "perfection" of which M. Saisset here speaks is not that of Herder or of Turgot, but of his favourite Augustine.]

[1] "I do not deny," says M. Saisset, "that in the Old Testament, and especially in the Psalms, many passages may be found of quite a different character; *ex. gr.*, Psalm cxlv. 18, 19, Amos ix. 7, contrasted with Deut. iv. 7. [See also specially I. Kings viii. 41. 43.]

[2] I do not here distinguish the Mahometan population from the Christian nations, properly so called. Is not the Koran, in fact, as it

I would say as much on the score of morality. The idea of human fraternity is a *Christian* idea. (See also in the Old Testament, Exodus xxiii. 9; Deut. xxiv. 17; Levit. xix. 34.) It is true that the Stoics had elevated themselves to it, just as Plato, before our Lord, had attained to the unknown God, the God who is a Spirit, of the Gospel. But Christianity alone has made the dogma of universal charity known to the *human race*.

Yet what can be more natural or reasonable than to believe in the one God, who hath made men all brethren? Certainly, it *is* natural and reasonable, that is to say, conformable to the purest inspirations of nature and of reason. But these sublime instincts would remain dormant within us, without a regular and assiduous cultivation. This culture is given by civilisation, and the two forces employed by civilisation in this grand work, are religion and philosophy.

To speak at present only of religions, surely it is incontestable that they have fulfilled, and are even yet fulfilling in the world an eminently civiliznig action. What but its religious institutions made the greatness of the Jewish people? Where is the source of the unconquerable vitality of that race which neither Babylon, Greece, nor Rome could destroy; but in the strong religion which Moses collected at Sinai, under the dictation of Jehovah? On what monument is Jewish civilization, with its poetry, its institutions, its history,

has been so well called, a defective edition of the Gospel? [In days of greater theological accuracy than ours, Mahometanism was always reckoned among *Christian heresics*. See *Lambert Danæus' Edition of August. De Hæresibus*, lxcvi.]

its manners, graven in lasting characters? It is a religious monument, the Old Testament. What gave Greece her arts, her literature, her liberty, her philosophy, but the religion of Orpheus and of Hesiod? Try to understand Æschylus and Sophocles, Ictinus and Phidias without the Greek religion. Plato himself would have no meaning without it.

The philosophy of religion, received by the eighteenth century, appears infinitely more false and wretched when we come to speak of Christianity. Who, at this time of day, will venture seriously to dispute that Christianity has civilized the modern world? What was natural religion in the days of Clovis and Charlemagne? Find, if you can, its principles among the barbarous hordes who thronged the soil of Europe. Who then spoke to men of a spiritual, just, and holy God, of a free and immortal soul, of love and charity? Was it Christianity, or the fantastic religion of nature which was dreamed of by the philosophy of the eighteenth century?

The eighteenth century did not know itself. It cursed Christianity, of which it was the legitimate child. . . . It is certain that natural religion, as conceived by the eighteenth century, in the name of which that age contended with Christianity and philosophical systems, is the product of Christianity. Let us explain this curious connection at sufficient length.

Man is born with two needs, at once distinct and inseparable, the *moral* and the *religious* instinct. Free, he yet feels that there exists a law which should regulate his will. Capable of intelligence and of love, his mind and his heart require an infinite object. Every man possesses the instinct of the Good, and the instinct of the Infinite, in a word, the instinct of the Divine. Every one who can live without faith in the Divine, or who has smothered that sublime faith within him, does not belong to humanity.

The moral and religious instinct, the instinct of the Divine is primordial in man, anterior and superior to every religion and every philosophy, the aliment and the foundation of every religious belief and of every philosophical speculation. This alone is common to all men, savage or civilized, ancient or modern, of the Mongolian or Caucasian race. This alone constitutes the unity of mankind. . . .

The common foundation of every religion as of every philosophy, is the invincible need which pushes man on to develope the instinct of his nature, the instinct of the Divine. . . . A day came, prepared by Divine Providence, when all the religions of the world became acquainted, and finding themselves diverse and opposed, engaged in strife, and, so to speak, broke each other in pieces, to give place to a religion which collected and organized their fragments. We may mark that day by a date which the human race will never forget—the birth of our Lord.

. . . Why did all the religions of antiquity bear in their very heart the germ of inevitable death? Because no religion before Christianity had succeeded in determining the essential conditions of the moral life of man. Because it solved this problem, Christianity comprises all essential truths. It is the heir of all religions and of all philosophical systems. It has fused together all these apparently discordant elements, Moses and Plato, the wisdom of Memphis and Delphos, and the wisdom of Athens and of Alexandria. It has borrowed from Greece its metaphysics, from Stoicism its morality,[1] from Judea its traditions, from the East its mystic breath, from Rome her spirit of government; and it is thus[2] that Christianity has succeeded in uniting all the conditions of the moral life of humanity in one body of durable doctrine. . . . Those who speak of a new religion do not perceive that Christianity is not *a* religion like others. . . . It has solved once for all the problem of positive religions. . . .

The eighteenth century was wrong about the nature of religions in general, and about the Christian religion in particular. It believed that religions were the work of credulity and imposture, while they are the natural and regular product of the moral and religious instincts of the human race. It was deceived about Christianity, because it believed that Christianity was a religion like any other, and that it was radically contrary to natural religion and to reason.

This is a capital mistake. What the eighteenth century called natural religion is the foundation of Christianity. This position is sufficiently proved by looking attentively at the three chief attempts which were made in the eighteenth

[1] [This statement requires much qualification. It was his intense perception of the distinction between the haughty morality of stoicism and the doctrines of grace, which finally won the great intellect of Maine de Biran to the cross.]

[2] [M. Saisset's mode of statement here is, I think, objectionable. If Christianity collected all truths, it was not by an eclectic process, but by a Divine *unification*.]

century to systematize natural religions. These attempts are connected with the three chief philosophical schools of the time—the schools of Kant, Rousseau, and Reid. I put aside the Encyclopéde, the Materialists and Atheists, who, after having collected natural religions and natural law, end by telling us that morality consists in self-preservation, and religion in believing in nature.

The three schools in question profess a great contempt for philosophical systems, and much independence in respect to religious creeds—what, however, with the Scottish thinkers is consistent with the sincerest faith in Christ, with Kant goes no further than respect, and with Rousseau sometimes proceeds to hostility.

But upon collecting the fundamental articles of natural religion, in Kant's *Critique of the Practical Reason*, in Rousseau's *Profession de foi du Vicaire Savoyard*, and in Reid's *Essays*, what do we find? The same truths that Christianity had for the first time united in a system appropriate to the human race, and which modern philosophy, the genius of Descartes, Malebranche, and Leibnitz, had established upon the ground of reason.

Examine, in fact, the fundamental dogmas upon which Christianity reposes. They may be reduced to three—the Trinity, the Incarnation, the Atonement. We need not now enter into the depths of these dogmas; we shall say but little, and that strictly confining ourselves within the limits of our subject. But what is the most evident meaning of these dogmas?

The dogma of the Trinity establishes, in the first place, the absolute unity of God, His spirituality, His incommunicable and absolute perfection. This God, considered in Himself, is not, however, an inert and lifeless being, an abstract and undetermined power, which can only actualize by developing itself, and become real by its works. He is a God in whom perfection and personality are inconceivably united. He knows and loves Himself. He lives in Himself, with a life that is free and independent, beyond time and space. From personality, He excludes nothing but its miseries; He contains the principle of it, life with intelligence and love. The unity, personality, and independence of God, are implied in the dogma of the Trinity.

This God does not remain in the mute depths of His eternal existence. He is love. Love counsels Him to expand His perfection without Himself. He creates. He fills space and time with the marvels of His power. He reflects Himself in a free and intelligent being, made in His likeness, capable of comprehending and adoring the Eternal.

This supreme creation is finished by the filling up of the chasm which separates the finite from the infinite. God hides himself, so to speak, in nature, under the fatality of its laws. He manifests himself in man. He tabernacles in our nature, and is well-pleased with it. More: He wills to unite Himself to our nature by the closest and most incomprehensible of ties. He is made man, and is Incarnate.

Man separated from God is little but a more perfect animal, the child of time, and made to be devoured by it, a weak and wretched part of that infinite circle of existences, which are incessantly produced and destroyed. By the Incarnation, he becomes a being of a different grade, capable of understanding, loving, and possessing eternal things. But his intellect is yet weak, and his will is subject to failure. Man knows sin, and he is separated from his first principle. To ransom and restore him, he wants infinite mercy to give infinite value to his repentance. This is the mystery of redemption.

God has taken the manhood into God. He died for all. He wills that all should be saved, because all are His children,—furnished with the same gifts, submitted to one law of love. Hence that sublime morality, which has surpassed the purest conceptions of ancient wisdom, and regulated for ever the relations and affections of man. Reasonable love of one's self, as made in the image of God: love of one's neighbours, as members of Christ; all our affections directed towards the general love of God;—such is the eternal code of morality, founded upon the eternal code of religion.

We are not ignorant of many objections which may be raised here, and we cannot discuss them now. Suffice it to say that we have not written a word which is not conformable to the exactest text of the most rigorous orthodoxy, and at the same time to the most enlightened reason.

Such is the natural religion which Rousseau developes so eloquently in the Savoyard vicar's *Profession de Foi*, whose principles Kant interlinks with superior strength in his *Critique of the Practical Reason*, which the Scotch school, in its turn, promulgated to the eighteenth century in a form at once less severe and less eloquent, but with admirable good sense and honest conviction. Some have thought that in writing the Gospel of natural religion, Rousseau destroyed that of Christianity. By no means. He merely traced a fine commentary upon it.

II.

Substantial agreement of Christianity and the Platonic Philosophy in reference to certain metaphysical problems.[1]

THE first problem which metaphysics proposes to itself is that of the existence of God.

St. Augustine solves it like a genuine disciple of Plato. The Atheists may be confounded by excellent processes of discursive reasoning. Plato himself has perfectly succeeded in proving[2] that Atheism is the negation of the simplest and most evident principle of reason—the principle of causality. But in the estimation of a true philosopher, the existence of God is a verity so self-evident as to have no need of demonstration. In truth, the mind does not attain to God as the last consequence of anterior principles. It is raised to

[1] [Translated from M. Saisset's *Introduction to St. Augustine, De Civitate Dei*. Pp. 72-102.]

[2] [De Leg. x.]

Him as the First Principle of all principles, by a natural and irresistible movement.

There are, however, two degrees which may be distinguished in this ascending movement of reason.

Just as the sun of the visible world appears to us first as the centre of light, so God is to us, in the first place, the absolute Truth, the one Truth, in which all truths are identified, the universal reason which enlightens all intelligences. He is, says Plato, the sun of the intelligible world. Here is His first claim upon our adoration and reverence.

But the material sun is not only the centre of light; it is also the source of heat and life. So God is not only the principle of intelligence, reason, and truth; He is also the principle of being, the Idea of ideas, absolute unity, Good in itself, in short the ultimate root of all that exists.

We have seen St. Augustine in his *Confessions* elevating his mind to God as the eternal Truth and the uncreated Word. In the *De Civitate Dei* he places himself with Plato at a still loftier elevation. He demonstrates God as the Being of beings, infinitely above all bodies, above the soul, above all sensible and intelligible forms; in a word, as the first and immutable form of all life and of every existence. I cite the whole chapter, one of the finest in the work, when judged by that severe metaphysical beauty, whose noblest attractions are force and precision.

"Those philosophers, therefore, whom we have seen not undeservedly preferred to all others in glory and renown [the Platonists] clearly perceived that no body was God; and therefore, in their search after God, transcended all bodies. They perceived that whatever is mutable is not the Most High God; and, therefore, in seeking Him, they transcended also every soul and all mutable spirits. They then perceived that every form in any mutable thing, by which it is what it is, whatsoever its mode and nature may be, cannot be, except from Him who truly exists, because He exists immutably. And thus, whether they considered the body of the universe, its figures, qualities, ordered motions, its elements, arranged from heaven even to earth, and whatever bodies are in them; or, again, all life, whether that which nourishes and sustains itself, as in trees, or that which both does this and is sentient, as in beasts; or that which both has these properties and understands, as is the case with man; or, finally, that which does not want nutritive sustenance, but only maintains itself, is sentient, and intelligent, such as is life in the angels; they have seen that none of these can be, save from Him who simply is. For to Him existence is not one thing, life another, as though He could exist without life; nor is life one thing to Him, intelligence another, as though He could live without intelligence; nor, again, is His intelligence something different from His blessedness, as though he could be intelligent, and not blessed—but life, intelligence, blessedness, is with Him the same as being. On account of this immutability and simplicity, the Platonists understood both that He made all things, and that He could not have been made of any. For they considered that whatever is, is either body or soul; that soul is somewhat better than body; that the form of the body is sensible, and the form of the soul intelligible. Hence they preferred the intelligible to the sensible form. We call those things sensible, which can be perceived by corporeal sight and touch—those things intelligible, which can be understood by the look of the soul. For there is no outward beauty, whether in the posture of the body, such as its shape, nor in motion, such as is the modulation of music, of which the mind does not judge. Which certainly could not be the case, unless there were in it this better form, without the swelling of bulk, without the clamour of sound, without space of place or time. Here, too, unless this form were mutable, no one man would judge better than another of sensible form. In this respect the ingenious would be no quicker than the slow of wit, the experienced than the inexperienced, the ignorant than the educated; the same person when he is making progress would have no better judgment, in any way, after than he had before. But that which is susceptible of greater and less is unquestionably mutable. Whence those who are gifted with genius and learned in these points have readily come to the conclusion, that the first form cannot be in those things, in which the property of mutability is easily proved to exist. Since, therefore, in their view, both the mind and the body have forms that are more or less fair, and if they had no form would have no existence, they saw that there was something where there is that prime, immutable, and therefore incomparable form; and they most justly believed that the principle of things was there, because it is not made, and all things are made by it. Thus hath God showed unto them, that which may be known of God,[1] since the invisible things of Him are clearly seen, being understood by the things that are made, even His eternal power and Godhead."[2]

God is then at once the principle of truth and the principle of being, the primitive unity, rendered visible to itself and to every intelligence by that splendour of the eternal reason which is the characteristic of its essence.

But why has this God manifested Himself outwardly, who manifests Himself eternally to Himself in the interior light of His word? Why has this perfect and self-sufficing Being, gone forth from Himself to produce the universe? Is it by caprice or chance? is it by a necessity inherent in His nature? is it by an act of His will? It will readily be understood that Plato and St. Augustine could not admit either chance and caprice on one hand, or indigence and necessity on the other, without giving themselves a direct contradiction, and breaking their metaphysical systems to pieces with their own hands. Chance and caprice may be met with in wretched and imperfect beings like men, and even they are subjected to secret laws; but applied to God, the immutable Being, caprice and chance are unmeaning words. Can God have need of His creatures, and in creating can He be supposed to obey the necessity of completing His being and His life? But God is perfect. He possesses and knows Himself. He enfolds in His being the elements of a blessed life,

[1] Romans i. 19, 20. [2] *De Civ. Dei*, Lib. viii. C. vi.

and of a perfect felicity. If then God becomes fruitful, if He wills to be the Father, if He wills to communicate life and being—it is because God is good. He is not only the Perfect Being and Perfect Intelligence,—He is also Perfect Goodness. Let us listen alternately to Plato and St. Augustine.

"Let us state the cause which has led the Supreme Ordainer to produce and to compose this universe. He was good, and he who is good has no kind of envy. Exempt from envy, He willed that all things should, as far as possible, be like Him. Whoever, instructed by wise men, shall admit this as the principal reason of the origin and formation of the world will be right."[1]

St Augustine accepts unreservedly this explanation of the *wherefore* of creation. He takes up with sympathy, and interprets like a true philosopher, the touching and sublime image of God, which Plato presents to us, when he pictures the Father of the universe as full of joy at the spectacle of His work in life and motion. St Augustine recognises in this trait the God of Genesis, and expounds forcibly, in opposition to a false theology, those much controverted words of the Bible, "And God saw that it was good."

"What else are we to understand in the sentence which is repeated through all the works of the six days[2]—*and God saw that it was good*—but

[1] [*Timæus*, 29, 30. See the original passage quoted in the note, volume I., p. 230. This passage contains the germ of the *optimism* of Leibnitz. cf. *Essais de Théodicée.*—Part 1. 8.]

[ὡς δὲ κινηθὲν αὐτὸ καὶ ζῶν ἐνενόησε 'ο γεννήσας πατὴρ ἠγάσθη τε καὶ ευφρανθεὶς. κ. τ. λ.—*Timæus*, 36.]

[2] [*Per omnia.*—The statement is not made, however, of the second day of the Demiurgic Hexaemeron.—Gen. i. 6-8.]

approbation of the work which was wrought after that art, which is the wisdom of God? But God was so far from *learning* that it was good when it was made, that none of those things would have been made at all had this been unknown to Him. When, therefore, He sees that that is good, which would not have been made at all had He not seen it before its creation, He *teaches*, and does not *learn*, that it is good. And Plato, indeed, ventures to say more—namely, that God was full of joy when the universe was completed. Where he was not so insensate as to suppose that God was made more blessed by the novelty of His work, but wished to show that that which had pleased his divine Artificer when it was purposed to be created by His art, pleased Him when it was actually produced; not that the knowledge of God admits of any variation, so that the things which are not yet, those which are, and those which have been, are different in it. For God does not, in our way, foresee the future, or see the present, or look back to the past; but in another manner profoundly different from the way of our thoughts. He does not pass by a change of thought from one thing to another, but sees immutably. Those things which are done in time, both those which are not as being future, and which are as now present, and which are not as now past, He comprehends them all by His abiding and eternal presence. He sees not one way with His eyes, another with His mind, for He is not compounded of soul and body. He does not see one way now, another in the past, yet another in the future, since His knowledge is not changed like ours by the difference of the present, the past, and the future, *with whom is no variableness, neither shadow of turning.*[1] For He, to whose incorporeal *contuition* all which He knows is present at once, does not pass with an effort from thought to thought, since He knows time with a knowledge unconditioned by time, just as He moves temporal things without undergoing temporal motion. He, therefore, saw that what He made was good, where He saw that it was good to make it. Nor, in seeing it actually made, did He double, or in any way increase His knowledge, as though he were of less knowledge, before He made what He was to see, seeing that He could not work so perfectly unless He wrought with a knowledge so perfect that nothing could be added to it from His works. Wherefore, if it were only intended to teach us who made the light, it would have been enough to say—*and God said, Let there be light, and there was light*—that we might have known not only that God made light, but that He did so by His word. But as it was meet that three most important points of knowledge about creation should be intimated to us—who made it, by what agency, and why—Scripture states: *God said, Let there be light, and there was light. And God saw the light that it was good.* If, therefore, we ask who created, the answer is God; by what means? *He said, Let there be, and there was;* why? because *it was good.* No author can be more excellent than God; no art more efficacious than God's word; no cause better than that that which is good should be created by the God who is good. Plato also affirms that

[1] St. James i. 17.

this is the most just cause of the creation of the world, that works which are good should be wrought by the God who is good; whether he had read these things in the Bible,[1] or happened to learn them from those who had read them; or whether by his penetrating genius he beheld the *invisible things of God as understood by the things which are made*, or whether he had learned from those who had so beheld them."[2]

St. Augustine is so fully satisfied with the Platonic explication of the *wherefore* of creation, that he cannot comprehend how certain theologians, especially Origen, ventured to repudiate it. He refutes them with much warmth, and to finish the task of reducing them to silence, he asks them whether, in refusing to see the ultimate reason of creation in the wisdom and goodness of God, they do not fail to recognise the God of the Christian Trinity in Unity, who necessarily acts according to that which He is, that is, at once as being, intelli-

[1] [Josephus, the Jewish historian; among the Christian fathers and apologists, Justin Martyr, Tatian, Theophilus of Antioch, Clemens of Alexandria, Tertullian, Minutius Felix, Origen, Lactantius, and Theodoret, have dwelt upon the unacknowledged obligations of the ancients to divine revelation. The 10th Book of Eusebius' *Evangelical Preparation* is taken up with an attempt to prove that Plato and other philosophers borrowed the best part of their theology and ethics from Scripture: the 11th, 12th, and 13th books specify the particulars in which Plato may be supposed to agree with Holy Writ.—See Waterland's Charge, *The Wisdom of the Ancients Borrowed from Divine Revelation*, vol. v., 1-29. We may agree with Berkeley's beautiful saying, that "perhaps these sublime hints, which dart forth like flashes of light in the midst of a profound darkness, were not originally struck from the hard rock of human reason, but rather derived, at least in part, by a divine tradition from the author of all things" (*Siris*, sec. 298-301-360); but we may admire all the more St. Augustine's honesty, in confessing that it was chronologically impossible for Plato to have been a pupil of the prophet Jeremiah, or to have studied the Septuagint version of the Scriptures.—*De Civ. Dei*, Lib. viii., c. xi.]

[2] *De Civ. Dei*, Lib. xi., c. 21.

gence, and love. And, in fact, he says: "When in the case of any created thing it is asked who made it, by what means, and why, and the answer is given, that God made it, by His word, because it is good; it might be proved, indeed, though only by a voluminous investigation, that there is nothing to hinder our understanding this part of Scripture in such a way that, in the mystic depth of this answer, the Trinity is intimated to us, that is, Father, Son, and Holy Spirit."[1]

Here a new and perilous question, which had often occupied the mind of St. Augustine, presents itself to him—a question of which he has given a very remarkable solution in the *Confessions* and *De Civitate Dei*, that of the eternity of creation. When St. Augustine explained so well how God must necessarily have known His creatures before producing them, he met a difficulty which he did not solve. The difficulty is this: can it be conceived that there is in God, the Eternal and Immutable Being, a before and after?[2] St. Augustine has powerfully proved that the intellect, like the essence of God, is above the viscissitudes of time; that with Him foresight, sight, and retrospect (so-called) are all one; that He embraces the present, the past, and the future, with one immutable regard. But how is this consistent with the admission that creation had a beginning in time, that is to say, that God passed at a given moment from repose into action, to subside into repose again? Is not this to conceive God as a being subject to

[1] *De Civ. Dei.* Lib. xi., c. 23.

[2] [See the passages from Scaliger, Boethius, and Kant, quoted in this volume. Page 173.]

change? Is it not like assimilating His activity to our laborious effort, and abasing to the level of the creature the degraded majesty of the Eternal Creator?

There is no more difficult problem in metaphysics, there is none upon which St Augustine has reflected more profoundly, and thus, without completely withdrawing himself from Plato—his usual guide, he has left here the living impression of his own peculiar genius.

Let us, with St Augustine, take in succession the two alternatives which this problem presents to our reason. On one side there is an eternal and immutable God, who, at a definite moment, enters upon a course of action to produce that which did not previously exist. On the other side, there is a world which always existed, a chain of ages which has no first link, a creation co-eternal with the Creator. The more we think of it the more terrified the mind becomes at being forced to choose between two conceptions, which are equally full of insoluble difficulties. I will venture to say, that there are few philosophers who have not, at least at moments, believed that which Emmanuel Kant systematically professed—namely, that the problem of creation contains one of these antinomies which will always be the rock on which metaphysics must strike.

St Augustine was perfectly acquainted with the difficulties and perils of each of these contrary alternatives. It is sometimes asked, he says, what God was doing before He created the heavens and the earth? "I will not," he continues, "make the answer which is said to have been jestingly made by one who eluded the serious difficulty of the question in replying. *He was preparing hell fire for those who curiously pry into His deep things.*"[1] The saying is more or less pointed, but the question remains. The more we meditate upon God, the more we recognize that immutability is one of the most essential characteristics of His nature. Perfect and fully self-sufficing, there is in His being "no variableness, neither shadow of turning." To pass from rest into action, and from action into rest, is the peculiarity of an imperfect nature, which tends with painful effort to a greater perfection, is fatigued, and takes breath to begin again. In God there is nothing of this kind. His will, like His essence, must be immutable, and instead of unfolding itself, like ours, in a series of successive efforts, it is concentrated in one sole, simple, eternal act.

Hence, continues the philosophical theologian, when it is said that God rested the seventh day, we must only see in it a human and symbolical expression.[2] In the same way, the days of creation mark the hierarchy of beings, and the successive epochs of their appearance upon the face of the earth. But the action of God cannot be decomposed into epochs. It is one, hence it is perfect. How then can we understand that God did not act during an infinite series of ages?

[1] ["Alta," inquit, "scrutantibus gehennas parabat."—*Confess. Lib.* xi. C. 12.]

[2] [This expression is, I think, not quite accurate. St. Augustine's words are worth quoting:—"Cum vero in die septimo requievit Deus—nequaquam est accipiendum pueriliter, tanquam Deus laboraverit operando. Sed requies Dei requiem significat eorum qui requiescunt in Deo, sicut lœtitia domus lœtitiam significat eorum qui lœtantur in domo. Quanto magis, si eadem domus pulchritudinæ suâ faciat lœtos habitatores

Here St. Augustine comes into collision with the philosophers of the Alexandrian school, Plotinus, Porphyry, and Iamblichus, who were deeply penetrated with the principle of the divine immortality, and deduced from it the eternity of creation. St. Augustine cannot consent to be associated with such a doctrine, but he is too discerning and too honest to confound it with that of the Epicurean materialists, who maintain that only the forms of the world change, but that matter and atoms exist externally, and of themselves. To these philosophers the world is uncreated; there is no Creator; the question of creation does not exist at all. The error of the Alexandrian philosophers is of a less gross order; they admit that the world does not suffice to itself, and that it is the work of God, only they refuse to believe that the world ever began, and see in it the eternal manifestation of eternal activity.

"Even apart from the witness of the prophets," he says, "the world itself, by its most regularly-ordered mutations and revolutions, and by the exquisite beauty of all visible things, proclaims in a certain sense, in its very silence, both that it has been created, and that it could not have been created but by a God ineffably and invisibly beautiful." So far for the Materialists;[1] but, adds

ut non solum, eo loquendi modo lœta dicatur, quo significamus per id quod continet, id quod continetur, sicut theatra plaudunt. Sed etiam illo quo significatur per efficientem id quod efficitur, sicut læta epistola dicitur, significans lœtitiam corum, quos legentes efficit lœtos.—*De civ. Dei.*, Lib. xi. c. 8-31., cf. ibid. c 7, and *De Genesi ad Litteram*, lib. iii. iv.]

[1] [The sentence just quoted is the refutation of the Epicurean Materialists; that which follows, of the Alexandrian school.]

St. Augustine, "Those who confess, indeed, that the world was created by God, but who maintain that it had not a beginning in time, but merely a commencement of its creation, so that in some way, which can scarcely be construed by the intellect, it was always created, have certainly something to say; whence they seem to themselves to defend God as it were from the imputation of chance and caprice, lest that which had never before occurred to him should be supposed to have come into His mind (namely, to create the world), and that a new will happened to Him who is no respect mutable; but I do not see how this theory can stand in other respects."[1] In fact, follow the necessary chain of consequences. If you admit that the world is infinite as to duration, you must necessarily admit that it is infinite as to extension. Otherwise it will be asked, why God created nothing in these immense spaces that the mind conceives beyond the whole finite universe, as we have just now heard the Alexandrian philosophers ask those who make the world finite as to duration, why God did nothing during that succession of ages that the mind conceives before all determinate duration. Here, then, is a world infinite as to duration and extension. Is not that to make it independent of God? Is it not to make God useless, and the universe divine.

Such are the difficulties which seem inseparable from each of the two alternatives of the problem of creation—reason cannot be satisfied either with

[1] *De Civ. Dei*, lib. xi. c. 4.

a world co-eternal with God, or with a God who has created the world in time.

There is but one means to disentangle this inextricable knot; that is, to deepen our apprehensions of eternity and time. St. Augustine applies himself to it with ardour, and we shall see him display in this difficult research a very superior acuteness and power of analysis. The notion of time, says he, is one of the most familiar; it is met with in all that we say. There is no man, however ignorant, who does not understand what is meant by a longer or shorter period of duration, such as a century, a day, a minute. What, then, is time and duration? There is nothing more difficult to define.

Time has three modes—the present, the past, and the future. Now the past is that which exists no longer; the future is that which has not yet been; the present alone seems to have a positive existence. But what is the present? Is it an age, a year, a day, an hour? But even an hour is a space of time which can be decomposed into parts; some parts which exist no longer, others future, which have yet to be. How shall we grasp, how shall we define that indivisible portion which constitutes the present? The present alone really exists; and it hardly is, before it is no more. Enclosed between two nothings, the past and the future, it has but a fugitive being, which it is impossible to arrest.

But it may be said that time is the motion of the celestial spheres. Doubtless this motion helps us to divide and to measure time, but it does not constitute time. Let the stars cease their revolutions; provided the potter's wheel continue to go round, it will give me the idea of time. Then it may be affirmed that time is in general the motion of bodies. But the motion of bodies is made in time; it does not constitute time, it supposes it. It is with the assistance of time that I measure the motion of bodies, that I call it quick or slow, equal or unequal. Therefore I must have a measure for time independent of corporeal motion.

To understand time and its measure, we must disengage ourselves from the confused impressions of our senses. We must enter into the depths of our consciousness. "It is in thee, O my soul, that I measure time. Confuse me not by objections; which means, confuse not thyself by the thronging din of thy sensual prejudices. In thee, I say, I measure time. It is the affection or impression which things, as they pass, make in thee, and which abides when they have passed away—it is this which is present that I measure, not those things which have passed away, that it might remain. This I measure when I measure time. Wherefore, either these things are time, or, if not, I do not measure time."[1]

It is, then, if I understand St. Augustine aright, in our own consciousness, and with the assistance of memory, that we find the first notion of duration. The mind itself is the type and measure of duration, and it is by adding to the consciousness of our present life the recollection of our past life, and the prevision of our future life, that we form the idea of time. There are, says St.

[1] *Confess.:* Lib. xi., c. 27. ["Ergo, aut ipsa sunt tempora, aut non tempora metior."]

Augustine, three simultaneous acts of the mind—expectation, attention, and recollection. The mind expects the future, grasps the present, recollects the past. *Et expectat, et attendit, et meminit.* By expectation the future becomes present to the mind; recollection renders present the things that are past; and by attention, the mind gives, in some sort, extension and fixedness to a present, that can never be grasped.[1] The result of this acute and ingenious analysis, in which St. Augustine anticipates and equals the profoundest investigations of modern psychology,[2] is, that if time is not the motion of bodies in general, or more generally still, the change in created things, yet time supposes that change. It is not by the external senses that the notion of time is acquired, but by the inward sense, and it is the mind, the Ego, which is to us the primitive model of the substance which endures; but mind, superior as it is to the body, is itself a created and changeable substance. It flows on incessantly from the present which passes, and is swallowed up in the past. It goes toward a future which soon will be effaced in its turn. It is thus with all being, even with angels. St. Augustine, in the *Confessions*, had admitted that the angelical nature, although made from nothing, is united to God in a manner so perfect that the simple act of this union escapes from the law of time.[3] But later reflections modified this thought, and in the *De Civitate*, which was

[1] *Confessions*, lib. xi. ch. 28.

[2] See the admirable fragments of M. Royer-Collard on the *Notion of Duration*, published by M. Jouffroy, in Vol. iv. of his translation of the Works of Thomas Reid.

[3] *Confessions*, Book xii. ch. 11-15.

the work of his full maturity, he declares that the angels themselves, in spite of the perfection of their happy life in the bosom of God, remain subject to change, and to the vicissitudes of the present, the past, and the future.[1] God alone is eternal, because God alone is immutable, because God alone is uncreated, because God alone is God. How should there be the flow of duration in God, since His perfect and simple being exists always identical with itself.

All thy years, O my God, are but a single day. It is not a succession of several days, but a perpetual to-day, which does not pass on to give place to a to-morrow, which has not succeeded to a yesterday; and this to-day is eternity.[2]

Who does not recognise in these words the perhaps somewhat feebler, but faithful echoes of those grand passages of the *Timæus*?[3]

Here, then, according to Plato and St. Augustine, are the real notions of time and eternity. Eternity is the incommunicable attribute of God; time is the law of all creatures. Eternity is immutable and simple; time is moveable and divisible.

Let us now return to the problem of the creation, and perhaps we shall be able to see more clearly by the light of these better defined notions.

If time supposes change, and if change supposes changeable beings, creatures whose successive conditions give birth to the present, the past, and the future, it follows, that when thought does away

[1] *De Civitate*, lib. xii. ch. 25. [2] *Confessions*, lib. xi. ch. 4.

[3] [See passage cited in note to page 239 vol. I. *Timæus*, cxxxviii.]

with creatures, it destroys time with the same blow. Therefore, to imagine a certain time which has preceded the world, that is to say, which has existed before the collection of creatures, is a contradictory idea, and to ask what God was doing before the creation of the world, is a meaningless question, since the voids before the world suppose a time anterior to the world, that is to say, a time independent of every creature and of all change, which means a void time, a time in which there is neither present, past, nor future, which is a palpable contradiction. In like manner, to say that the world and time are co-eternal with God, is to make use of unintelligible language; for between the world and time, which, by their nature, change and pass, and God, who is an immutable being, there is a radical opposition.[1] Therefore we must say with Plato, that the world and time were created together by the eternal Architect. God precedes the world, not by a priority of time, for that would make Him analogous to time, but by a priority of nature and of essence.[2] Here St. Augustine objects to himself. How has God always been the Lord, that is to say, how has God always been adored, if there were not always creatures? St. Augustine cannot consent to give up the principle that God has always had the quality of Lord, and that He has always been adored. If it were otherwise, the quality of Lord would be a novelty in God, it would begin at the moment when He began to be adored. Nor on the other hand can we lay down that the human race has always ex-

[1] *Confessions*, lib. xi., ch. 13. [2] *Confessions*, lib. xii., ch. 29.

isted. Evidently no Christian could admit this; besides, setting aside authority, reason agrees with the book of Genesis in overthrowing the hypotheses of certain philosophers, who admit untold revolutions of ages, perpetually reproducing and bringing back the same beings, the human race included.[1] Reason and faith, then, agree that there must have been a first man, although this apparition of a new being in time contains a profound mystery, and is very difficult to reconcile with the unity of the creative act and the immutability of the divine will.[2]

Now, if man is new upon the earth, how could God be Lord before the formation of man? He was adored by angels, says St. Augustine, but then returns this difficulty: Angels then have always existed, and if this be so, how is it that they are not co-eternal with God?

"What shall we answer to this?" says St. Augustine. "Shall we say, both that they always existed—since they existed in all time, as they were created together with time or time with them—and yet that they were created? For we shall not deny that in a parallel sense time was created, though no one can doubt that time existed during all time. For if time did not always exist, there was a time when there was no time. Who is foolish enough to affirm this? We may say rightly enough, there was a time when Rome, Jerusalem, Abraham, man did not exist, and so on. Finally, if the world was not made contemporaneously with the commencement of time, but after the lapse of some time, we may use the pro-

[1] *De Civitate*, lib. xii., ch. 13. [2] *De Civitate*, lib. xii., ch. 12 24.

position, There was a time when the world did not exist. But the assertion, There was a time when there was no time, is just as incongruous as the statement, Man existed when there was no man, or, The world was when there was no world. . . . As, therefore, we say that time was created, while yet it is asserted that it always existed, because time was through all time: so it does not follow, as a necessary consequence, that if there were always angels, the angels were therefore uncreated; so that they may be said to have always existed, because they were through all time, and they were through all time because time could not have been without them. For where there is no creature, by whose mutable motions time is formed, there can be no time. Hence, though they always existed, they were created, nor if they always existed, are they consequently co-eternal with their Creator. For He always existed by His immutable eternity; they were made. They are said always to have existed, because they were in all time, and time could not have been without them. But since time passes on by mutability, it cannot be co-eternal with immutable eternity. And hence, though the immortality of the angels does not pass in time, nor is past as though it did not now exist, nor future as though it were not yet, yet their motions of which time is composed pass from the future into the past; and therefore they cannot be co-eternal with the Creator, of whom it may not be said, either that He has been what He is not now, or that He will be what He is not yet."

Here, then, is the conclusion of St. Augustine:

"Wherefore, if God was always the Lord, He always had creatures subject to His dominion—creatures, not begotten of His substance, but made by Him out of nothing—not co-eternal with Him, for He was before them, though at no *time* without them, preceding them not by a transitory interval of time, but by an abiding eternity."[1]

It is thus that St. Augustine has resolved the problem of the eternity of creation. Did he succeed in conciliating the eternity of creative action with the dependence of things created? Did he disarm beforehand the dialectic of Kant? We dare not affirm so much; but what seems incontestable is, that he has touched with a bold and delicate hand one of the deepest mysteries of the human mind, and that to all his glorious titles he has added another, that of an ingenious psychologist and an eminent metaphysician.

To complete the exposition of his Theodicea, we have now only to point out, in a general way, the principle of his optimism. If God is essentially good, if He creates the world through goodness after His eternal wisdom has represented to Him the world ideally as a faithful representation of His own perfection, it follows that the world is essentially good, and that evil cannot have an absolute existence. He who is perfect in goodness, says Plato, could not, and cannot do anything that is not very good. He found that among all visible things He could absolutely make no work finer than an intelligent

[1] [*De Civit. Dei*, Lib. xii. c. 15. This remarkable chapter illustrates the train of thought by which Leibnitz seems to arrive at the conclusion of a world infinite in duration.—See Volume I., P. 240, note.]

being, and that in no being could there be intelligence without a soul. Therefore He placed intelligence in the soul, and the soul in the body; and He organised the universe so that it should be by its constitution the finest and the most perfect of works.[1] We find the same doctrine and the same language in the 10th book *De Legibus*. "The King of the world imagined, in the distribution of of each part of it, the system which He judged the best, so that the good should be uppermost and the evil undermost in the universe. It is in relation to this view of the whole that He makes His general combination of the places which each being ought to occupy, according to his distinctive qualities."[2]

In this fine passage Plato does not speak of effective and absolute, but of purely relative evil. For it is his express doctrine that good alone is positive, whilst evil exists merely negatively. St. Augustine is here still full of Plato, and we feel that he finds a pleasure in conciliating without violence, the revered inspirations of the beloved philosopher with the express doctrine of Christianity.

"In fact, there is no nature originally bad, and this term only indicates the privation of goodness. But from earthly to heavenly things, and from things visible to those which are invisible, there are some good things better than others, unequal for this very reason that they might exist at all. But God is in such sense the great Artificer in great things that He is not less in small things; and these small things are not to be measured by their greatness, which is nought, but by the wisdom

[1] Plato Timæus.

[2] *De Leg*, lib x.

of their Framer. As in the visible form of man, if one eyebrow be shaved off almost nothing is subtracted from the body, but much from that beauty which does not consist in bulk, but in similarity and proportion."

"They (certain heretics) do not attentively consider how these things (fire, cold, wild beasts, &c.,) are excellent in their own places and natures, and disposed with admirable order; and how much beauty they add to the sum-total of things, each for their own part, as to their common country, or how much use they are to us, if we are willing to employ them wisely and well. So certain poisons which are injurious when unfitly used, if properly employed, are changed into wholesome medicines, whilst, on the contrary, even those things by which men are delighted, such as food and drink, and even light, become hurtful by an immoderate and improper use. Whence Divine Providence warns us not to find fault with things foolishly, but rather to search diligently into their real use; and where our wit falls short, or our weakness fails, to believe that that utility is hidden, just as some things were which we were barely able to discover. The very concealment of their utility is either an exercise in humility, or a diminution of pride."[1]

"It is ridiculous to condemn those defects in animals and trees, and other things mutable and mortal, which are destitute either of sense, or intellect, or life, and by which they are subject to dissolution and corruption; these creatures have

[1] *De Civ. Dei*, lib. xi. c. 22.

received that mode of existence by the will of their Creator, that by their failure and succession they may make up that lower and temporal beauty which is suitable in its kind to the parts of this universe. Things earthly were not to be made equal to things heavenly; nor was the superiority of the latter a reason why the former should be wanting to the universe. When therefore in those places where it was suitable that these should exist, some spring up as others fail, and the less yield to the greater; and those which are vanquished acquire the qualities of their conquerors: all this is the order of passing things. The beauty of this order does not please us, because, linked as we are in virtue of our mortality to a portion of it, we cannot take in that universe to which the portions that offend us agree with sufficient fitness and congruity."[1]

"All natures, therefore, since they exist, and consequently have their own mode, species, and inner peace and harmony, are assuredly good; and since they are where they ought to be by the order of nature, they keep what they have received; and those things which have not received the gift of perpetual existence, are changed for the better or the worse, according to the need and motion of those things to which they are subjected by their Creator's law, tending by Divine Providence to that end, which the mode of the government of the universe includes; so that not even such corruption as brings on our mortal and mutable natures to dissolution, so makes that which existed to be non-existent, that it does not

[1] *De Civ. Dei*, lib. xii. c. 4.

become in succession what it ought to be. Whence God, who exists in the highest sense, and by whom for this reason all essences are created, which do not exist in the highest sense (because that ought not to be equal to Him which is made out of nothing, and indeed it could not exist at all were it not made by Him), God is not to be blamed through offence at any defects in created objects, and is to be glorified upon the due consideration of all natures."

III.

Philosophy and Religion.

I HAVE said, in one place, that M. Saisset's work, in its second part, leaves the impression upon my mind, that he would have us to consider philosophy as the προσαγωγὴ to God. Such access to God (ἡ προσαγωγὴ) is in Scripture assigned to Christ alone.[1] I am the more bound, in justice to M. Saisset, to cite the following equally Christian and philosophical account of the passage of Augustine from philosophy to Christianity:—

"The reason of Augustine began to gain strength. Could he find repose in the noble doctrines of Platonism? His soul was appeased, it was not satisfied. Philosophy was insufficient for him, religion alone could give him unbounded

[1] Rom. v. 2; Eph. ii. 18; iii. 12; 1 Pet. iii. 18.

serenity. Augustine tells us the reason of the insuffiĉiency of spiritual philosophy. Philosophy can enlighten the reason, but it only acts imperfectly upon the will. It teaches us speculative truths, but it does not bestow upon us the strength to transform them into practical verities. It reveals to us, indeed, on one side, a soul spiritual, free, yearning after virtue, perfection, and happiness; on the other, a God who is the true God, since He is the principle of all truth, holiness, and happiness. But how shall this soul, at once so sublime and so miserable, attain to this God? Here is what philosophy never taught. Augustine brings out, with wonderful depth and energy of thought, the enormous void which is left in the heart of man, and which religion alone can fill. He gives us his entire conception in these strong words: 'Plato made me know the true God, Jesus Christ showed me the way to Him.' This way is Jesus Christ Himself, the God-man, who unites and reconciles the two natures which the voluntary fall of man had separated. This is the idea which Augustine has conquered for Christianity. Plato had revealed to him the Logos, the Divine Word; but that the Word was made flesh and dwelt among us, Christianity alone could teach him."—*Introduction to De Civitate*, p. 30.

INDEX.

CPSIA information can be obtained
at www.ICGtesting.com
Printed in the USA
LVHW040430110522
718423LV00002B/382

9 783375 006662